To Pat & Will

Allan McHughen

Sidetracked

Allan Michael Hardin

iUniverse, Inc.
New York   Bloomington

Sidetracked

Copyright © 2008 by Allan Michael Hardin

All rights reserved. No part of this book may be used or reproduced by any means, graphic, electronic, or mechanical, including photocopying, recording, taping or by any information storage retrieval system without the written permission of the publisher except in the case of brief quotations embodied in critical articles and reviews.

This is a work of fiction. All of the characters, names, incidents, organizations, and dialogue in this novel are either the products of the author's imagination or are used fictitiously.

iUniverse books may be ordered through booksellers or by contacting:

iUniverse
1663 Liberty Drive
Bloomington, IN 47403
www.iuniverse.com
1-800-Authors (1-800-288-4677)

Because of the dynamic nature of the Internet, any Web addresses or links contained in this book may have changed since publication and may no longer be valid. The views expressed in this work are solely those of the author and do not necessarily reflect the views of the publisher, and the publisher hereby disclaims any responsibility for them.

ISBN: 978-0-595-52417-4 (pbk)
ISBN: 978-0-595-51186-0 (cloth)
ISBN: 978-0-595-62471-3 (ebk)

Printed in the United States of America

For Doug

Chapter 1

The bullet clipped the tip of the pine bough a foot from Kinslow's right ear. In the split second it took for the dust to rise from the severed branch, he was off his horse with rifle in hand and diving for cover behind the aged pine. With his mount positioned between the shooter and himself, he hit the ground, shoulder rolled beside the big tree, and quickly manoeuvred into a defensive position behind it. He took several deep breaths and listened intently for another shot or any other sound that might give away the bushwhacker's position.

He waited several seconds, but nothing else happened, which surprised him. He removed his dusty, sweat stained Stetson, gently set it on the ground, and tentatively peeked around the tree. Twenty years of tracking killers, thieves, and other scum had honed his hunter's skills to perfection. With only a quick glance, he was able to form a mental picture of the terrain from whence the bullet had come.

The high trail he was using followed the top of the ridge. Fifty feet ahead, it turned sharply to the left and began a steep descent to the river valley below. A huge deadwood log situated at the turn, on the downside of the trail, provided excellent cover. From behind it, a man had a perfect view of anyone who came along.

Kinslow sighted his Winchester on the log. He levered and fired three rounds as quickly as he could, the bullets sending chards of rotten wood flying into the air. He rolled back behind the cover of the pine and waited for return fire. None came. He took another quick glance from the other side of the tree, but he still couldn't see or hear anything.

Interesting, he thought.

"I am a U.S. marshal! Kinslow's the name. Step out from behind the log with your hands over your head and I won't kill you," he shouted with authority. He sat upright with his back against the pine, reloaded his rifle, and then sat still and listened. "Kinslow? Woodrow Kinslow?" came the questioning reply.

Kinslow was surprised the shooter knew his first name. He positioned himself again and rang another three shots off the top of the log. He sat back against the pine, reloaded, and hollered out again, "This is your last warning! Come out unarmed, with your hands over your head, and do it now!"

A reply came back, instantly, "Don't shoot, Woodrow. For God's sake, don't shoot! It's me, Ansen Miller. You remember — Abilene?"

Kinslow put on his hat, stepped out from behind the tree, and bounced another bullet off the top of the log. A rifle flew end over end and landed on the trail, kicking up a small cloud of dust. Miller shouted, "Stop shooting, goddamn it! I'm coming out."

He stepped out cautiously from behind the log and inched his way up the embankment to the trail, his eyes fixed on Kinslow, except for the odd glance downward to see where he was going. When he reached the trail, he stopped and squinted at Kinslow. He still wasn't sure who he was dealing with. "Woodrow, is that really you?" he asked, tentatively.

Kinslow gave Miller a quick once over. There was nothing extraordinary about the man. He had an average build and was of average height, maybe five foot ten, or so. He was attired in well worn dungarees supported with suspenders overtop a pair of red long-johns. A weather beaten sheepskin coat and a hat that looked like it had gone through a cattle stampede, completed the ensemble. His face, covered in a healthy set of whiskers, was as weathered as his coat.

"Hands in the air, I said!" emphasized Kinslow.

Miller's arms flew up, exposing the old Navy Colt pistol tucked in his pants.

"Take that pistol out very slowly with two fingers of your left hand and toss it. Do it quick, or I'll shoot you where you stand," ordered Kinslow.

Miller took the pistol out and threw it to the ground.

"Hit the dirt! Face down! Hands behind your back and do it now!" commanded Kinslow.

Miller didn't hesitate. Down he went, as ordered. Kinslow hurried to the prone man and took up a position astride him. With his rifle in one hand, he padded Miller down with the other, in search of a hidden pistol or knife. Finding nothing, he stepped around in front of Miller and ordered him up.

Miller rose, dusted himself off with his hat, looked at Kinslow, and said, "God, I'm sorry Woodrow. I didn't know it was you, I swear! I'd never have —"

"You always shoot first and then make acquaintance?" interjected Kinslow.

"It's not like that at all, Woodrow. They're out to kill me and I thought you was one of 'em. I swear, as God is my witness," replied Miller, almost pleading.

"Whoa, whoa, slow down. Who's trying to kill you and why?" asked Kinslow, softening his tone somewhat.

"Rancher named Birk," replied Miller and then changing the subject, he said, "Listen, I'm stove up in a line shack just around the corner, yonder. Why don't we go down and talk. Beans are warm and the coffee's hot. What do ya say?"

Kinslow thought for a moment. He always trusted his gut and now it told him this wasn't a trap. He looked back up the ridge, gave a shrill, two-fingered whistle, and hollered, "Knothead." A big chestnut bay appeared and trotted over to him. Kinslow picked up Miller's pistol and rifle. The six shooter, he stuck in his belt. The rifle, he emptied and tossed back to Miller. He picked up the cartridges, mounted his horse, and said, "Lead on."

They had gone about a hundred yards when the trail took a sharp ninety degree turn to the left. Another two hundred yards brought them to a sloping meadow with a ramshackle cabin in the middle. It was a typical line shack used in roundups, covered with clapboard and shingles, which kept out most of the rain and wind.

On one side of the building was an extension with a roof and no walls where horses were fed and kept. Miller's pinto was tethered there. Kinslow dismounted, removed the two rails in the gate of the make shift corral, and scooted the bay inside. Normally, he would have taken the saddle and gear off, but he wasn't planning on staying long. He could go for something warm to eat and coffee sure sounded good. Besides, his curiosity was aroused about this man he hadn't seen in over a dozen years.

Kinslow followed Miller into the shack. His hunter's eye for detail took in the interior in one glance. It was one big room with a wood stove in the middle, double bunk beds against one of the walls, a plank table, four wooden chairs, and various tools and utensils hanging on the walls; traps for varmints, shoeing irons, several ropes, an axe, a buck saw, and harnesses in various stages of disrepair.

"Set yourself down," said Miller, motioning to the table. Then he fed the stove two pieces of wood and he stirred, what Kinslow assumed, were the beans. He reached up to the warming shelf, took down two tin cups, and with the other hand lifted the coffee pot from the back of the stove. He set a cup in front of Kinslow and the other across the table. As he poured the coffee, he said, "Hope you take it black. Ain't got no sugar or such."

Kinslow didn't respond. He watched Miller as a hawk might watch a potential prey. Miller poured his own coffee, set the pot back on the rear of the stove, and sat down across from Kinslow. After a momentary pause, Kinslow said, "Well, let's have it."

"What? Oh yeah. Well, I thought you was one of Birk's men and you found me. I was just defendin' myself, is all," Miller said, almost as a matter of fact.

He looked into Kinslow's eyes and gave a quick downward jerk of his head. The nod was an exclamation point that said, "*And that's that!*" He took a long pull on his coffee, got up, took a pair of tin plates from the shelf above the stove, and set them on the table. He picked up the pot of beans and doled out generous helpings on each plate. He dropped a spoon on top of Kinslow's food and then, in one continuous motion, took his place again and began shovelling the beans in, as if he hadn't eaten in a week.

As he continued to watch Miller closely, Kinslow took a bite of the beans, which turned out to be surprisingly good. He hadn't quite made up his mind about Miller's story, and he needed more information. "Keep going. I want to hear the whole thing. What sort of trouble are you in?" he asked.

Miller stopped eating, looked up at Kinslow, and replied, curtly, "Trouble? No trouble! Try to be neighbourly and look what it gets you!" He returned his attention to his food.

Kinslow was getting annoyed with the run around. "Look, give me some straight answers, or I will let you explain to the local law why you tried to bushwhack a U.S. marshal."

Miller looked up from his plate and grinned. "Federal marshal, eh? You've come a long way since Abilene, Woodrow. Last I recall, you was just a snot-nosed deputy."

"That was a long time ago," retorted Kinslow. "Looks like things haven't changed much for you. You're still looking over your shoulder for someone on your trail!"

Miller, having finished his beans, pushed the plate into the middle of the table, tipped his hat back, and said, "I still owe ya for savin' my hide back then. I ain't forgot, but it don't give you no call to badmouth me."

"Sorry, didn't mean for it to come out like that. Calm down and tell me the whole story from the beginning," Kinslow said as he sat back in his chair, prepared to listen.

Miller was speaking but Kinslow wasn't hearing him. His mind had drifted back to the time in Abilene when he had pulled Ansen Miller out of the clutches of three drunks that would have beat him to death if he hadn't interfered.

"Marshal? Kinslow — are you listenin'?" asked Miller, interrupting Kinslow's trip down memory lane.

"Oh, I'm sorry," apologized Kinslow. "What were you saying?"

"I was sayin' it weren't my fault. It was an accident."

"What wasn't your fault?"

"Killin' the Birk kid. It was an accident."

Kinslow shook his head and said, "Slow down. Start over from the beginning and don't leave anything out."

Miller sighed and began again, "I was checkin' fence, day before yesterday. I got a little place down by the river, about forty acres. Butts right up to Birk's spread. That son-of-a-bitch owns most of the valley and he is begrudgin' me my little scrap of dirt." There was a momentary pause, as if Miller was deep in thought, and then he continued. "Anyway, I come across a downed calf. It had the Birk brand on it. The bastards cut my fences again and the calf was all tangled in the barbed wire.

"I just got the poor thing untangled when up ride the Birk boys, Andy and Mark. Andy, the younger one, asks me what the hell I was doin'. I look up and tell him to get off his ass and help me, seein' how it was their calf and how it was them what cut the wire in the first place. Mark, the older one, says somethin' about teachin' me some manners. He charges at me. I sidesteps, reaches up, and pulls him off his horse. Well sir, we both go down, me on the bottom and the youngin' on top.

"I realized right away somethin' was wrong, 'cause he weren't movin'. I crawled out from under him and what I saw caused me to leave my breakfast right there. The kid went head first into a busted fence post and the splintered end went through his throat. He was bleedin' like a stuck pig."

There was a long pause. It seemed to Kinslow that Miller was through talking. "So, what did you do next?" he asked, prompting Miller into telling more.

"After I got my head about me again, I pulled the young lad off the post and laid him down on his back. Woodrow, he looked up me with the saddest look I have ever seen. I think he knowed he was gonna die and he was scared as all get out. I killed him, Woodrow! I killed him!"

"Sure sounds like it was an accident to me. Nobody can lay blame on you," said Kinslow, trying to be convincing.

"That ain't the way Birk sees it. I killed his boy and he means to do the same to me," replied Miller.

"So, you take to the hills, set to bushwhack anyone that comes your way!" said Kinslow.

"Well, what in hell would you have done?" retorted Miller, rather indignant. "Come on, Mr. Big-shot Marshal, what do I do now?"

"Let the law handle it," replied Kinslow, just as indignant. "And since I represent the law, I guess that'd be my job!" He waited for a reply from Miller, but none was forthcoming. Kinslow continued, "I'm expected in Greeley. Picking up a prisoner for transport. You'll come with me to get him and then we'll all head to Fort Collins. There's a territorial judge there and we can tell him your story."

Miller shook his head and replied, "No. No, I ain't goin' nowhere where Birk and his men can get at me. I'll stick it out right here, thank you very much!"

Kinslow leaned in towards Miller and said, firmly, "I'm not giving you a choice. You are coming with me. Now get saddled. We can still make a lot of miles before dark."

Chapter 2

Several days before Ansen Miller took a shot at Kinslow, Johnathan Birk was leaning against a corral rail, watching one of his wranglers trying to gentle a feisty mare.

"Marks dead! Mark's dead! He killed Mark!"

He turned his head in the direction of his son's voice. He thought he'd heard Andy shouting that Mark, his older son, was dead. His mind told him this couldn't be true. Andy was either drunk, or was out in the sun too long. Likely as not, Mark's horse threw him, perhaps knocking him unconscious and Andy had panicked. Mark was fine and walking back to the ranch right now, cursing out Andy for riding off and leaving him. Dead? Not a chance!

As Andy Birk galloped his mount towards the corral, he was met by his father, who grabbed the reins and said, "What the hell are you yelling about? Make some sense!"

"Pa! Pa! That sodbuster, Miller — he's killed Mark! I saw it with my own eyes! Mark's dead, Pa!"

"Get off the goddamn horse and stop talking crazy. I swear if this is some kind of prank."

"Ain't no prank, Pa. Mark's dead!" Andy insisted.

Johnathan Birk was a full six foot four, lean and lanky and most of it was legs. As soon as Andy dismounted, he put his hands on the boy's shoulders, looked into his eyes, and said, "Now Andy, take a deep breath. Take two, if you need to, but slow down and tell me exactly what happened." He was still convinced Mark was alright.

Andy took two deep breaths. Johnathan loosened his grip on the boy's shoulders and Andy began to relate his news. "We was checking the south section along the river, Pa. We was at the crossing and we looked over and we see Miller cutting a calf. He must have seen us coming 'cause he had a shotgun pointed at us when we come up on him, so we had no chance to draw our pistols. He told us to throw our guns in the dirt. Mark was gonna have no part of it and he spurred his horse at him. Miller shot him with both barrels, Pa. Damn near blew his head off! I didn't have my gun and he was reloading the shotgun, so I hightailed it back here as fast as I could. We gotta go back and get him, Pa!"

Johnathan Birk started barking orders to several men who were within earshot, "— and you, Willie, get my horse saddled and bring it to the porch, pronto!"

He crossed the forty feet between the corral and the ranch house in a dozen long strides. Inside, he got a Winchester from the rifle cabinet in the foyer and his Colt Peacemaker and holster from the oak desk in his study. He loaded the rifle and the ammunition belt from the boxes in the desk drawer, strapped on the holster, and headed for the door. "Got business, Maria. Don't hold supper," he said to his housekeeper, not knowing or caring whether she heard him or not.

Out on the veranda, he scanned the yard and bellowed, "Willie, where's my goddamn horse?" A second later, one of the ranch hands came out of the barn, leading a big black stallion. Johnathan stepped off the veranda, strode to the waiting horse, and mounted, all in one swift motion. He looked at Andy and said in a commanding tone, "Let's go see what the hell happened. Lead the way."

It was a good mile or so to the south pastures that ran alongside the river. Both of them rode in silence. Andy was still in a state of shock and Johnathan's mind wouldn't let him believe his older son was dead. *Andy was wrong. Fool kid doesn't know what he saw. Yeah, that's it. It had to be. It just had to be,* he thought, denying the worst.

Johnathan thought about the day his darling Cora gave birth to their first son, Mark. What a glorious day that was, full of celebration, with drinks and cigars all around. Not so with Andy, two years later. Cora died in childbirth. Complications the doctor called it. Complications, hell! The quack was drunk and his beloved Cora had bled to death. He came very close to killing the doctor and if it wasn't for some friends physically restraining him, he just might have.

He told himself he never blamed Andy for Cora's death, but throughout the years he never held the same feeling for Andy as he did for Mark. Outwardly, he treated the boys the same, but inside he felt affection for Mark that he just didn't have for Andy.

After Cora's passing, he devoted all his energies to the ranch. He took a dozen sections of Colorado wilderness and turned them into one of the finest and most respected cattle ranches in the territory. The name Johnathan Birk carried a lot of respect and weight in this part of the country.

A few years ago, the Government opened the range that bordered on the south end of his land for homesteading. There were a few minor skirmishes with some of the homesteaders who decided to set up shop in places that they weren't supposed to. Birk had the power and the guns to chase them off his prime land. He lost a couple hundred acres south of the South Platte River, but the huge majority of his land, north of the river, was not designated for homesteads and the squatters soon got the message that if they stayed on the south side of the river, they would have no trouble with Johnathan Birk.

Once the boys were old enough, they took on the physical work of running a big spread. They oversaw the fence checking, the roundups, and the branding, while Johnathan ran the business end. Mark felt the sodbusters were still a class below ranchers and at every opportunity he harassed them with little things such as cutting their fences and riding on their land to look for strays. This often led to confrontation, but until now nothing serious had happened.

Johnathan thought he knew Ansen Miller. He wasn't the friendliest man in the world, but he never caused Johnathan any grief. He had set up a small place adjacent to the south end of the Birk ranch, with the upper waters of the South Platte River between them. Not that the river was any deterrent. Most of the summer you could ride across it and not get your feet wet, but it was a well defined border and served its purpose, until now.

"Down there Pa! — Pa, ya hear me?"

The sound of Andy's voice brought Johnathan's focus back to the present. They were atop a bank that gently sloped to the river some twenty feet below. Johnathan quickly surveyed the area for any sign of his older son. Mark's roan was across the river grazing and Johnathan thought he saw someone or something on the ground nearby.

He spurred his horse hard and it took off down the embankment and across the shallow river at full gallop. As he came up and over the south bank, Johnathan could see Mark laying face up, some ten feet away, near the fence. He wasn't moving and the large red puddle around his neck and shoulders sent a shiver through Johnathan. His instincts told him the worse, but his rational mind still refused to believe what he saw.

He dismounted and was at Mark's side in one swift motion. He put his ear to the boy's chest and listened hopefully for a heartbeat. There was none. As he lifted Mark's head, it tilted backwards exposing the gaping hole in his throat. He hugged the boy close and emitted a low guttural sound like a cat growling which slowly escalated into a full fledged scream of unabated anguish.

Jonathan was still shouting "No! No!" through clenched teeth, when the sound of Andy's horse caught his attention. He turned and glared up at his younger son, who in his entire life had never seen his father so angry.

"See, Pa. It's just like I told you. He —"

"You say Ansen Miller did this?" interrupted Johnathan.

"Yes Sir, I saw it with my own eyes," said Andy, anxiously awaiting the next question.

"With a shotgun?"

"Yes Sir," replied Andy, his lower lip quivering.

"That's a mighty big hole, even for a shotgun," Johnathan said with a questioning tone.

He laid his dead son's head back on the ground, rose up, and began inspecting the area. Thirty year's experience tracking wayward cattle, cunning cougars, and wily wolves taught him to read sign well and quickly. He noticed there been a lot of activity in the immediate area around Mark's body. His eye caught the splintered fence post with blood on it.

He thought for a moment, looked up at Andy, and asked, "You ain't lying to me, are you, boy?"

"No, Pa! I swear to God! Miller shot Mark and run off like the coward that he is!"

Johnathan mulled it over in his mind for a moment. The sign he was reading and the facts, according to Andy, didn't seem to fit. For instance, if Miller was butchering a calf, where was the blood or other signs indicating it happened? Johnathan also noticed Andy's pistol was in his holster and not on the ground, like he claimed. But it didn't matter. Someone had killed his son and that someone was going to pay for it, by God. "Get back to the ranch and tell Willie to come with a buckboard and blankets. Don't kill your horse getting there, either. We're in no hurry now," he said.

Andy broke Johnathan's gaze, turned his horse, and disobeying his father, spurred it into a gallop. Johnathan watched him ride out of sight, shook his head, and looked down at his dead son once more. "Jesus, Mark! What did you do now?" he said to the body on the ground. Looking towards the sky, he said, "God, I'm so sorry Cora. I'm doing the best I can."

He stood looking around for a moment and his eyes welled up with tears. He decided on his next move. *Maybe that son-of-a-*

bitch, who murdered Mark, is at home and I can settle it right now, he thought. He mounted and rode southwest along the fence line towards Miller's place, which was about a half mile upstream from the crossing.

Johnathan never pushed his horses hard unless it was absolutely necessary. This felt like one of those times and in a few short minutes he was in a grove of aspen, about a hundred yards from Miller's farmyard. He took a long look around and saw that everything seemed quiet, maybe too quiet. He edged his mount out from the cover of the trees and slowly rode towards the farmhouse, checking in all directions for any sign of movement. As he got closer, he could see a woman hanging clothes on a line. He stopped and carefully looked all around, again. There was nothing but a mangy mutt asleep on the porch and a few hens scratching in the dirt.

He rode into the yard and as the woman looked up, he touched his hat brim and said, "Ma'am".

"Saw you come out of the trees. What can I do for you, Mr. Birk?" Beth Miller asked, without stopping her work.

"Well, I was hoping to see your husband. Got some business I need to discuss with him," Johnathan replied as he turned in the saddle and looked around once more.

"Don't expect him back 'till dark. He's out checking fences. Seems like a lot of them is fallen down lately, like the wire was cut or something. 'Course, you wouldn't know anything about it, would you, Mr. Birk?" she said, with a hint of sarcasm.

"No, I wouldn't," he stated emphatically. He leaned forward in the saddle for effect and said through clenched teeth, "Tell your murdering husband I've got business with him. Killin' business." He turned the stallion's neck sharply, spurred him once, and trotted off the way he had come.

When she was sure Birk had left, she called out, "He's gone, Ansen. You can come out now."

Ansen Miller emerged from the outhouse, rifle in hand, and said, "I told you he wasn't gonna listen to reason. Does he sound like he thinks it was an accident? He wants my hide and he aims to get it."

"What are we going to do, Ansen?" she asked as she curled her arms around him and held him close.

"I don't know, Bethy. I just don't know," he said. "I need some time to think. I saw an old line shack over near Hansen's Ridge. It's on the old trail that goes over the pass. Nobody uses it any more since they built the stage road. I'll hole up there for a few days until Birk calms down and I can think my way out of this mess."

"But — but, Ansen. What if they come back here?"

"Just stick to the story, Bethy. You ain't seen me and you're gettin' worried."

"Alright, Ansen. I can do that."

"Good girl. Now, let's get me some grub."

Chapter 3

"Mister Marshal, Sir — do you think we could stop long enough to relieve the pressure on these old kidneys of mine?" asked Miller, his tone dripping with sarcasm.

"Sure, the horses could use a rest," answered Kinslow, not letting himself get caught up in Miller's foul mood. "That looks like a good place just ahead," he added, as he pointed to a spot where the trail widened out.

Once he was in the open area, Miller dismounted quickly and scurried to the privacy of a clump of willows to do his business. Kinslow dismounted, loosened his horse's cinch, reached into a saddle bag, and brought out a large carrot. He broke it into two pieces, giving his horse the larger half. He loosened the cinch on Miller's mount and gave it the other piece of carrot.

Miller came out of the willows, buttoning up his pants. "Ah, that sure feels better," he remarked.

Kinslow looked up from the cigarette he was rolling, licked the paper and pulled the draw string of the tobacco pouch closed with his teeth. He tossed it to Miller and said, "Have a quick smoke and we'll get going."

"Why are you in such an all fired hurry?" Miller asked.

"I gave my word to Sheriff Claxton that I would be there today and I like to keep my word. It's just the way I am."

Kinslow finished his cigarette, threw the butt on the ground, and squashed the embers dead with his heel. He retighten his horse's cinch and said to Miller, "Cinch up and let's get going."

Miller took a long pull on his just-lit smoke and threw the rest of it into the dirt in disgust.

They rode in relative silence with just the occasional complaint about his sore back voiced by Miller. Kinslow liked to think when he rode. He believed Miller's story and he would make sure Miller got to tell it to the judge in Fort Collins. Johnathan Birk worried him, though. He had seen it a dozen times before; men who tamed the country, fought hostiles, predators, and weather to carve out a place for themselves and when civilization caught up to them, they protected what was theirs, the only way they knew how, with tenacity and force. As often as not, they either were the law, or they took the law into their own hands. Miller, without a doubt, would have had a date with a rope or a bullet if he hadn't come along.

"How did you end up here, Ansen? It's a long way from Abilene," Kinslow asked, with genuine interest.

"Why do you care?" replied a disgruntled Miller.

"Don't, all that much. Just making conversation," Kinslow remarked, as he gently spurred his horse and rode ahead of Miller.

Miller wasn't exactly proud of his life for the past twenty years. He drifted for most of it, working as a ranch hand, prospector, trapper, a flunky on a river boat and the list went on. Four years ago, he had hooked up with a wagon train headed for Oregon as a hunter and scout. Here, he met Beth, his future bride-to-be, and she and Ansen hit it off right away.

Miller had gone to Denver for supplies where he heard about the Government giving away land. He quit his job. He and Beth were married and they registered a homestead adjacent to Johnathan Birk's property.

Miller caught up to Kinslow and said, "Sorry, I don't mean to be such a miserable son-of-a-bitch." I been doin' a lot of things, since Abilene. Got married about four years back and like I said before, my place is about ten miles southeast of where you and I got reacquainted, right next to Birk's place. Birk was pretty angry about havin' neighbours, but as long as we stayed on the south side of the river, he left us pretty much alone. It wasn't until them youngin's of his grew up that the trouble started."

"What kind of trouble?" Kinslow asked.

"There's three of us got places that butt up against the river. Well sir, the grass along the stream is pretty lush, so when the Birk cattle ate up all there was on their side of the river, the boys decided to help themselves to the grass on our side. They cut our fences and run our cattle off so theirs could graze. I went to see old man Birk about it a few times. He said he'd look into it, but nothin' was ever done."

"You should have gone to the law," said Kinslow.

"Can't afford to be away from the place for two days at a time and besides, it wouldn't do any good. Birk has got the law around here in his hip pocket," Miller retorted.

Kinslow gave him a puzzled look, decided not to push the issue, and turned his attention to the trail in front of him.

About two miles ahead was a row of low rolling hills. Kinslow remembered the town of Greeley was just over the crest. The town was typical of many small communities in the west. They all had a main street with false front buildings. There were usually a couple of hotels, several saloons, a mercantile, a blacksmith shop, a livery stable, and the stock yards, of course. They usually had a church, which doubled as the town hall. They all had a sheriff's office with a jail in the back and a graveyard marked *Boothill.*

As they rode down the main street, Kinslow thought how, after awhile, these towns all started to look the same. The sheriff's office was most of the way down the street, next to the dry goods store. Kinslow and Miller dismounted in front of it, tied their horses to the rail, and went inside. It was a dusty, one-room space with a big wood stove in the center of the room and a couple of cells with large steel bars off to one side, each containing a small cot adorned with only a stained mattress. A man was standing in the far cell, looking out through a tiny window.

Off to the right of the cell area was a huge oak desk littered with papers, dirty dishes, and a partially dismantled rifle. Behind the desk sat Jed Claxton, reading one of those dime novels Kinslow had no use for. He looked up as the door opened, squinted, recognized Kinslow, sprang up, and stepped towards him. He started to extend his right hand, withdrew it, and wiped it several times on his shirt front before offering it again.

"Woodrow Kinslow, sure good to see you and right on time, as always," Claxton said, as he shook Kinslow's hand. Seeing Miller, he asked, "And who is this — your deputy?"

"No, ah — no, he's just riding along to Fort Collins," Kinslow replied, as he glanced at Miller. The look on Kinslow's face told Miller to keep his mouth shut. Miller merely nodded and tipped his hat towards the sheriff.

Claxton stared at Miller and said, "Big rancher name of Birk is in town lookin' for a fella who looks a lot like you. What'd you say your name was?"

Miller didn't answer. After an uncomfortable pause, Claxton motioned in the direction of the cells and said, "This here fine looking gentleman is Max Boudreaux. He's a half breed Ute and a cold blooded killer. Cut a young man's privates off and then slit his throat for good measure."

Kinslow took a few steps towards the cell and quickly looked Boudreaux over. Their eyes met and they stared at each other for the longest time. "Have him ready to travel at sunup," Kinslow ordered, as he turned and headed for the door.

Once outside, Miller caught up to the long legged Kinslow and said, "I think he knows who I am."

"Nothing to fret about," replied Kinslow. "I could use some supper and a drink. How 'bout you?"

"I wouldn't say no to either," replied Miller.

"Let's see to these horses first," Kinslow said. They led their mounts to the livery at the end of the street and turned them over to the owner. Kinslow removed two sets of saddle bags from his horse. He took out two carrots from one of them and told the livery man to give one each to the two horses.

Fitzgerald's Hotel & Dinning Emporium was across the street and a few doors down from the sheriff's office. Kinslow stayed and ate there, whenever he was in town. He never met anyone named Fitzgerald and inquiries about the name of the hotel only brought shrugged shoulders. Kinslow doubted there was such a man. He concluded someone had just picked a name out of a hat.

While Miller waited in the lobby, Kinslow checked them in for the night, took the stairs two at a time, found room number three, opened the door, and dropped his saddlebags inside. He dashed back down the stairs, motioned to Miller, and they both headed into the dining room. Kinslow picked a table in the far corner where he sat with his back to the wall, so he could see everyone and everything in front of him. It wasn't paranoia, simply a good vantage point for observation. Miller sat down to his left.

A skinny, freckle faced kid, about fourteen or fifteen, clad in a food stained apron, approached their table, and said, "We got beef soup, beef steak, beef stew, and apple pie. What'll ya have, gents?"

Kinslow spoke first, "I'll have the steak with some fried onions, a double shot of that horse liniment you call whiskey, and a coffee."

"Sounds good," said Miller. "I'll have the same, but throw in a chunk of apple pie, too."

The waiter went behind the bar, filled two glasses with generous shots of whiskey, brought them to the table, and set them down without breaking stride, as he headed for the kitchen.

Miller picked up his glass, tipped it towards Kinslow, and toasted, "Here's to those who wish us well." He knocked back three quarters

Sidetracked

of the drink, set the glass down, and looked at Kinslow as if he was expecting the marshal to do the same.

Kinslow took a sip of his drink, swished it around, swallowed it, and returned Miller's gaze. "What's on your mind, Ansen?" he asked.

"Nothin'. Just can't figure you out. You've helped me again and I'm not sure why. Lawmen in these parts usually don't do that sort of thing."

"All lawmen should enforce the letter of the law, but it doesn't mean they can't use the common sense the good Lord gave them to temper the law with justice," Kinslow answered, as he took another sip. "Take your case. I believe your story, but the law says there is a death to account for. We are going to Fort Collins to do just that. It is also my duty to see you get there alive."

"Well, I am in your debt and I give you my word, you'll have no trouble from me," Miller said with sincerity. He smiled at Kinslow, finished his drink, wiped his mouth with his sleeve, and scanned the restaurant for the waiter. He was thinking another drink sure would go down real nice.

They small-talked about ranching, homesteading, horses, and law enforcement for about fifteen minutes when the waiter, who was probably the cook as well, emerged with their steaks. He set the plates down and scurried off to the kitchen again. He came out a few seconds later with a coffee pot, two cups, and a huge slab of apple pie, all on a tray. As the waiter poured their coffee, Miller requested another whiskey. He looked to Kinslow for approval, who nodded '*yes*' and smiled.

They both ate hungrily and in relative silence. They had just finished their steaks and Miller was starting on his pie, when movement out in the lobby caught Kinslow's attention. He was positioned so he could see everything through the restaurant entrance. The hotel door swung open as five men came in led by a tall, lanky, older gent, who looked all around the lobby and then made his way to the restaurant entrance in three strides and scanned the interior. He was followed by Sheriff Claxton and what Kinslow thought were three cowhands, but one of them seemed rather young.

The tall man saw Kinslow and Miller and came straight to their table with his entourage in tow. He set his knuckles on the edge of the table, leaned in toward Miller, and said, "Here you are, you murdering scum." He turned to Sheriff Claxton and said, "Take him to the jail. We'll hang him in the morning."

Before Claxton could take his first step, Kinslow spoke, "He's not going anywhere. He is my prisoner and I'll be taking him to Fort Collins."

"Like hell!" Birk said, as he drew his pistol. "He is a murdering son-of-a-bitch and we can take care of him right here and now."

Andy Birk and Jed Claxton followed the older Birk's action and drew their guns. The two cow hands looked at one another, thought it would be best to back the boss's play, and drew their pistols as well. Miller slid his chair sideways so he was facing Birk and slowly lifted his hands.

Kinslow didn't flinch. He took a sip of his coffee, looked Birk right in the eyes, and said, "I'm only going to say this one more time — the man is my prisoner. I am a U.S. marshal and I have jurisdiction. You are interfering with a federal case and subject to arrest yourself. Isn't that right, Sheriff Claxton?"

The deflection worked beautifully. All eyes were on Claxton, who mumbled and stumbled and managed to say, "Uh, well — I don't know — you see. It's —"

The click of Kinslow's pistol being cocked brought everyone's attention back to him. Johnathan Birk began to say, "Now, look —"

He was immediately cut off by Kinslow, "I hear one click of a hammer going back and I'll shoot you where you stand, Birk." He turned his gaze to Claxton and added, "And you're next." He shifted his eyes back to Birk and then spoke in the direction of Andy and the two cowhands, "And I'm pretty sure I'll get a least one, or maybe even two of you."

Birk stood for a moment, wavering. Kinslow knew he was deciding whether to chance it, or not. Kinslow eased his left hand to the edge of the table. His mind was already formulating his next move which was to shoot Birk first, put another quick one in Claxton, tip the table over, use it as a shield, and make his play with the other three. A split second before Kinslow was ready to put his plan into action, Birk lowered his gun and put it back in his holster. The others glanced at one another briefly and followed suit.

"Alright, I'll fold this hand, but the game ain't over. No sir, not by a long shot," Birk said, with a bit of quiver in his voice. "I'm offering a thousand dollars to the man who kills Ansen Miller. He'll never make it to Fort Collins! When the word gets out, there will be enough gunslingers and bounty hunters on your trail to make sure the job gets done."

Kinslow stood up, smiled, shook his head, and spoke "Mr. Birk, I just told you if you interfered with me, you would be subject to arrest. One shot! Anybody takes one shot at me on the way to Fort Collins and when I am through I will come back here with an arrest warrant for you and I don't care if I take you dead or alive. It will be up to you. Do I make myself clear?"

Birk replied, "You're a tough man, Kinslow. I don't doubt you mean what you say, but my son is dead." Pointing to Miller, he continued, "That man killed him and I aim to see justice done."

"Justice? Sounds like vengeance to me. He's going to Fort Collins to present his case to a judge. That's how justice works," retorted Kinslow. "In fact, why don't you tag along, Mr. Birk? I'm sure the judge would like to hear your side of the story."

"My side of the story is quite simple. That pig farmer gets caught butchering my calf on my property. My boy Mark steps up to stop him and gets both barrels of a shotgun in the throat for his trouble. Hanging offence, plain and simple," replied Birk, without any emotion.

Miller, who had been a silent observer in the action to this point, jumped up from his chair, kicking it backwards as he rose. He took a step towards Birk before speaking, "You lyin' skunk. That calf was caught in the wire your boys cut in the first place. I was tryin' to get it loose, dagnab it. Shotgun? Hell, I don't even own one. The boy tried to run me down. I pulled him off his horse and he fell face first into a busted fence post. It was an accident, goddamn it." He pointed to Andy and continued, "Just ask the boy, there. He saw it all. He'll tell you what happened."

Birk replied, the distain apparent in his voice, "He already has."

Realization hit Miller, "Why you lyin' little —"

Before Miller could do anything stupid, Kinslow fired a shot into the floor. All eyes turned to him and he said, "Looks like we got two different stories, here. Sure sounds like something for a judge to work out, don't it?"

Birk stared at Kinslow. For a moment, Kinslow thought he was going to go for his gun, but instead Birk turned to his son, gave him a very stern look and then barked, "Let's go!" He marched out of the restaurant, through the hotel lobby, and outside with the rest of his troop right behind him.

Ansen Miller turned to Kinslow and said, pleadingly, "I didn't murder the boy, Woodrow. That kid is lyin'. I swear on my dear Bethy's life."

Kinslow replied, as he holstered his gun, "I believe you. Let's get you to the judge. Birk has an opportunity to bring the boy to testify, but I'll bet you a steak dinner he won't. I'll give the judge my deposition and everything should be fine."

"Thanks for everything, Woodrow. I mean it," said Miller.

"Don't thank me yet," said Kinslow. "We still have to get there. Now, let's get some shuteye."

They left the restaurant and climbed the hotel stairs to the second floor. Once inside the room, Kinslow noticed Miller glancing at the single bed with a look of concern. "You get the floor," said Kinslow with a grin. "Expenses only cover a single room. The steak and pie you ate for supper ran us out of money for the day."

Outside the hotel, Johnathan had Andy's shirt front in his big fists. They were face to face and Johnathan glared at the boy with bulging eyes and reddening face. Andy was convinced he was about to get the beating of his life.

Johnathan spoke slowly and deliberately, "I think you're lying, boy, but it's no matter now. We got to finish this thing." He relaxed his grip on Andy and continued, "You ride for the ranch just as hard as you can go. Get Willie out of bed and tell him I need extra mounts for five men and provisions for a week. Bring Sanchez. We'll need him for any tracking we might have to do. With some hard riding, you should be back here by mid morning. Don't you dally. In fact, don't you even stop for a piss! You hear me?" He shoved the boy in the direction of the livery then turned and headed across the street to the Gold Dust Saloon.

Chapter 4

Kinslow woke to the soft morning light, seeping through the tiny pinholes in the green canvas window blind. He stretched his legs, arched his shoulders and back, cranked his neck, and sat up, groaning. As he looked around the room, his memory kicked in and told him when and where he was. He tossed what passed for a pillow at his roommate, catching him in the head. Miller moaned, sat up, rubbed his eyes, and grumbled, "What time is it? Feels like the middle of the night."

Pulling on his boots, Kinslow said, "Time to get going. We're wasting daylight."

"Next time, I get the bed. This sleepin' on the floor is for younger fellas. It causes a terrible ache in my old bones," complained Miller as he threw Kinslow's pillow and the one he was using back at him.

"It's all good training. We'll be sleeping on the ground for the next few nights with only a ground sheet and a blanket with a saddle for a pillow. I could sing you a lullaby, if it would help," Kinslow said, turning his head so Miller couldn't see his devilish grin.

Kinslow reached under the pillow that was still on the bed and pulled out a small calibre, four barrel, single shot derringer called a pepperbox. The idea being, when the trigger was pulled, all four barrels went off at once. It was very effective for maximum damage at short range. He tucked the derringer inside his vest pocket, making sure Miller didn't notice. He stood, retrieved his gun belt from the bedpost, and strapped it on. He picked up his saddle bags from the corner of the room, took out a pistol, and tossed it to Miller, who was still sitting on the floor.

Miller looked up in surprise. "Why — why this is my gun. What the hell?"

"You're going to need it, if you are going to be my deputy," said Kinslow, trying to hide a smile.

"Deputy? I don't understand," replied Miller, even more surprised.

"Look Ansen, I have given this a lot of thought. You may not want the job, but I see it this way; anyone Birk hires is less likely to try something if we let it be known you are my deputy. The other reason is a selfish one. It ain't easy watching two prisoners on the trail. I'd rather have you with me than against me. If that doesn't suit you, I can leave you in Claxton's jail while I take Max Boudreaux to Fort Collins and then come back for you. I don't think I can guarantee your safety under those circumstances. Guess you could say we need each other."

Miller thought briefly and replied, "You're sure takin' a chance on me. Yeah, I'll back your play, but I trust you to set this Birk thing right with the judge."

"You have my word on it," Kinslow said, as he extended his hand. "You also have my promise if you cross me, I won't hesitate to shoot you."

Miller stood up, accepted Kinslow's hand, and said with sincerity, "You've got my word, Woodrow."

Kinslow added, "Besides, it pays fifty cents a day plus expenses. Next hotel, you get your own room."

Miller laughed, as he said, "That alone is worth it, if I don't have to listen to you snore."

Kinslow wondered if he was doing the right thing to trust Miller. His gut told him he'd made the right decision. He didn't need any help taking the prisoner to Fort Collins, something Miller didn't need to know.

Kinslow took something else from his saddle bags, picked up the Bible from the small table by the bed, held it out to Miller, and said, "Put your left hand on the Bible and raise your right hand." Kinslow waited for Miller to do so and then continued, "Do you swear to uphold the laws of the United States of America and to carry out your duties as a duly appointed officer of the law, to the best of your abilities, so help you God?"

Miller, grinning from ear to ear, took the oath. Kinslow pinned an oval badge on his shirt front and shook his hand once more in congratulations.

"A lawman! Don't that beat all," beamed Miller. "Now, how's about some breakfast? On my expenses, of course!"

"Breakfast will have to wait. We need to get geared up to go," responded Kinslow.

"No coffee?" Miller wasn't smiling any more.

"No coffee," said Kinslow.

"Bad state of affairs when a man can't have a cup of coffee first thing in the mornin'," muttered Miller, as he pulled on his boots and rolled up his bedding.

A few minutes later, they were out on the street headed for the livery. Fred Larson, the livery man, a big, bulky Swede, was forking hay when Kinslow and Miller approached. Larson took a break by leaning on his pitchfork and said with a heavy accent, "You'll be wanting your horses, I think. They are just finishing up their morning feed."

"At least somebody's gettin' fed," mumbled Miller.

Kinslow ignored him and said to Larson, "I didn't expect to see you up this early, Fred. I'm glad I didn't have to wake you."

"No sense wasting daylight," said Larson.

Miller looked at Larson and interjected before Kinslow could respond, "You sure you two ain't related?"

Kinslow and Larson both looked at each other confused and then Kinslow caught the inference, shook his head, and got back to the business at hand. "Yes thanks, Fred. We've come for our mounts. I'd also like to rent a mule and some packs. How much would it cost?"

"Depends how long you want them for and where you are headed," replied the Swede.

"Going to Fort Collins. Three days, if I'm lucky. Four would be a better bet," said Kinslow.

Larson lifted his head and looked skyward, as if he was looking for an answer to come from above. After a moment he lowered his head and said to Kinslow, "Way I see it, a fair price would be two bits a day for the mule and a nickel a day for the packs. For eight days, that comes to two dollars and forty cents. Another fifty cents you owe me for putting up your horses over night, brings it up to two dollars and ninety cents. Make it an even three dollars and I'll throw in some feed for the trip. Since I know you and trust you, I'll wave the five dollar deposit."

"Eight days? I said four," objected Kinslow.

"You have to bring the mule back. That's another four days," reminded Larson.

Kinslow gave Miller a look of embellished astonishment to which Miller shrugged his shoulders and said, "He's got a point."

"You're a big help," remarked Kinslow. He turned to Larson and said, "You should have a mask on if you are going to be robbing people. Is there any way I can leave the mule and packs at Fort Collins for you to pick up?"

"Oh sure, I can do that, but it will cost you more," said Larson.

Kinslow sighed and asked, "How much?"

Larson looked up again. This time Kinslow followed his gaze, just to make sure there really wasn't something up there. Larson lowered his head and said, "That would be a dollar and twenty cents for four days, by our first figuring, fifty cents for your horses for the night and fifty cents a day for me to send a man for the mule. Comes to five dollars and seventy cents. Make it six dollars and I'll throw in all the feed for the trip."

Kinslow stood with his hands on his hips looking at Larson for a moment. He wasn't quite sure if the numbers were right, but he wasn't going to argue. He shook his head and then muttered loud enough for Larson to hear, "Might be cheaper just to buy the goddamn mule."

Larson laughed, hung up the pitchfork, and said to Kinslow, "Could let you have one for seven, maybe eight dollars."

Kinslow replied quickly, "Seven dollars? Throw in the packs and some feed and we have a deal." Before Larson could argue, Kinslow shook his hand and added, "Oh, and I'll need a receipt."

Larson frowned and said, "Mules are in the side corral. I will pick out a good one and we'll get it rigged."

Kinslow took several steps toward the door when he noticed three other horses in the stalls. He turned and asked Larson, "Whose mounts are these?"

"They belong to Johnathan Birk and a couple of his men," Larson replied.

Kinslow said to Miller, "Go give him a hand, will you Ansen? I have something to do in here."

Miller followed Larson out to the corrals while Kinslow carefully examined the horses. He wanted to be able to recognize them from a distance if he needed to. Satisfied, he went outside to the corral and helped Larson and Miller finish with the mule. Kinslow paid Larson, shook his hand, and bid him farewell. They walked the horses and mule to the Greeley Mercantile, a short distance up the street from the livery. Kinslow left Miller holding the animals while he bounded up the stairs to see if the store was open. He tried the handle of the door and was mildly surprised to find it unlocked.

"Tie them up and come on in," he said to Miller as he entered. He quickly gave the place the once over. It was like a hundred other stores he'd seen in just about every town in the territory, filled with everything imaginable, from a huge wood burning stove to the penny candy on the counter.

He didn't see anyone about. He closed the door, took a few steps inside, and spoke aloud, "Hello, — hello. Anyone here?"

A woman stood up from behind the counter. She was very tiny, barely five feet tall. She had greying hair, a blue flowered gingham dress, and spectacles. "Oh my goodness, you startled me," she said, somewhat flustered. "I didn't expect anyone here this early."

Kinslow apologized, even though he wasn't sure what for. He took a crumpled piece of paper out of his shirt pocket and handed it to the little woman. "My name is Woodrow Kinslow, Ma'am. I am a U.S. marshal. Me and my deputy are taking a prisoner to Fort Collins and we'll need provisions for three men for four days, if you please, Ma'am."

"My goodness, so polite. You can stop *Ma'aming* me. My name is Abigail, but you can call me Abby." She took his list and gave it a quick read, "It'll be a few minutes. Help yourself to some coffee. It's on the stove, yonder."

Kinslow was on his way to the stove when Miller came in. He said, "It's going to take a while for the store keep to round up our supplies. There's coffee." He took two tin cups from the heating shelf at the rear of the stove, poured the coffee, and handed one to Miller.

"Thank you," said Miller. He sauntered to the jars of candy on the counter and took a couple of licorice pieces, which he stuffed in his pocket and a peppermint stick, which he used to stir his coffee.

"You paying for those?" asked Kinslow.

"Breakfast! Goes to expenses, don't it?" said Miller.

Kinslow shook his head, "I got a feeling I may regret putting you on as a deputy."

They both sat down at a small table by the stove and talked about the up coming trip. Part way through their second cup of coffee, Abby started piling supplies on the counter. "If you boys are through sitting and jawing, I could use some help here," she said in a school marm tone.

Miller and Kinslow jumped up like scolded school boys and set to work. They brought the goods out from the store room, set them on the counter and while Abby checked them off the list, they took the supplies outside and put them in the packs that were on the mule.

With the packing complete, Kinslow went back into the store to settle the bill. Abby and he went through the list, the usual fare; bacon, jerky, sugar, beans, coffee, flour, tobacco and papers. Abby had thrown in a couple jars of her homemade apple sauce, free of charge, because she thought Kinslow was a nice boy. Kinslow also bought a new coffee pot, two tin cups and a couple of tin plates, some .45 calibre ammunition for his Peacemaker, and some .44 calibre for his Winchester carbine.

"Is that it?" Abby asked.

"My deputy took some licorice and a peppermint stick."

"That will be another three cents."

Kinslow paid Abby, folded and put away the receipt in his right shirt pocket, tipped his hat, and wished her well.

"You boys be careful out there," Abby said, as Kinslow closed the door behind him.

"To the sheriff's office next, I'm guessin'," remarked Miller, as they stepped out of the store.

"Yep," was the only reply.

They walked the animals next door to the sheriff's office and tied them to the rail. This time Kinslow waited for Miller to catch up and said, "Keep your hand on your pistol. If there is anyone in the office other then Claxton, watch my back. I don't trust him."

They entered the office cautiously and much to Miller's relief, there was nobody there but Max Boudreaux in one cell, still looking out the window and Claxton snoring on a cot in the other. Kinslow stamped his feet as he walked toward the sheriff. The noise got Boudreaux's attention, who merely turned and looked at Kinslow, but it had no effect on Claxton. Kinslow kicked the cot several times before Claxton opened his eyes, sat up, and groaned, "Christ, what time is it?"

"Time to get going. Have a late night, did you?" asked Kinslow. He could smell the whiskey on Claxton and he added, "Birk must have been buying."

Claxton looked up and gave him a dirty look. Kinslow waited patiently while he got up, staggered to the wash basin, submerged his face in the cold water, towelled off, and ran his fingers through his matted, greasy hair. When he was done, he checked the potbellied stove for any signs of life. It was stone cold. "Guess coffee will be a while," he remarked.

"It's alright, we won't wait," said Kinslow.

Claxton stretched, yawned, and said with a grin, "Might as well wait, you won't get him," nodding in Miller's direction, "to Fort Collins alive."

It happened so quickly, neither Miller nor Claxton saw it coming. Before the sheriff could utter another word, Kinslow grabbed him and backed him up against the wall. His arms were crossed in front of Claxton's throat and he was crushing the sheriff's windpipe. He brought his face directly in front of Claxton's, so their eyes were level and inches apart. Kinslow stared into the frightened jailer's face for what seemed an eternity before speaking very slowly, "Listen to me you tub of guts. I know you are in Birk's pocket. I'll tell you the same thing I told him, in case he didn't pass it on to you. Anything happens to my deputy, I am coming back for anyone I think might have been responsible and that includes you." He cold-stared into Claxton's eyes for emphasis and then relaxed his hold. "Now, move your fat ass and get my prisoner ready for travel."

Claxton gulped and took a couple of deep breaths. He went to the desk and opened a side drawer. Instinctively, Kinslow's hand went to his pistol. At the same time, he glanced at Miller and saw he already had his pistol drawn and had the sheriff well covered. Claxton's trembling hand came out with a ring of keys and a set of wrist irons. He handed them to Kinslow and said, "All yours."

Kinslow took them, passed the irons to Miller, and said, "Watch him close," indicating Claxton. He unlocked the cell door, ordered Boudreaux out, and had him put his hands behind his back. He told Miller to put the irons on Boudreaux and watched until Miller was done, then ordered Claxton into the cell.

"What? Now wait a minute. You can't do that. I'm the sheriff, damn it," complained Claxton.

Kinslow pushed him into the cell and locked it. As he was turning away, he said, "Oh, one more thing. Where is the prisoner's horse?"

"Horse? He didn't have no horse," replied Claxton.

Kinslow looked at Boudreaux and asked, "That true?"

Boudreaux shook his head *no*.

Back to Claxton, Kinslow said, "Horse thief, too. Charges are starting to add up. You know, you are starting to annoy me. I'll ask you for the last time before I come in there and take you apart, where is the prisoner's horse?"

"In the corral behind the jail. The little paint mare."

"His saddle and gear?"

"In the small shack at the back of the corral. Anything else?"

"Yes, come to think of it. What were the circumstances around this man's crime?"

"He got arrested for murder. Cut a bank clerk's throat."

Kinslow took a deep breath and continued, "And the motive? Why did he do it?"

Claxton shrugged his shoulders, "Don't know. Never asked." He lay down on the cot and turned his face to the wall. "Now, if you'll excuse me, I have some sleep to catch up on."

Miller opened the rifle cabinet and helped himself to a Winchester and a box of .44's. He said to nobody in particular, "I am borrowin' this here rifle in the name of the U.S. Government, bein' a deputy and all. Need it for the job."

Kinslow went to the desk, rummaged about until he found a pencil and a piece of paper, and wrote out an I.O.U. for the rifle and ammunition. He said to Miller, "We don't borrow anything. We pay our way. Let's go."

Outside, Kinslow left Miller with the animals while he took Boudreaux out to the corral, undid the handcuffs, and recuffed him to a gate post. He gathered Boudreaux's gear and got his horse ready to ride. He retrieved the prisoner and they went back to the front of the jail, with Boudreaux walking in front and Kinslow close behind, leading the painted mare.

Miller kept his freshly loaded rifle on Boudreaux while Kinslow removed the irons and took a short piece of rope from one of the packs. He tied the prisoner's wrists securely behind his back and then tied the loose end to his belt, greatly restricting any arm movement. He helped Boudreaux mount, got on his own horse, drew his gun, and told Miller to get mounted. Kinslow gave the street one quick glance. The only sign of life was a cowhand leaning against one of the porch posts of the saloon, smoking a curly. Kinslow spurred his horse and led the way out of town, at an easy gait.

The smoking cowhand turned and rushed into the saloon. "Mr. Birk, looks like they're leavin'."

Johnathan Birk walked quickly to the saloon entrance and watched as the Kinslow party disappeared over the hill just to the west of town. As he turned to go back in, he heard his name called. Turning in the direction of the voice, he saw a man approaching. He focused for a moment and then recognition eased his apprehension. It was Tom Sanders, a local gun for hire, who wasn't fussy about the kind of jobs he worked. "Mr. Birk, can we talk?" said Sanders when he got closer.

Birk knew what Sanders wanted. Johnathan had always fought his own battles and had no use for men like Sanders, but as they say, *"desperate times call for desperate measures"* and Birk thought it wouldn't hurt to hear him out. "Sure, let's talk over a drink," he said as he led the way back into the saloon.

"Little early for a drink, but why not?" said Sanders.

Birk went to his table, motioned Sanders to a chair, and poured two drinks. "Now, what can I do for you," he asked after a sip of the whiskey.

"I heard you are offering a reward for Ansen Miller. Is that dead or alive?"

"I want him alive. I want to kill him with my own hands."

"A thousand dollars is what I heard. Is that right?"

Birk thought for a moment and then said, "Tell you what. I'll make you another offer. You ride with me and my boys and if we can get Miller alive, you'll get fifteen hundred dollars. If you have to kill him, it's only worth five hundred to me. You see, Mr. Sanders, this way it is in your best interests to take him alive. Still interested?"

Sanders knocked back the rest of his drink, extended his hand to Birk, and said, "We have a deal. When do we leave?"

"As soon as my son gets here with a tracker and spare horses, we'll gear up and head out. Should be here in a couple of hours."

"Then I'll see you in a couple of hours," Sanders said as he got up and left.

Wes Manion, the cowhand who'd been standing guard, spoke up, "Boss, I don't know about this. I just don't like it."

Birk was more than half drunk. He'd been brooding and drinking all night. He jumped up and back handed Manion across the face, knocking him backwards. "The bastard killed my son and he is damn well going to pay for it and if you don't have the stomach for it, then you can get what's owed you and get out of my sight," screamed Birk.

"Sorry, Mr. Birk. I'll do just that. What you're doing ain't right," said Manion.

"What do I owe you?" inquired Birk.

"Wages for two months and some. Twenty two dollars, I reckon."

Birk took a twenty dollar gold eagle from his pocket and flipped it at the cowhand. "Here's twenty. Consider yourself lucky to get that much. Now get the hell out of here."

The cowhand pocketed the coin and hurried out of the saloon. Birk poured another drink, as three men at a corner table watched with interest.

"Well," remarked one of the men, "sounds like easy money to me. You fellas in?"

The other two nodded agreement, finished their drinks, gathered up the playing cards and coins from the table, and followed the cowhand out of the saloon.

Chapter 5

A short distance out of town Kinslow reined in his horse, stepped off the trail, and said to Miller, "Ansen, go ahead."

Miller moved to the front, leading the mule and Boudreaux's horse, which were tethered together. Kinslow took up a position in the rear where he felt much more comfortable with everyone in front of him.

The trail headed westward, up and over a row of low lying hills. Once they were over the first knoll and out of sight of the town, Kinslow halted them. He dismounted, pulled some field glasses out of one of the saddle bags, and walked the short distance back up the hill. Near the crest, he hunched over and stayed low until he reached the top, where he positioned himself behind an old pine tree and surveyed their back-trail, looking for anybody who might be following. There was no sign of anyone. He scanned the town and again saw no activity. The only signs of life were three riders on another trail heading to the northwest. Even though they were some distance away, Kinslow could tell they were driving their horses pretty hard. He folded the field glasses and went back down the hill.

"See anythin'?" Miller asked.

"Nothing that concerns us. Nobody moving except for three riders heading sort of northwest. Do you know where that trail goes?"

"Nope, 'fraid not," replied Miller. "You think it was Birk?"

Kinslow looked at Boudreaux and asked, "Do you know where that trail heads?" Boudreaux stared at Kinslow for a short time, smiled, and turned his head away. Kinslow focused his attention back on Miller "I don't think it was Birk. I think he sent the young one back to the ranch for more men, but I'm sure we haven't seen the last of him."

Kinslow remounted and took up his position in the rear. They all rode in relative silence, partly because of the distance between them, but mostly because not one of them had much to say. Miller was worrying over his predicament. Max Boudreaux was trying to figure out Kinslow, who was focused on the country around him.

The trail was an easy one on the horses. It was an old Indian route that followed the Poudre River Valley to Fort Collins. The flora in the valley was quite diverse. Trees included ponderosa and lodge pole pines, cottonwood, aspen, and juniper. Fir and spruce trees occupied higher elevations; lots of good places to set up an ambush. Three hours riding brought them to one of the many shallow crossings of the Poudre. There was a small meadow just before a short descent down an embankment into the river.

"Time to rest the horses," Kinslow said, as he dismounted. He loosened the cinch on his horse, helped Boudreaux down from his mount, walked him to the grassy bank, and sat him down. While Miller finished with the other horses and mule, Kinslow pulled a couple of carrots and a large chunk of beef jerky from one of the packs. The carrots, he broke into pieces and gave one to each of the animals. He cut a large chunk of the jerky and gave it to Miller. He sat next to Boudreaux on the bank and cut several bite size pieces of the jerky to feed to him. He ate several bites himself and then rolled a couple of smokes, one of which he lit and put between Boudreaux's lips. Miller joined them and Kinslow passed him the makings.

"We'll rest a few minutes. Let the horses graze on this nice grass a bit," Kinslow said.

"We sure are takin' our sweet time gettin'' there," commented Miller. "Birk will be on us in no time."

"What do you suggest? Run the horses into the ground and walk the rest of the way?" asked Kinslow.

"No, it's just —"

Kinslow cut him off, "Don't worry about Birk. I've handled his kind before."

"I don't doubt you have, Woodrow, but you don't know Birk. I do! He ain't gonna let this thing die," replied Miller.

"I didn't think he would," said Kinslow as he turned his attention to Max Boudreaux. "So, Mr. Boudreaux, what is your story?"

Boudreaux gazed at Kinslow for a few seconds, as if he didn't know what to make of him. "Why would you care, or are you just making conversation?"

"I don't really care all that much. I just believe every man deserves a fair shake. This is your chance to prove to me you are worth standing up for," said Kinslow.

Miller interjected, "He is an honest lawman. With him on your side, you'll get a square deal. Trust me, I know."

Boudreaux looked at Miller then back at Kinslow and said, "Let me ask you a question, Mister Lawman? If this Birk fella kills your little buddy here, will you take him in for a hanging?"

"As sure as I'm sitting here," countered Kinslow.

Boudreaux thought for a moment and continued, "My story isn't much different. I set things right because the law wouldn't and now they are going to hang me for it."

Kinslow wasn't sure if Max was done talking or not, but he pushed for more. "What happened?"

"I've been watching you closely and I'm guessing you are a fair man. This judge fella, would he listen to you?" asked Max.

I'm not guaranteeing your situation would get any better if I talk to him, but yes, I'm pretty sure he will listen to me," Kinslow replied with conviction.

"I want you to understand, I am not like Birk. He lost a son and he replaces his grief with anger and blind vengeance. The man I killed needed to die. There was no other way," said Max.

"What did he do?" interjected Kinslow.

"He was attacking young girls. He would lay in wait outside the camp until the men left and then he would grab the first young girl he saw, drag her into the trees, and assault her. We talked to the Indian Agent, but he would not listen. We went to the law. They laughed at us and told us it was not a crime to rape squaws. So, we took matters into our own hands. We set a trap for him. We caught him and justice was served, as you white men like to say."

"You killed him?" asked Kinslow.

"What does it matter? It is done," replied Max.

"It matters a lot, if you didn't actually do the killing. Could mean the difference between a rope and some jail time"

"The young women he attacked got their justice. The law you value so much means nothing to me. They arrested the first Indian they recognized from the ones who were doing the complaining, yours truly," said Max, rather sarcastically.

"The law is not at fault, it's those who misuse it for their own purposes," argued Kinslow.

Boudreaux looked at Miller and said to Kinslow, "Why don't you deputize me like you did him and I'll go arrest them." He laughed out loud as he added, "Yeah, a half-breed with a badge. That's funny."

Kinslow ignored his comment, "If what you're telling me is true, I'll back your story with the judge."

Boudreaux smiled and chuckled. Miller said, "Don't you be scoffin' at this man. If he says it, he means it. Like I said before, he's a man of his word."

Kinslow said, "Thanks Ansen, but I think Max has to decide that for himself. Let's get going."

They checked the packs, re-cinched the animals, and took them down to the river for watering. After they drank their fill, Kinslow helped Boudreaux back on his horse and checked his restraints. Boudreaux said to Kinslow, "Just so you know, the northwest trail hooks up with this one about six miles ahead. Good place for those three fellas to jump us."

Kinslow looked up at Boudreaux and said in all sincerity, "Thanks, Max. That's good to know."

At about the time the Kinslow party stopped to rest, Johnathan Birk heard the sound of hoof beats pounding down the street. He jumped up and hurried to the saloon doors. Andy, leading a string of horses and Carlos Sanchez, one of Birk's top horse handlers and an excellent tracker, pulled up in front of him. "Where the hell you been? I expected you an hour ago," Johnathan bellowed.

"We got here as fast as we could, Pa. No sense killing the horses," replied Andy, nonchalantly.

As Andy started to dismount, Johnathan stepped forward enraged, "Why you little —"

Andy swung his leg back over his horse and was back in the saddle. Johnathan stopped. There was a look in Andy's eyes that told him not to push it. He ignored it. "You little bastard, I'm going to beat some respect into you!"

Tom Sanders' appearance on the boardwalk interrupted Johnathan, "Trouble, Boss?" asked Sanders.

"Nothing I can't handle," replied Johnathan.

Andy seized the opportunity to deflect his father's attention, "Who's this asshole?"

Sanders shot Andy a hateful stare and stepped forward, his hand on his pistol. "Man insults me, best he be prepared to back it up, Sonny," he threatened.

Andy ignored him and said to his father, "We're using hired killers now to do our fighting? Thought we handled our own affairs."

Johnathan went into a tirade, "Your brother is dead, goddamn it! Doesn't it mean anything to you? I'm going to see his killer pays for it, if it's the last thing I do and no gunslinger with a badge is going to stand in my way. Sanders just evens the odds. Insurance, you might call it. Now find yourself some backbone and let's get this thing done. They already have a three hour head start."

Sanders drew his pistol, did a couple of fancy spins, and re-holstered it. He pointed at Andy with the forefinger and thumb of his gun hand, mocking a shot. The younger Birk gulped. Sanders smiled and said to Johnathan, "I'll get my horse and gear and catch up."

Johnathan and Andy were still glaring at each other. Johnathan broke the uncomfortable silence and said to Sanders, "We have some horses and gear at the livery. We'll meet there." He strode off in the direction of the stables along with Jim Trueman, the other of the two cowhands he'd come to town with. Thirty minutes later, they were all provisioned, saddled, and on their way.

Chapter 6

The three of them were short on experience when it came to bounty hunting. Todd and Billy Clagg were trappers, attired in the fruits of their labour; loosely sewn fur caps, tanned deer hides for coats, and rabbit fur leggings, covering their knee-high moccasins. Todd, the older and larger of the two men, sported a bear claw necklace, while Billy preferred to travel lighter with only a magpie feather stuck in his cap. Both of them had a large hunting knife strapped around their middle and tucked in each of their belts was a Navy Colt pistol, both so old and worn there was no guarantee they would even fire.

Adam "Fancy" Ingram, on the other hand, was the exact opposite of the brothers. He wore a black shirt, black pants, black boots, and a black hat, the band of which was encrusted with dollar sized silver medallions. A white bandana was tied around his neck. He wore silver spurs and his gun belt, equipped with two ivory handled pistols, was adorned with the same silver medallions as his hat band. His jet black hair and pencil thin moustache completed the ensemble.

The Clagg brothers spent all of their lives just getting by. They prospected, trapped, and worked just about every menial job known to mankind. They were creatures of opportunity and weren't above breaking the law, if it looked like a sure thing and they were relatively certain of not getting caught.

It was about a year ago when Todd came up with the idea of bounty hunting. How hard could it be? Most of the posters said, *Dead or Alive*. It was all perfectly legal. Find the wanted man, shoot him from behind cover, and get paid good money for it. However, they soon found out bounty hunting wasn't as easy as it seemed. In over fourteen months, they managed to bring in one measly horse thief for a hundred dollar reward.

Sheriff Claxton almost arrested them for murder because the poster said, *alive*. The brothers claimed self defence and Claxton couldn't prove otherwise, so he paid them. As they were leaving the sheriff's office, Billy noticed a poster tacked to the wall. It read, "*Wanted — Fancy Ingram — for suspicion of murder — $200.00.*" He tore it off the wall and showed it to Todd. "Ain't that the fella was standin' in front of the saloon smokin' one of them little ceegars?"

Todd looked closely at the likeness. "By golly Billy, I think you're right. Let's get rid of this business first," he said, indicating the corpse on the pack mule.

With the departed horse thief resting peacefully at the undertaker and the bounty money in their pockets, the brothers headed to the saloon for a drink. As they entered, they paused at the door and looked the place over. It was empty, except for the man dressed all in black and silver, whom they suspected to be Fancy Ingram. He was working on a drink at the far end of the bar. They approached the bartender and Todd ordered a bottle of whiskey and two glasses. He pulled the cork, poured two drinks, and passed one to his brother. He looked down the bar and spoke, "You there, can we buy you a drink?"

Fancy looked up, thought for a moment, and slowly made his way toward the brothers. He leaned his right elbow on the bar, holding the empty shot glass, and faced them. His left hand was on his gun as he stared directly at Todd and said, "Sure, I could use another."

"Name is Todd Clagg. This here's my brother Billy," said Todd as he poured the whiskey. "Who might you be?"

"My friends call me Fancy," he said as he knocked back the drink and turned to leave.

"What's the rush? Have another," urged Todd, holding out the bottle.

Fancy turned and looked at the brothers, first one and then the other, and said, "If you are after the bounty money on me, you have already lost the advantage of surprise. Getting me drunk won't lessen the odds of you dying. I'll kill you both before you can even think about getting those pistols out of your belts." After a short pause he added, "Now, I'll have another drink."

Todd filled his glass and glanced at Billy. He could see the fear in his brother's eyes and immediately came to the conclusion that bushwhacking Fancy in a dark alley was the only way they were going to see the bounty money. "Bounty? On you? Didn't know. Me and my brother just come to town for a drink, is all."

"You're a liar. I was watching you when you brought the body into the sheriff's office," retorted Fancy.

Todd stammered, "Well — yeah — but, ya see, we do some bounty huntin' when we're short of cash, but we didn't know you was wanted — is what I meant to say."

Fancy thought for a moment. Todd wasn't sure if he bought the story or not. He broke the tension by changing the subject, "So, what brings you to town?" he inquired.

"Funny you should ask," answered Fancy. "I was just passing through when I heard this rancher is offering a thousand dollars for the man who killed his son. I'm headed to the table over yonder to wait until he comes back. Bring your bottle. We'll play some cards. Get to know each other. A thousand dollars, split three ways, is a lot more than the two hundred you'd get for me and probably a lot safer for you two."

A short time later, Johnathan Birk stormed back into the saloon, having just had his run in with Kinslow in the restaurant. He got a bottle and two glasses and he and one of the cowpunchers, who'd ridden in with him, sat down at one of the tables. As the night wore on, Fancy caught little bits of what Birk was saying. Seems his kid went back to the ranch for horses, supplies, and a tracker. When the kid got back, they were going to go after this marshal who was taking the killer to see a judge in Fort Collins. Apparently, the marshal had made him a deputy, or something? Fancy didn't understand it all, but he concluded it was Ansen Miller that Birk was after.

He listened to the small talk as the saloon began to fill up with the regular nighthawks and drifters. Turns out, the marshal had backed the entire Birk bunch down in the restaurant and Birk had left with his tail between his legs. Fancy figured when the others got here, they would follow the lawman and make their move somewhere down the trail. He and the Clagg boys would just have to get there first.

****

Max Boudreaux had told Kinslow the truth. The trail wandered away from the river for a few miles and then headed back down to the stream. They'd gone about six or seven miles when they came to a small plateau overlooking the river. From this vantage point, Kinslow had a good view of what lay ahead. Their route crossed the river and connected with another trail coming from their right, about a hundred yards upstream. Max Boudreaux indicated this was the trail on which they had seen the three riders, as they were leaving town earlier. At the junction, the trail disappeared from view, covered by the willows and brush growing along the river banks. Kinslow figured if the three riders got to this spot head of them, it would be an ideal place for an ambush.

"Let's give the horses another rest and we'll talk about our next move," said Kinslow. He dismounted and helped Boudreaux down, walked him to a large poplar, and sat him down against the tree. He motioned Miller over and said. "I have an idea on how to draw these bushwhackers out."

Kinslow's plan was to work his way upstream, on this side of the river, to the other trail, where he would cross the stream and come up behind any potential ambush. Miller was to wait a few minutes and then continue on up the original trail, walking the mule. Hopefully, the waiting assassins would assume he was a lone prospector and not who they were looking for, which would give Kinslow and Miller the element of surprise.

Kinslow took a long piece of rope from one of the packs. He wrapped it around Boudreaux several times and tied him tightly to the tree that he was sitting against. He tied the horses securely to a small pine, pulled his Winchester from the scabbard, and levered a shell into the chamber. He took out his revolver, opened the cylinder, and rolled it to make sure it was fully loaded. He knew it was, but habit made him check every time. He said, "Alright, I'm on my way. Give me a ten minute start and then come ahead. Take your rifle out and have it ready to fire. If they are waiting for us, things could happen real fast. Good luck, Ansen."

"Yeah, you too," replied Miller as he watched Kinslow sprint away on foot. He waited for what he figured to be about ten minutes and then untied the mule, got his rifle from his horse, levered a shell into the chamber and left the hammer cocked. After checking on Boudreaux, he headed down the embankment and across the stream, on foot, leading the mule, and singing very loud and extremely off-key. While he seemed nonchalant, he was carefully scrutinizing each side of the trail for any sign of movement.

It didn't take long to travel the short distance to the junction of the trails. He could make out fresh tracks in the dust where the trails converged, but he didn't dare stop to check them closely. To anyone watching, why would a crazy old prospector care about tracks? He didn't have time to think about it, however. Todd and Billy Clagg stepped out from behind cover with guns drawn. "You there, pilgrim.

I want to see them hands holding sky real fast, or you're a dead man," commanded Todd.

Todd Clagg didn't know it, but he'd just uttered his last words. Miller pulled the mule's reins down and across his own body, from left to right, forcing the mule to step between him and the Claggs. At the same time, he brought the cocked Winchester up and fired across the mule's back, hitting Todd Clagg with a chest shot, dead center. Panic overtook Billy Clagg. He emptied his pistol in Miller's direction as he ran for the horses tethered in the brush, a few yards away. One of his wild shots dropped the mule and another clipped Miller's hip.

It wasn't quite what Fancy Ingram expected. He'd stationed himself on the stream side of the trail while the Clagg brothers found cover on the opposite side. This way, whoever came down the trail would be between him and the brothers. The Claggs would challenge from the front and he could approach from behind without being noticed.

He was fooled by Miller's prospector imitation and had relaxed. Miller's rifle shot startled him, momentarily. He drew both his pistols and was all set to cut the prospector in half, when a hail of bullets from Billy Clagg came his way. He ducked back behind cover and when the shooting stopped, he waited a moment and then ventured a look from behind the tree. He saw the prospector on the ground, holding his side and writhing in pain. He heard a horse galloping away and he figured it was Billy Clagg, running scared. He was about to step out and finish the prospector off, when the lights went out. He didn't know what hit him and it would take days to get rid of the headache Kinslow's rifle butt had given him.

"Where are you hit, Ansen? Let me have a look," said Kinslow, with genuine concern.

Miller removed his hand from his right side. There was a lot of blood and after a closer look, Kinslow smiled and reassured him, "Just a little nick. You'll be sore for a couple of days and you'll have to sleep on your left side."

"Sure, sure, I get myself shot to pieces and you make jokes. You can keep this marshallin' business. And another thing, I better get a raise in pay for this," said Miller, rather indignant.

Kinslow chuckled as he checked the rest of the scene. Fancy was out cold. The mule had been head shot and was dead. He cocked his Winchester and approached Todd Clagg. He saw the blood seeping from the hole in Clagg's chest right above the heart and assumed he was dead. Two decades of law enforcement, however, taught him, at times, things weren't always what they seem. He was always cautious until he proved to himself what his eyes were seeing was, indeed, fact. He gave Clagg's boot a hard kick and looked for any signs of life. There were none.

He lowered the hammer of the rifle just as a horse whinnied from the brush a few yards away. He'd seen the third man ride off, but again caution took over. He didn't relax until he was sure there was no one else around, just the two mounts tied to a sapling. He untied the horses and brought them close to Miller and handed him the reins. He told Miller to hold the mounts while he unloaded the packs from the dead mule and put them on one of the horses. He used a piece of pack rope to bind Fancy Ingram's legs at the ankles and his hands behind his back. He picked up Fancy's inert body and laid him face down across the other horse.

Supporting Miller's weight with one arm, while leading the horses with the other, he headed to a large pine tree where he sat Miller against the shady side and then tied the horses to a low branch. He took off Miller's bandana and stuffed it tight, inside his pants, against the graze to stem the superficial bleeding.

He picked up Miller's rifle, chambered a shell, and handed it to him. "I'll go back and get our horses and our prisoner. Won't be long." Glancing at Fancy, who was still unconscious, he added, "He'll be out for a while. Even if he comes to, he ain't going far."

"Don't you worry 'bout me, Woodrow. I'll be fine, even though I'm bleedin' to death," whined Miller.

Kinslow took a few steps, stopped, turned back to face Miller, and said, "You did a hell of a job, Ansen. Can't think of anybody I'd rather have backing me. Thanks."

Miller forgot all about any further complaining. He felt good, real good. "Maybe this marshallin' isn't such a bad deal after all," he told himself as he watched Kinslow running back down the trail.

It took Kinslow all of ten minutes to get back to the spot where he left Boudreaux and the horses. He mentally sorted out the numerous hoof prints in the dusty trail. There were two sets of fresh tracks; one was those of the mule Miller was leading and the other belonged to a horse travelling in the other direction. He was following the fresh prints carefully. He didn't know if the rider would stop where he'd stowed Boudreaux. He thought not for two reasons; one, Boudreaux and the horses were far enough off the trail and well hidden and two, the man in question was running scared. He would be travelling too fast to notice anything. Kinslow was right. The tracks didn't veer off the trail.

Kinslow cocked his rifle and approached the spot where he'd tied Boudreaux to a tree. The prisoner was still there, as were the horses. After one last glance around, Kinslow retrieved the horses, freed Boudreaux, and helped him mount, leaving his wrists tied behind his back.

Once on their way, Boudreaux spoke, "So, you're still alive."

"Why? Were you hoping different?" asked Kinslow.

"No, I figured when I heard the horse go by, hell bent for leather, I would see you again," replied Boudreaux with a hint of a smile.

"Glad to oblige," replied Kinslow.

They looked at each other for a moment. Boudreaux broke the awkward silence by smiling, which prompted Kinslow to turn and spur his horse into. In a few minutes they were at the ambush spot. Miller was up and adjusting the packs. *Tough hombre,* thought Kinslow.

Fancy Ingram was just coming to. Kinslow dismounted and tied off the two horses. He looked up at Boudreaux and instructed him to stay put. "How's the hip, Ansen?" he asked."

"Hurts some, but I think I'll live."

"Good. We'll put in a couple more hours in the saddle and then find a spot to stop for the night," said Kinslow.

Miller thought for a moment and said, "You know Birk is not far behind us. If we don't ride like hell, he is gonna catch us soon."

"Ansen, I figure he is going to catch us anyway. We'll deal with it when the time comes. Right now, I have tired horses and a wounded deputy to worry about," said Kinslow.

"Oooooh, my head. What the hell?" Ingram moaned, as he returned to full consciousness.

Kinslow grabbed Ingram by the back of his belt and unceremoniously pulled him off the horse. Ingram landed hard on his back and groaned again. Kinslow bent down and lifted his face, so he was looking directly into Ingram's eyes and said, "Listen up, bushwhacker. You had a meeting with my rifle butt. I'm a U.S. marshal and you are under arrest for attempted murder. I am taking you to Fort Collins and if you give me one ounce of trouble, I'll use the other end of the rifle this time. Do we understand each other?"

Ingram didn't say anything. Miller interjected, "Better listen to him, Sonny. He's a man of his word. Trust me, I know."

Kinslow untied the rope around Ingram's ankles and helped him mount up. He tied Ingram's horse to one of the packs on Clagg's horse and secured Boudreaux's mount to the other side of the same pack.

They set off, with Miller leading the entourage and Kinslow in the rear, where he could watch the two prisoners.

A short time later, Billy Clagg was still running his horse into the ground. His fear and panic were replaced by a whirlwind of thoughts churning through his mind; T*odd was dead. That bastard prospector had killed him. Why did he do that? We just wanted to talk to him.*

He came around a slow curve in the trail and saw the group of riders coming his way. He slowed down to a trot and as the riders came close, he reined his horse to the edge of the trail, stopping to let them pass.

Johnathan Birk halted his men as they approached Billy Clagg. "Who might you be?" he asked.

"Just on my way to town," replied Clagg.

"I didn't ask you where you were going. I asked who you were. Now, once more, who are you?" demanded Birk.

Clagg sensed Birk was in no mood for banter. "Clagg. Billy Clagg," he said, trying to hide his fear.

"Where did you come from?" inquired Birk.

"Fort Collins," Clagg lied.

Sanders rode forward, stopped next to Birk, and said, "He's lying, Mr. Birk. I saw him in town yesterday, him and another scum sucker. Bounty hunters, I think. They had a body on a horse in front of Claxton's office."

Birk turned back to Billy, "Should we try this again, Mr. Clagg? Once more then, where did you come from?"

Clagg thought for a moment about sticking to his story, but something told him it was not the right thing to do. He focused on Sanders and answered, "The man you called a scum sucker was my brother. He's dead. Shot by some crazy prospector. All we wanted to do was talk and he up and shoots Todd for no reason."

"Where was this," Birk demanded.

"I — I don't know — uh, up the road — 'bout two — three miles, I reckon," stammered Billy.

"Show me!" demanded Birk.

"I can't. I gotta get to town and tell the sheriff and get poor old Todd in the ground. Besides, I am pretty sure I got him, that no good bushwhacker."

"I said you are coming with us," Birk said to Clagg and then to Sanders, "If he tries to run, shoot him."

Although Birk usually cared a great deal about the stock in his stables, he was not thinking of his horse's well being right now. He was

Sidetracked

a man on a mission and nothing or nobody was going to stand in his way. He spurred his horse hard and the others followed his lead. A short time later, they all arrived at the crossing of the trails; Johnathan and Andy Birk, Sanders the gunslinger, Sanchez the tracker, Jim Trueman the cowhand, and last but not least, Billy Clagg.

Birk first noticed the dead mule and as he rode closer, he saw a body on the ground. He dismounted for a better look. "This one is dead, alright. He smells like you," he said to Clagg. "Must be your brother."

Sanchez had already dismounted and was checking the ground. He walked the trail back and forth, scrutinizing the tracks. He went back up the northwest trail a short distance and returned.

"It's all pretty mixed up, Senor, but I think I got it figured out. Seems three hombres come from there," he said, pointing to the trail on the right. "Three maybe four riders come from here." He pointed back in the direction from which they had just come. "Looks like a horse with no rider, also."

He indicated the spot where the Clagg brothers stepped out to confront Miller, "Somebody standing here, by the dead one." He walked to the spot where Miller had fallen, "Looks like the hombre standing here was wounded. There is blood on the ground."

He stood up, looking somewhat puzzled, "There is something I am not understanding. One man, he follows the three from this trail on foot. It looks like someone is hiding here," pointing to where Fancy had hidden himself. "It looks like one man rides back to the east and the rest go to the west."

Birk edged his horse near Clagg's. "You want to clear up some details for us?" he demanded.

"Sure, Mr. Birk, sure. It's like he says. Me and Todd waited right here and a fella name of Fancy was on the other side. We was hoping to get Miller and the marshal between us, when this old prospector come up with his mule. We was just gonna talk to him, when he up and blasts Todd. I don't know why Fancy didn't back our play, but I emptied my pistol at the prospector. I guess I killed the mule and winged him, too."

"You got cow shit for brains," Birk snorted. "That was Miller, you idiot!"

Clagg pondered a moment, "Oh, so if he dies, does it mean I get the reward?" he asked in all sincerity.

Birk looked at Sanders, "Escort our friend here down the trail and make sure he heads to town."

Sanders grabbed the reins of Clagg's horse and rode back down the trail leading him. Birk and the rest of the bunch started up the trail, following the Kinslow party's tracks. After a couple minutes, two shots rang out and a little while later, Sanders caught up to them, with Clagg's horse in tow.

Andy Birk rode up to Sanders and said, "You murdering son-of-a-bitch. There was no call to shoot the man."

Sanders smiled, "He drew first. Tried to bushwhack me. Self defence, I'd call it. Besides, we can use the extra horse."

Johnathan Birk broke up the confrontation. "Andy, just let it go," he said and to Sanders he added, "I've had just about enough of you. You do one more thing without orders from me, our deal is off. You got it?"

"Sure, Mr. Birk, whatever you say," was Sanders' snide reply. He gave Andy a hateful stare and rode off. Andy gave his father a similar look. The older Birk ignored him and turned his horse back up the trail.

Chapter 7

Kinslow's intent was to slow Birk down by leaving the trail several times and creating numerous false leads for him to follow. To that end, they rode alongside a creek for several hundred yards, entered the water, doubled back upstream, crossed the main trail to the other side, and rode forward through the brush. They rode into the trees in dozens of places, leaving false trails and then circled back to the main trail. It would take hours to follow them all. Satisfied they'd done enough to make it very difficult for anyone tracking them, they rode downstream in a creek for a couple of miles until they arrived at the eastern outskirts of an old mining camp.

The camp was typical of the dozens of abandoned mining settlements in the area. Gold fever spread like a prairie fire when some tinhorn prospector claimed he found a bit of yellow in one of the creeks. Before long, there were hundreds of claims filed in every stream for fifty miles, but no one found so much as a flake of gold. There was even talk of lynching the prospector who made the original claim.

The hordes of humanity disappeared as quickly as they came, leaving behind sagging sluice boxes, makeshift wheel barrows, broken pick handles, and other remnants of human activity. There were only a few permanent structures left standing. The largest was a reddish, clapboard, rectangular, single room building. Several other smaller structures, which housed a variety of enterprises, adorned the lone street. Scattered about the hillsides were dozens of square, wooden frames with pine laggings for trusses. Large canvas tarps had served as walls and roofs. When the occupants left, the tarps went with them, along with their shattered hopes and dreams.

As they entered the camp, Kinslow's keen eye spotted a fenced pasture off to his right. He said to Miller, "Ansen, I think this will do for the night. We only have an hour of daylight left, anyway. Might as well put up here. I think we've slowed down our tag-alongs."

Kinslow rode the perimeter of the fenced pasture, checking for broken or downed rails. "Looks good," he said to Miller. "Let's turn them loose. There's lots of grass and there's water in the trough. We'll give them some oats later."

Kinslow helped Max Boudreaux off his horse and sat him down in the dirt with his back against one of the rail posts. He did the same to Fancy Ingram while Miller stood vigilante with his rifle cocked. He unsaddled and took all the gear off the horses and then stood watch while Miller attended to his mount. "Keep an eye on these two while I check this place out," said Kinslow. Looking at Fancy Ingram, he added, "If he moves a muscle, shoot him. Try not to hit anything vital."

Kinslow made his way down the center of the street. When he came to the large, red, rectangular building, he peered inside through a broken window where once there was a pane of glass, a sign of anticipated permanence. A couple of long strides brought him to a set of double doors. Some of the leather straps, used for hinges, were rotted through and had broken in the wind, causing one of the doors to lay hanging at an odd angle. Kinslow struggled with it, set it upright, and then left it open.

Once inside, he saw a long pine log table with benches for seating, running down the entire center of the one large room. Along one wall was a huge stove, perhaps twice the size of any he'd ever seen, with a sizeable pile of split wood on one side. Shelves, built from equipment crates, lined the wall behind the stove. On them were a few odds and ends the miners left behind; an old lantern with the glass broken, a number of small pots and pans, a couple of sealer jars with God-knows-what in them, some lifters and pokers for the stove, and an old hat with a big hole in the brow. Kinslow stuck his finger through the hole and remarked to himself that there had to be a story there.

Offset from another wall, was a makeshift saloon area consisting of two stacks of large nail barrels piled together about eight feet apart with two long planks between them that served as the bar.

Kinslow gave the place one last look and returned to the pasture. "Looks like home for the night," he said to Miller. "Let's get these two settled and then I'll come back for the gear."

Kinslow got Boudreaux and Ingram to their feet and escorted them into the big building where he sat them down at one end of the long table, across from each other. Under Miller's watchful eye, he took two pieces of rope, reached under the table, tied their ankles tight, and then tied the ends of the two ropes together, so the two of them were bound to each other. It would be impossible for either one of them to get to their feet and cause any trouble. Kinslow stood guard while Miller brought the gear in. He piled it all in one corner with the exception of a ground sheet and saddle that he set up near the stove, as per Kinslow's instructions.

"Figure we'll take turns sleeping and watching," suggested Kinslow. "I'll get a fire started if you want to fill the coffee pot with some water from the pump outback." Miller nodded assent and left while Kinslow dug out the equipment and supplies needed to make some bacon, beans, and biscuits. They weren't really biscuits, just some flour, water, and bacon fat mixed together and fried in a hot pan. They were barely edible, but filling.

It wasn't long before Kinslow had a hot fire going. On one side of the stove, there was a pot of coffee brewing and supper, such as it was, was burning nicely on the other side. He untied the ropes around Boudreaux's and Ingram's wrists and dished out three plates of food, one each for the prisoners and one for Miller, who asked, "Ain't you eatin'?"

Kinslow answered, "There are only three plates and besides, these two need our full attention. The best way to avoid trouble with prisoners is to never give them an opportunity to try something."

Miller pondered on that bit of sound advice for a moment and then turned his attention to the food. After a couple of bites, Fancy Ingram put his spoon down on his plate and knocked the whole thing onto the floor. Boudreaux and Miller were startled by the sudden clatter of the tin plate, but Kinslow didn't move a muscle. Miller looked to Kinslow for an indication of what he should be doing.

Kinslow smiled and said to Miller, "You see, Ansen, I'm supposed get real mad and rush over to pick up the plate and while I'm bent over, our little gunman here is going to jump me. He seems to have forgotten he is tied to Mr. Boudreaux at the ankles and couldn't do much anyway, but why don't we see." Kinslow walked up behind Ingram, grabbed a fistful of shirt at the back of his neck, and forced his upper body down as far as it would go, his face just inches above the floor.

"Pick it up!" commanded Kinslow. Ingram stretched as far as he could. His fingertips barely caught the edge of the plate and he was able to grab it. Kinslow sat him upright and took the plate from him, "Looks like you're done," he said.

"I'm going to kill you before this is done," Ingram promised, through glaring eyes and clenched teeth.

"You're going to have to get in line," replied Kinslow. He shifted his gaze to Boudreaux. When their eyes met, Max Boudreaux just smiled and went back to the business of eating his bacon and beans. Kinslow watched him for a moment and thought to himself that blowhards like the kid in black, he understood. It was the quiet, smiling ones he could never figure out. It was like the smile meant they knew something you didn't and they weren't about to tell you what it was.

Kinslow scraped off the bit of food that was left on Ingram's plate and refilled it. He sat down next to Boudreaux, facing Ingram. "What's your name?" he asked Ingram between bites.

Fancy didn't answer.

"I'm only going ask this one more time. What is your name?"

"Why do you want to know?" snarled Fancy.

"Need to write something on the tombstone when they hang you," Kinslow said, with complete indifference.

Ingram lost his air of confidence for a split second and a hint of apprehension appeared on his face. He gathered his composure and replied, "Name is Adam Ingram. Most folks call me *Fancy*. Guess it's 'cause I'm pretty fancy with a gun." He waited for a reply, but there wasn't one forthcoming. Kinslow's focus was on his food.

Ingram tried another approach. "You can't arrest me. I didn't do nothing. I was just doing my duty, trying to bring in a killer."

Kinslow sopped up the last of his beans with the last piece of biscuit, cleaned his big handle bar moustache with one long swipe of this right sleeve, got up, and poured himself a cup of coffee before he spoke. "The man you tried to shoot in the back, Mr. Ingram, is a duly appointed U.S. deputy marshal. Conspiracy to commit murder against a federal officer is a hanging offence."

"What? No. No! That's not true — he — wait just a —" stammered Fancy.

Kinslow cut him off, "Tell it to the judge!" To Miller he said, "Clean up here will you, Ansen. I'm going to check on the horses."

"I filled up the trough, so they should have drunk their fill," Miller said.

"Thanks Ansen. I'm going to give them a little oats and maybe a bite of carrot."

Kinslow went out and Miller said to no one in particular, "Thinks more of them horses than he does most people."

Fancy saw an opening, "So old timer, can you really trust a man like that?"

"Like what?" asked Miller.

"Hey, you just said it yourself. He cares more about dumb horses than he does people. You think a man like him is really going to care about what happens to you?" pressed Ingram.

Miller felt himself swelling up with anger. He wasn't mad at Ingram. He'd seen a dozen Ingrams and they never bothered him. He was angry at himself because he listened to Ingram and he allowed doubt to enter his mind. "Listen you sack of sheep shit, Woodrow Kinslow gave me his word that I would get a fair shake from him and the judge and it's good enough for me. Yes sir, that's good enough for me!" He busied himself gathering dishes and pots to get himself away from Ingram.

There was no conversation for the longest time. Miller was occupied with clean up while Ingram and Boudreaux really had nothing to say to each other. Ingram found the silence uncomfortable. He turned his attention to Boudreaux. "Hey Indian, how about you? You think Kinslow and some white judge are going to give you a fair shake?"

Boudreaux grinned and shrugged his shoulders, "Whatever comes, will come. I don't worry about it."

"What did you do to get yourself arrested?" asked Ingram.

"Killed a white man who asked too many questions," replied Max with a grin.

Miller let out a boisterous laugh. Boudreaux smiled, pleased with himself. Ingram, seething, said, "Ah, both of you go to hell! First chance I get, I'm cutting loose and I'll kill anyone who gets in my way."

Miller responded, "I'll be watchin' you real close, Sonny. One sign of trouble and I'll smash your gun hand with a rifle butt. We'll see how big you talk then."

"Yeah old man, I'm going to enjoy watching you die," retorted Ingram.

Miller dropped the pot he was cleaning onto the stove top and started towards Ingram. He intended to beat some sense into this big mouth, but Boudreaux stopped him when he said, "Don't listen to him. He's just trying to rile so you don't think too clear. If you get close when you're not thinking, you might just give him a chance to jump you."

"Thanks," Miller said, "he almost had me."

Kinslow cleared his throat to announce his presence. "Trouble, boys?"

Miller responded, "Nothin' I can't handle."

After a momentary pause, Kinslow said, "Horses are fed and watered. They're good for the night. Now, I suggest we all get some shuteye. We've got some hard riding tomorrow." He got a blanket from the gear pile and folded it several times to make a pillow which he handed to Boudreaux. "I'm going to have to leave you tied up. Sorry, but this should help." He turned his attention to Fancy Ingram, "You can make out the best you can. Maybe, if you're tired enough, you'll be easier to handle."

Miller asked, "You want me to take the first watch?"

"No, I can't sleep just yet. You go ahead, though. I'll wake you later," replied Kinslow.

Miller retrieved his bedroll from the pile, made himself a bed using the ground sheet and saddle he'd set up earlier and before long, he was snoring. Kinslow sat at the other end of the long table where he could watch the two prisoners. Boudreaux positioned the blanket, folded his arms and laid his head on them. Ingram started to say something, but Kinslow shut him up when he said, "Sleep, not talk!"

Johnathan Birk reined in his horse and raised his arm in a halting gesture. In the fading light, he'd caught site of the mining camp as he rounded the corner. Kinslow's plan to slow them down was somewhat effective, but Birk remembered the mining camp was near by from a time when he and a friend from Denver had done some sheep hunting in the area. His instincts told him the camp would be a good place for Kinslow to spend the night. Based on that and because it was getting dark, he said to Sanchez, "Never mind finding their damn trail. I know where they are. See the buildings down there? I'm thinking we have found what we were looking for. Go down on foot and have a look around. We'll be waiting back up the trail."

Sanchez dismounted, handed the reins to Birk, and set off. Birk turned his mount back in the direction they had come. "Let's rest 'em, boys," he said as he rode back up the trail. He remembered that a short distance back was a widening in the trail with a small meadow on one side, a good place to camp for the night. Once there, Birk dismounted and started barking out orders and assigning tasks. Andy Birk got the job of cooking up some grub for everyone which, of course, didn't sit well with him.

With everyone doing their part to gather up some fire wood, it didn't take Andy long to get a fire going, the coffee brewing, and the beans and biscuits cooking. Everyone found a comfortable place to sit within the vicinity of the fire. They were holding their plates and hardware in anticipation of something to eat. Andy took the pot from the fire and was heading to feed his father first. As he passed by the men, Sanders stuck his foot out and tripped him. Andy stumbled and then caught his balance. He didn't fall, but he did spill some of the beans.

Sanders slowly raised his gaze and said, "Kinda clumsy aren't you, boy?"

Andy scowled at him for a few seconds and then continued on his way.

"Hey boy, you forgot my grub," said Sanders.

Andy turned and pointed to the beans on the ground, "There's your share. Enjoy."

Sanders jumped to his feet, his hand on the butt of his pistol, as he spoke to Andy's back, "Boy! You've pushed it a little too far. Now pull your iron."

Andy turned slowly, set the pot down on the ground, and started back towards Sanders. He kept walking until he was only a few feet away and spoke in a calm, steady tone, "You can kill me where I stand, Sanders. Everybody here knows it, but what you have to ask yourself is this; are you going to get out of here alive? Look around."

Sanders quickly glanced at the others. Johnathan Birk's Winchester was cocked and pointed at him and Jim Trueman was standing with his pistol drawn. For a split second, Sanders was actually thinking about calling their play, but Sanchez's timely return broke the tension.

"What did you find out?" asked the elder Birk.

"You were right, Senor. It is them. They are in the building with the smoke. Horses are unsaddled and put up for the night. Looks like they are staying."

"Good. Thanks Carlos. Get yourself something to eat," said Birk.

"Strange thing though, Senor Birk. I count four men," continued Sanchez.

Birk counted out loud, "The marshal, Miller, the half breed — who's the fourth?"

"I look in the window and I see the marshal has two hombres tied up. I am thinking this is the third man who was with the brothers."

Birk pondered a moment and then concluded, "Well, this might just be to our advantage." To the men he announced, "We're here for the night."

While Carlos Sanchez was scouting out the camp, Kinslow refilled his coffee and sat back down at the table. He was taking a sip of the hot, black brew when he caught some movement out of the corner of his eye. He slowly reached for his pistol and set it on the table in front of him, hammer back. He waited a couple of minutes then turned slowly and looked at the window frame, his hand on the Peacemaker.

He moved quickly to the door and peeked out, checking the boardwalk in both directions. Most people would have concluded their eyes were playing tricks on them, but not Kinslow. He trusted his senses and he was convinced he'd seen something.

He took a quick glance back inside at the sleeping beauties and then eased out onto the boardwalk, keeping himself flat against the wall to avoid detection by anyone watching.

He stood listening for a few seconds and was all set to go back inside, when he heard the horses snorting and neighing. He quickly made his way to the edge of the big red building and took a look around the corner. A small building, which once served as a bathhouse, stood between him and the pasture. Kinslow covered the short distance to the small building and stuck his head out far enough to see the entire pasture. His sharp eye caught the silhouette of a man standing on the bottom rail of the fence, observing the stock. The shadow stepped down from the fence, made its way to the far end of the pasture, and disappeared into the bushes.

Kinslow waited several moments and then assured the man was gone, he made his way back to the red box building. Once inside, he rousted Miller, who sat up, rubbed his eyes, and said, "My turn already?"

"No," replied Kinslow, "We've got company. We are going to do some night riding."

Full consciousness returned to Miller. "What do you mean? What company? Who?" he asked.

Kinslow explained, "Can't say for sure, but I'm betting it's Birk. Probably up the trail a bit, waiting for daylight. We'll just give him a little surprise. We'll be long gone when he gets here."

While Miller went out to gather the gear and saddle the horses, Kinslow loaded up the stove with as much wood as it would hold. He figured, from a distance, Birk would see the smoke and assume they were still inside. When Miller came back in and announced everything was ready to go, Kinslow took him aside and cautioned him, "I figure some time soon, Fancy is going to make a move. I'll handle him, but no matter what happens, don't take your eyes off Boudreaux. I think I can trust him, but I'm not a hundred percent sure."

Miller took a defensive position off to one side of Max Boudreaux, while Kinslow woke Ingram up. "Time to ride, gentlemen," he announced as he knelt down and untied the rope around Ingram's ankles and the piece connecting him to Boudreaux. Kinslow hoisted Ingram up and laid him face down on the table while he retied his wrists behind his back. Under Miller's watchful eye, he knelt down again and untied Boudreaux's ankles and retied his wrists, only he didn't force Boudreaux face down on the table.

Ingram noticed this and remarked, "Hey, how come he don't get treated as rough as you're treating me?"

"Because I like him," was Kinslow's reply. He looked at Miller, "Ready, Ansen?" Miller nodded assent and they walked the two prisoners out into the street.

Kinslow brought Ingram's horse to him, tied a short piece of rope to Ingram's right ankle, and helped him mount. As he was reaching under the horse for the rope to tie Ingram's ankles together, Ingram thought he saw an opportunity. He spurred his horse. It was the last thing he remembered doing before he was knocked cold. As soon as Kinslow saw movement, he gave a tremendous pull on the piece of rope he was holding. The rope was attached to Ingram's right ankle and the momentum of the yank pulled him sideways from the horse. He hit the ground with a bone shattering thud. While he was semi-conscious, Kinslow tied his ankles together, retied his wrists in front of his body, hoisted him up, and threw him face down across the saddle. He finished up by tying his wrists to his ankles with a rope that went under the horse's belly.

Kinslow, adrenalin still pumping, turned to Boudreaux and said, "Your turn."

Boudreaux said as pleasantly as he could. "No trouble here, Sir."

Kinslow began to tie the rope to his right leg when Boudreaux spoke up, "Is that necessary? I ain't going anywhere right now."

"Right now?" asked Kinslow. "What does that mean?"

"It means if I get the chance, I'm gone. I know you believe I will get a fair deal from this white judge. I don't. Like I said, if I get the chance I'll go, but for now I will wait and see how this plays out."

"You mean you're hoping Birk will kill us and set you free," countered Kinslow.

"No. This is not true. If Birk kills you and Miller, I don't think he will want to leave any witnesses. If it comes down to a fight, you could use my help. Think about it."

Kinslow thought briefly and then coiled the piece of rope. He helped Boudreaux mount and said, "The wrists stayed tied."

He mounted and watched while Miller did the same. They rode out and picked up the trail again at the end of the camp. Kinslow rode up beside Miller and said, "If memory serves me right, this trail goes up and over this hill and into another valley. It continues over each row of hills in the same way. The miners used it as a short cut from one camp to the next. We'll take it and see if we can't shake Birk.

Boudreaux spoke up, "A little ways to the north, there is a trail that takes you to the top of the ridge. You can follow the tree line most of the way to Fort Collins."

Kinslow looked in the direction Boudreaux indicated. He couldn't make out much in the darkness, but if there was a higher trail, it would make sense to go that way. Even if Birk figured out which way they'd gone, the climb on the higher trail would certainly slow him down.

"Okay, Max. Sounds like a good idea." Kinslow untied his wrists and said, "Lead the way."

Miller started to protest, but Kinslow stopped him and said, "Ansen, I trusted you. Let's give this kid the same chance, okay?"

Miller replied, "Sometimes you're too damn trustin', Woodrow. One of these days it's gonna get you killed."

Chapter 8

The morning sun was creeping over the eastern horizon. As the black of night became an early morning grey, Birk rousted his men. He hadn't slept a wink all night. His irrational thinking convinced him killing Miller would get rid of the pain and emptiness he felt inside and nothing else mattered but that objective. "Let's go," he commanded, "We've got a job to do. Let's get it done!"

Jim Trueman was annoyed. He always liked to start his day with a coffee and something to eat, but he was not prepared to go against Birk's wishes. He and the rest of the men rose quickly, gathered their bedrolls, and saddled up. When they were all mounted, Birk led the way towards the mining camp.

A shallow, willow filled ditch crossed the main trail about a hundred feet from the eastern edge of the camp. A small wooden bridge spanned the gully, making it easier for wagon traffic to get across, but horse and rider could easily navigate it without the bridge. Birk and company rode down into the gully and dismounted. Sanchez gathered and tied off the horses while Andy Birk, Sanders, and Trueman positioned themselves along the bank of the ditch, facing the camp buildings.

With his rifle cocked, Johnathan Birk stood atop the embankment, scrutinizing the rectangular building where he assumed Kinslow was holed up. He hollered, "You in there — Marshal — it's Johnathan Birk." He waited a few seconds and then continued, "Marshal, all I want is the bastard who killed my son. The rest of you can go on your merry way." He listened for a response.

Convinced he was being ignored, Birk fired a shot through the open doorway and quickly ducked behind a clump of willows, fully expecting a barrage of bullets in reply, but none came. This surprised him somewhat. "Alright boys, let them have it," he ordered.

Lead from Winchesters and pistols hit the front of the building, sending splinters of wood flying in all directions. The sound of bullets ricocheting off something metallic inside could be heard. The bombardment continued for a few minutes and when most of the men stopped to reload, Birk yelled, "Hold it. Stop shooting."

Sanchez got Birk's attention. He pointed to the pasture and said, "The horses, they are all gone, Senor.

"Goddamn it," spat Birk, "go check the building. The rest of you keep him covered."

Sanchez made his way very cautiously to the front of the building, tentatively glanced inside, and when he saw the place was empty, he stepped in, still alert to the possibility someone could be hiding in the room. A good look around convinced him there was no one there. He stepped back into the doorway and waved a come-on sign to Birk, who sprinted to the building with the rest of the men in close pursuit. He ran directly inside and scanned the room, assuring himself the place was, indeed, empty.

Birk's mind was racing and he was calculating his next move, when Sanchez walked to the stove and using the lifter, raised one of the removable, round sections of the stove top and poked at the smouldering ashes inside. He said, "If they fill the stove to fool us and they go, I say they have been gone five, maybe six hours, Senor Birk."

There was no one else for Birk to vent his rage on, so he took two long steps towards Sanchez and backhanded him across the face so hard it knocked him to the floor. Birk stood astride the prone man and ranted, "You stupid greaser! I sent you down here to check things out and you told me everything was fine. You told me they were down for the night. Why weren't you watching to make sure this didn't happen?" He gave the cowering Sanchez a vicious kick in the midsection and continued, "I oughta shoot you right where you lay, you useless sack of shit."

Fearing his father, in his present state, might actually kill Sanchez, Andy stepped forward and spoke, "Leave him alone, Pa. It ain't his fault."

Taken aback, Johnathan turned his attention to his son. He left Sanchez on the floor, came face to face with Andy, and said, mockingly, "Oh, lookee here. Well, when did you suddenly grow a set?"

Andy ignored the personal attack, "All I'm saying Pa, is this thing is eating you up. You're not thinking too clear."

"Not thinking too clear?" Johnathan said each word deliberately and slowly. "Let's see now, things were going pretty good until you come along. My beloved Cora died giving you life, boy and then you go and get Mark killed. Oh, I'm thinking pretty clear, all right. My family is all gone and somebody has got to pay."

Father and son stared at each other for what seemed an eternity — Johnathan, realizing what he'd said in the heat of anger and Andy feeling like he was kicked in the chest. Johnathan swallowed hard and turned, "Why is everyone standing around? We got some hard riding to do," he said as he stormed out.

The same dawn light that spurred Johnathan Birk into action, found Kinslow and company high above the tree line, miles ahead of their pursuers. Kinslow stopped and looked in every direction. To his left, several hundred feet in elevation below, he could see the series of hills and valleys stretching to the horizon. To his right, the mountain they were on rose to the sky. Ahead, several miles, he could see that the trail would run into another mountain, which from this distance looked impassable. He turned to Max Boudreaux and asked, "Where does the trail go after it hits the mountain ahead?"

"It goes north — to the right — around the back of the mountain and then circles back south to the main trail we were on yesterday. It'll add a couple of days to the trip." Pointing to the rows of hills far below them, he added, "Or, we can go back down one of these valleys, head straight south, and hit the same trail. It would save a couple of days, but Birk would probably catch us."

Kinslow thought for a moment. "I'm thinking if we stay on this high trail, we stand a better chance of losing Birk. What do you think, Ansen?"

Miller answered, "Sounds good to me," and then added as an afterthought, "Just so you know, I ain't afraid of a fight with Birk."

"I know that, Ansen. Neither am I, but we have a responsibility to get these two prisoners to Fort Collins safely," replied Kinslow.

"Suits me," concluded Miller.

Fancy Ingram spoke up, "Am I supposed to ride like a sack of oats the whole way?"

Kinslow dismounted, undid the rope around Ingram's ankles and the one connecting his hands to his ankle and pulled him off the horse, dumping him on the ground. He lifted Ingram up by his collar and helped him mount. "If you try anything else, any little thing, you will finish the trip on foot tied to a horse's tail," Kinslow said with definite authority.

They started out again, Max Boudreaux in front, Miller leading Fancy Ingram's mount with the pack horse in the middle, and Kinslow as the rear guard. They hadn't traveled very long when Max Boudreaux stopped and said, "We better find some shelter quick. I think we are in for a good one."

Kinslow looked to the west at the deep purple clouds headed right for them. "Let's double back. I saw some big trees a little ways down the trail," he said as he turned his horse carefully on the narrow, rocky path and led the way. A couple of minutes later, he urged his horse over the steep embankment and down the few feet to a grove of large trees. The others were not far behind.

Kinslow gathered all the horses and tied them securely, while Miller watched the prisoners. A good old Rocky Mountain thunder storm had a way of spooking even the best horses. Kinslow pulled his slicker from his roll, as did Miller. Ingram and Boudreaux didn't have any rain gear and would have to tough it out.

Kinslow got Max and Fancy squared away under a huge tree, rolled a smoke, and got it lit before the rain hit. He found himself a nice spot under a big old granddaddy pine with a good view of the prisoners and settled in.

While Kinslow and company were finding shelter from the impending storm, Johnathan Birk grew increasingly impatient as Sanchez and Sanders tried desperately to sort out the dozens of tracks on the trail. "You're supposed to be such a good tracker! What is the problem? Which way did they go?" he shouted.

Sanchez rode to Johnathan. "Senor, I am sorry, but they have made so many tracks it is difficult to sort them all out," he said.

"Well damn it; give me your best guess. Which way do you think you might go if you were them?" insisted Johnathan.

"Senor, I really don't want to guess. They could have doubled back around us and are back on the main trail. They may still be going this way. This trail goes for miles over the hills. Every valley ahead of us has a trail going south to join the main one. They could take any one of them."

Sanders spoke up, "Mr. Birk, about a mile or so ahead, is another way. It's an old Ute trail that follows the tree line and then veers north around the big mountain to the west. It's the long hard way to Fort Collins. My guess is they went that way to lose us."

Birk pondered momentarily and then decided, "I like it, Sanders. I like it. That's the way we'll go."

They were just about at the turnoff to the tree line trail when the storm hit. The pelting rain mixed with pea-sized hail alarmed the horses. Andy Birk and Jim Trueman dismounted and led their mounts and the spares to what little cover there was under some trees. Johnathan Birk was shouting something about moving on, but nobody heard him above the wind and thunder. He galloped off, with Sanchez in close pursuit. Sanders hesitated, trying to decide whether to stay or go. He opted for the most profitable option, which was to stick with the boss.

The worst of the storm blew over in a very short time. Andy Birk and Jim Trueman mounted and rode out after the other three, with Trueman leading the string of spares this time. It was only a few minutes before they caught up to the rest, arriving just as Johnathan Birk, revolver drawn and cocked, fired a shot into his fallen black stallion's head.

Andy dismounted on the run and was shouting "Pa, Pa! What the hell?" as he ran toward his father.

Johnathan saw him coming and looked up. Andy saw the hurt in his father's eyes and the tear running down one cheek. The elder Birk wiped it off before he spoke, "Shadow broke his leg trying to get up this slippery slope. I had to shoot him. I had to. I didn't want him to suffer." After a pause he said, "Get me one of those mangy mustangs and let's get going."

Trueman dismounted, selected one of the horses from the string, and took it over to Johnathan. Andy stood silent for a moment and then addressed his father, "No, Pa. I'm done. I lied to you. That farmer didn't shoot Mark. It was our own fault. We were just having a little fun with him. Mark charged him and got pulled off his horse. He came down on a busted fence post, face first. It was an accident, Pa."

Johnathan was next to Andy in one of his long strides. He drove his closed fist as hard as he could into Andy's nose and sent him sprawling backwards. He drew his pistol and stood over his son. Andy shook off the sting of the punch and lifted himself up on his elbows, the blood from his bleeding nose mixed with the rain, running down his chin. He looked up at his father with an expression of pity and slowly rose to his feet. He reached down and picked up his hat, slapping the mud from it before he put it on. He turned his back on his irate father and began to walk to his horse, "Go ahead, Pa. Shoot me. You've hated me all my life. It's what you've wanted to do all along, isn't it?" He mounted, tipped his hat to the others, and rode off back down the trail.

Johnathan had actually cocked the pistol and aimed it at Andy's back. As Andy rode off, Johnathan let out a heart wrenching wail and fell to his knees. Sanchez knelt next to him and put his arm around his shoulders. "This is tearing you up inside, Senor Birk. Why don't we head back to the rancho?"

Johnathan took a couple of deep breaths before he answered, "No Carlos, I'm going to finish this. Accident or not, he killed my boy and justice is going to be served. Now find me their trail!"

Sanchez chose his words carefully, "The storm has made it very difficult to pick out new tracks from old ones. If I may offer a suggestion, Senor Birk?" He waited for some sign of permission. There was no indication from Birk, so he continued, "All these trails, the high one, the main one by the river, they all meet just outside of Fort Collins. With your permission, Senor, why don't we just go there and wait for this marshal and this Senor Miller? No matter which way they go, if we use the river trail, we will get there before them."

Johnathan Birk smiled and replied, "Good idea Carlos, but I have a better one. Why don't we just go talk to the judge?"

Andy Birk waited until he was well out of sight before he stopped, dismounted, and sat down on the trail embankment to compose himself. He was sure nobody would be coming after him and he needed time to think about what to do next. As his breathing slowed and he relaxed, his mind drifted back to a time when he and Mark were youngsters. Mark was twelve, so he would have been nine, well nine and a half.

Mark thought it would be a great idea to sneak one of their dad's pistols and a box of cartridges and have some fun. They took the six-gun and some tin cans and headed past the outhouse, which was just beyond the bunkhouse. Mark knew enough to set the cans on the fence facing the open field, so they wouldn't hit anything with stray bullets. Mark set six cans on the upper rail. He walked back twenty five paces and loaded the pistol. He held it with both hands, lined it up with a tin can, closed one eye, and pulled the trigger.

The recoil knocked him on the seat of his britches and the tin can survived. The loud report of the pistol scared the life out of Frank Lang, a cowhand who was doing his daily routine in the outhouse. Frank liked to take some reading material in with him and he was deeply engrossed in a dime novel when the shot rang out. His first instinct was to check himself to see if he'd been hit. Satisfied he hadn't, he listened for any more shots. None came, so he carefully opened the door a crack and peeked out. His apprehension turned to anger when he realized it was the Birk brats doing the shooting. He came roaring out, shouting at the boys as he tucked in his shirt and buttoned up his pants.

"We're just practicing shooting, Mr. Lang. Sorry if we scared you," Mark said casually, as he lined up another shot and pulled the trigger.

He knew what to expect this time and didn't get knocked over. He did, however, miss the can. The bullet ripped splinters from the rail just below the tin.

Before Frank could say anything, Mark fired again, this time hitting the can dead center. Frank was impressed. "Looks like we got a natural here," he said.

Mark smiled and was enjoying all the attention when his father and two of the ranch hands came running around the corner of the bunkhouse, rifles in hand. "What in hell is going on here?" demanded Johnathan Birk.

Mark looked up still smiling and announced, "Hey Pa, Mr. Lang says I'm a natural."

Johnathan found it difficult to sustain his strict demeanour. "That's great —uh —sure, let's see you try again," he said.

Mark lined up another can and squeezed the trigger, hitting it dead center. Johnathan, the proud father, put his hand on Mark's shoulder and praised him. Andy could see how proud his father was of Mark. He approached his brother, reached for the pistol, and said, "Can I try, Mark?"

As Mark was handing Andy the pistol, Johnathan reached in and took it. "You don't need to be playing with guns, boy," he said rather sternly. "Ain't you got chores to finish up, or something?"

That was one of many instances over the next ten years where a double standard seemed to be in place. Mark could do no wrong and he could do no right in his father's eyes. He didn't blame Mark for it. It wasn't his fault, but at the same time, Mark never said or did anything to ease the situation, either.

Andy's thoughts returned to the present. "To hell with him!" he said aloud. "Who needs the old bastard, anyway?"

Chapter 9

Nothing much surprised Kinslow anymore. Still, he was mildly curious as to why they hadn't run into Birk and his men. He really didn't believe they fooled the vengeful rancher even though Miller kept on about how they had outsmarted the son-of-a-bitch. Several possibilities crossed his mind; perhaps young Andy finally told his father the truth about his brother's death and Johnathan decided to let the law handle it, or more than likely, Birk had something else in mind.

After the big thunder storm passed, the rest of the three day ride to Fort Collins was uneventful. Fancy Ingram kept his needling up, but like all of his type, who were more gas than guts, he didn't try anything. Kinslow figured him for a smart one and he was convinced Ingram felt sure Birk would take care of matters and he would eventually be rescued. Max Boudreaux didn't say much, just the odd comment about what lay ahead on the trail, or an occasional inquiry about what there was to eat. Ansen Miller was another story. The man didn't stopped talking for the entire time on the trail. Kinslow now knew every detail of Ansen Miller's life since their encounter in Abilene. The man even talked in his sleep.

It was near noon on the third day when they descended into the High Central Plains. An hour later, they could see Fort Collins and roughly another hour brought them into the town.

My God, this place is sure growing, thought Kinslow. He remembered the last time he was in the town. It had to be at least a couple of years ago and there wasn't much more than a trading post and a livery then. Now there were signs of prosperity and growth everywhere. Residences, a church, and businesses that catered to miners, ranchers, and farmers of the area were springing up all over. Kinslow noticed there were two new hotels and several saloons. There was an official looking brick building near completion that would soon serve as the centre of civic administration. There was even talk of a railroad coming through in the next few years.

As they moved further down the main street, Kinslow's hunch about Birk being up to something was reinforced when he saw the lanky rancher, with a big grin on his face, leaning against one of the veranda posts of a local watering hole called the Black Nugget. Three men stepped out from behind Birk into the street and stood in front of Kinslow. Two of them looked like ordinary ranch hands. Kinslow thought one of them might be a Mexican. The third man wore a holster and gun that looked much too extravagant and expensive for an ordinary cowhand. He would be the one to watch.

Kinslow pulled up his horse and ignoring the three men in front of him, he turned sideways and addressed Birk, "We meet again, Sir. I hear tell you been out riding, enjoying the countryside, so to speak," said Kinslow with a conversational tone.

Birk's grin became a scowl as he said, "Nothing has changed, Marshal. I'm going to see justice is done in the matter of my son's death."

Kinslow leaned forward in the saddle to add emphasis to his statement. "Justice? Justice? Why does that word sound dirty coming from you?" He looked at the three men who were still blocking his way and then back at Birk and said, "Call the dogs off before they get stomped."

Sanders' hand moved slowly towards his holstered pistol as he looked to Birk for the go-ahead to drop this annoying lawman. Birk shook his head 'no', partly from common sense and partly because Ansen Miller's Winchester was pointed squarely at his chest. "Oh, I think you'll find out soon enough how we handle our own affairs in this part of the country," Birk said, rather smugly, as the grin returned to his face. He turned to the saloon entrance and as he went inside he said, "Come on boys, I'm buying the first round."

Sanchez, Sanders, and Trueman followed Birk into the saloon, leaving Kinslow and Miller in the street to wonder what just happened. Kinslow expected this to be the showdown and it didn't come. He couldn't shake the uneasy feeling that Birk was a puma waiting for the right opportunity to pounce.

He continued to dwell on it as they made their way to the town marshal's office. '*Office*' was just a word to describe a location. The truth was, it was once the army brig that had fallen into disrepair. Kinslow tied his horse up at the rail and told Miller to watch the prisoners while he went inside.

Kinslow had to stoop to get through the doorway. He stood for a moment while his eyes adjusted to the dim lighting inside. He saw a half dozen cells on the far wall, all vacant. Dick Quincy, the town marshal, was behind a huge cluttered oak desk, which was once in the commanding officer's quarters. He was a short stocky man with a huge bushy moustache, which hid any expression on his face. You could never tell if he was smiling or not. His feet were up on the desk and he was putting the finishing touches on the cigarette he was rolling. He put the curly into his mouth, took a match from his front shirt pocket, lit it on the desk top, and put it to the cigarette. He shook the match out and dropped it on the floor, took a big pull on the smoke, and as he exhaled, he pushed the brim of his hat up and looked at Kinslow. "Something I can do for you?" he asked in a rather sour tone.

Quincy's bitterness was caused by the army. At least, this was who he blamed. He got as far as the rank of Sergeant and was a damn good one until he got a dishonourable discharge for what the army called *'excessive force'* against a recruit. Damn panty-waist Colonel from the east didn't understand you to be tough with these recruits, or they would never survive the first encounter with any hostiles.

Kinslow stepped inside and made his way to the desk. "If you can spare the time, I have two prisoners for you. One of them is Max Boudreaux, charged with murder and the other is a young gunny calls himself Fancy Ingram. I'll file charges on him later." He reached in his back pocket and withdrew some papers, which he unfolded and threw on Quincy's desk. "Here's the paper work on Boudreaux."

Kinslow went back to the open door and hollered to Miller, "Bring them in, Ansen."

Miller ushered in Boudreaux and Ingram. Quincy opened a cell and was holding the door open. Kinslow took out his knife and cut the rope around Ingram's and Max's wrists, roughly shoved Ingram into the open cell, and indicating Max, he said to Quincy "Put him in a separate cell."

Quincy locked Ingram's cell and opened the next one. Max walked himself in and sat on the bunk. Quincy locked his cell and tossed the keys in the general direction of the big desk. "Anything else?" he asked as if there was some important business he needed to get back to.

"Tell me where I can find Judge Beams," said Kinslow.

"Well, if he ain't in his office next to Grady's Mercantile, he'll be at the Black Nugget. Judge likes his sauce, if you know what I mean," Quincy said, indicating a drinking motion with an imaginary glass.

"Thanks. Let's go, Ansen," said Kinslow

Quincy stopped them from leaving when he said, "Ansen Miller? There's a poster out on you for murder." He took a couple of steps towards Miller and said, "I'm afraid I am going to have to detain you until I can talk to —"

Kinslow interrupted him, "I don't think so. This man is my deputy and I will do any detaining that needs doing. We will clear the matter up when I see the judge."

Quincy smiled and said, "Oh, I'm sure you will."

Kinslow detected the sarcasm in Quincy's voice and he didn't like it. He was still thinking about it as they went back up the main street to the judge's office. The door was locked and there was no sign of life inside. Kinslow looked further up the street. Directly across from the judge's office was the Black Nugget Saloon. *Handy,* he thought.

They began to cross the street when Kinslow stopped Miller and said, "Ansen, I've got an uneasy feeling. Something is in the wind. It just doesn't feel right to me. Keep your eyes open and stay alert."

"What do you want me to do?" asked Miller.

"When we get to the Black Nugget, I'll go in first. You count to ten then come in and step to the side against the wall, with your gun ready."

Kinslow parted the swinging doors, stood for a moment, and surveyed the interior of the saloon. While his trained eye made note of the décor and the people dispersed throughout the establishment, he focused on finding the judge. As he looked to his right, he saw Birk seated at a table with a rotund, grey haired, stylishly dressed man. Kinslow did another scan to locate Birk's son and henchmen. Leaning against one end of the long bar, were the three men he'd just encountered in the street. He didn't see any younger men who could pass for Andy Birk. He took one quick glance at Miller behind him, nodded, and entered.

Kinslow made straight for the bar. The bartender stood wiping out a shot glass as he watched Kinslow approach. He set the glass in front of him and asked, "What can I get you, Marshal?"

"I'll take a shot of whatever it is you call whiskey and then you can point me in the direction of Judge Beams," said Kinslow.

The bartender filled the glass in front of Kinslow and pointed to the table where Birk was seated, "The gentleman in the suit and eyeglasses is Judge Beams."

Kinslow tossed back the drink, threw a dime on the bar, and walked slowly to the table. He tipped his hat to Birk and then addressed the other man, "Judge Beams?"

"Yes, how can I be of service, Marshal?" the judge asked.

Kinslow spoke slowly, "A couple of things, your Honour. I have two prisoners over in the jail. One is a half breed Ute who they say killed a white rapist to protect the young women in his camp. I would like to put a word in for him at his hearing. The other is young gunman who calls himself Fancy Ingram. I want to charge him with attempted murder and assault on a U.S. marshal."

"We can take care of this business first thing in the morning. And the other?" said Judge Beams.

Kinslow looked at Birk and then back to the judge, "Seeing who you have with you at this table, I'm guessing you have already heard his side of the story," he said.

"Yes I have," the judge replied "and I am about to issue an arrest warrant for Ansen Miller."

"On what charge?" demanded Kinslow, the anger starting to build in him.

"Murder!" replied Johnathan Birk, with a wry smile.

"Wait a minute. How can you issue an arrest warrant when you haven't heard all of the evidence?" spat Kinslow.

"I'm sorry Marshal, but there is no evidence in this case. It's Johnathan's word against Mr. Miller's," replied Beams.

"Johnathan? Kind of informal aren't we. Good friends I take it?" implied Kinslow.

Beams shook his head and said, "Sarcasm won't help your cause, Marshal. You can say your piece at the trail. Anything else?"

Kinslow rose slowly. Birk's three henchmen had moved around to the front of the bar and were leaning against it, facing the room. The one with the fancy pistol had his gun in his hand and was spinning the cylinder. Kinslow took a quick glance at the doorway for Miller. He wasn't there. Kinslow put his knuckles on the table and leaned in toward the judge before he spoke, "That kid of his is lying to you! It wasn't murder. It was an accident brought on by the two boys in the first place." Kinslow paused, looked around, and then continued, "Where is the kid? As the investigating officer in this case, I'd like to speak to him."

Birk spoke up, "Andy left us on the trail a few days ago. I told Judge Beams what Andy told me and my word is good enough in these parts."

Kinslow didn't move his body. He just turned his head, so he was facing Birk. "Well, it's not good enough for the law which seems to be under your influence in *these parts*," he said with emphasis. As he turned back to Beams, he continued, "Under the circumstances, I have decided, as is my jurisdiction, to take the two prisoners and Ansen Miller to a federal court in Denver."

As Kinslow stood up, Quincy and four other men, all well armed, a couple with rifles and the rest with shotguns, burst through the saloon doors, pushing Ansen Miller in front of them. Miller had a nasty gash across his right cheek, the result of a pistol barrel across the face. Quincy pulled back the hammers on the sawed-off, double barrelled, 12 gauge shotgun and centered it on Kinslow's chest.

Kinslow's resolve was unaffected by the grand entrance and he turned his attention to Judge Beams once more, "Like I said, my deputy and I will be taking the prisoners to Denver."

He stepped over to Ansen Miller, took his chin in his hand, and turned his head to get a better look at the wound. Quincy prodded Kinslow in the back with the barrel of the shotgun to get his attention and said, "He's my prisoner. Ain't anybody going nowhere. Well, maybe boot hill after the hanging." He started to laugh heartily at his own joke, but before he could get the second chuckle out, Kinslow spun his left arm up and under the shotgun and pulled it from Quincy's grasp.

"You the one pistol whipped my deputy?" Kinslow asked as he shoved the shotgun under Quincy's nose. Quincy didn't say anything, but Kinslow could see the answer in his eyes. He turned the shotgun and in one quick motion used the butt end to smash Quincy's nose with a short, powerful jab. Before he had time to think of his next move, something hit him like a mule kick in the back of the head. The last thing Kinslow saw before he passed out, was Sanders standing over him, cleaning his pistol handle with a handkerchief.

Quincy rose slowly. Holding his broken, bleeding nose with one hand, he kicked Kinslow repeatedly in the mid section. "Enough, enough," yelled Birk, "we don't want to kill him. That's all we need, is someone else to come around looking for him. Put him on his mount, take him out of town, and point the horse down the road and give it a good slap. Looks like Marshal Kinslow is going to miss the hanging party in the morning."

Quincy gave Kinslow one more half hearted kick and signalled two of his cronies to pick him up. He gave them instructions for disposing of the marshal, grabbed Miller by the shirt collar, and dragged him out of the saloon.

Birk stood watching the whole thing and when everyone cleared out, he sat back down at the table with Judge Beams. He poured another drink for the judge and one for himself. He raised his glass and waited for Beams to do the same. They clanked glasses and Birk gave his toast, "Here's to justice. Now my son can rest in peace."

Judge Beams seemed somewhat rattled. "I don't know Johnathan, I just don't know about this. We are really pushing the limits of authority here. A U.S. marshal —there could be serious repercussions. I just — "

"Don't worry, Ronald," Birk reassured him. He got up from the table and added, "It's his word against all of ours. Now, I've got to get some sleep. Got to get up early for a hanging in the morning."

On his way out, he tossed a twenty dollar gold piece to Sanders and said, "Drinks are on me, boys."

Chapter 10

As Kinslow slowly opened his eyes, he felt like he'd just awakened from a very deep sleep. At first, he didn't know where he was. Spinning glimpses of saloons, hotel rooms, and campfires flashed through his mind. The sharp, stabbing pain in the back of his neck brought him closer to clarity.

As awareness returned, he felt his horse beneath him. He straightened up in the saddle and looked around, trying to get his bearings. He came to the conclusion he'd been loaded on his horse and unceremoniously escorted out of town. He wasn't sure how far they'd taken him, but he sensed it wasn't a great distance. Unknown to his captors, even with a hard slap on the rump, Knothead would only have run as far as the first tasty clump of meadow grass and feeling no bit pressure, he would have stopped to munch.

Kinslow half fell and half climbed off his horse and after opening the canteen, he leaned his head back and poured water on his face, taking a couple of swallows at the same time. He tried to lift his left arm to check for damage from Sanders' pistol butt which brought on a jolt of pain that ran from his shoulder to his elbow. Using his right arm, he massaged his aching neck and then felt his tender ribs. Nothing was broken. He'd instinctively protected his midsection with his arms. Only one or two blows had gotten through to his chest. His left arm, which was bruised and sore, took the brunt of the kicks from Quincy. Thoughts of payback for Sanders and Quincy crept into his mind.

He took inventory. They'd taken his holster and pistol. The rifle scabbard was empty, as well, and he was missing his hat. You could replace a rifle or a pistol, but losing a hat was just plain inconvenient. No one really appreciates how long it takes to break in a new one. He felt for the knife he kept in his belt in the small of his back. It was still there. It was nothing fancy, a standard issue with a leather grip and an eight inch blade, honed to razor sharpness. He reached inside his vest pocket and felt a wave of relief, as his fingers curled around the Pepperbox Derringer. A quick check of a lower pocket in the vest yielded another hideaway, a small Remington .41 two-shot.

He remounted Knothead and headed back in the direction of town. He was correct about his horse not going very far. He wasn't riding for more than ten minutes, when he saw lights. In another few minutes, he was turning into a side street, one block off the main thoroughfare. He rode slowly, looking carefully into the doorways and shadows. Quincy and Birk obviously must have concluded he was no longer a problem, at least for tonight, because there was no one about. As near as he could tell, it must be near midnight. When he'd gone into the Black Nugget, the sun was just setting and by his internal clock, he guessed two or three hours had passed.

He made his way to the back of the jail and tied his horse to one of the rails of a makeshift corral. He edged his way along the side of the jail and peered out into the street looking in both directions, paying particular attention to the front of the building. There was no guard posted, so he made his way slowly along the boardwalk in front of the building until he came to one of the windows. He positioned himself below it in a crouch and carefully eased himself up, so he could see inside. The cell area came into view. There were two men in separate cells. *Where was the third? Why only two,* he wondered. He turned his attention to the big desk and the man behind it. He had his feet up, was drinking a cup of something, and the son-of-a-bitch was wearing his hat!

Kinslow stayed low as he made his way to the door. He stood up and tried the latch, very carefully. It was locked. Thinking quickly, he knocked. He could hear muffled crashing noises through the door. *The fool probably fell out of the chair,* he thought. He could hear heavy footsteps as the man crossed the plank floor and then a voice asked, "Who is it?"

Kinslow replied, speaking clearly and slowly, "Uh — it's Bill Blake. I work for Mr. Birk. He sent me over with a piece of paper for this Miller fella to sign. It's a confession, I think. Mr. Birk says we should use any means necessary to persuade him to sign it, if you get my drift."

Kinslow timed it perfectly. When the door opened a crack, he gave it a good swift kick. The man behind the door landed on his backside ten feet away and before he could get his bearings, Kinslow was on top of him, a knee planted in his chest and the Derringer shoved into one of his nostrils. "Little gun, but it makes a big mess," Kinslow said through clenched teeth. "Not a sound. Not one, or so help me I will blow the back of your head off. Whatever they are paying you, it ain't worth dying over. And one more thing, what the hell are you doing with my hat?"

"They — they give it to me. Said you wouldn't be needing it anymore," pleaded the man.

Kinslow stood up and took the man's gun out of his holster as he rose. He stepped away and said, "On your belly with your fingers locked behind your head." The man complied and Kinslow approached the cells. Max Boudreaux was in one cell and Ansen Miller in another. There was no sign of Fancy Ingram.

Kinslow searched the top of the desk for the keys to the cells. Not having any success, he addressed the man on the floor, "Hey, fat man, where are the keys?"

"Top drawer, left side. Look, I don't want no trouble. I'll do whatever you say. Just don't hurt me," he pleaded.

Tossing the keys on the floor next to the prone jailer, Kinslow instructed him to get up and open Miller's cell. He handed the Derringer to Miller and said, "Keep that peashooter on him, Ansen and if he makes one wrong move, shoot him in the belly." As a bit of an intimidation factor, he added, "God, but that's a slow and painful way to die."

"Bill Blake? You couldn't come up with somethin' better? Who the hell is Bill Blake?" asked Miller, in jest.

"It was the best I could do on short notice. It sounds like a cowpuncher's name, don't it? Bill Blake. Kinda has a nice ring to it." Kinslow turned serious and asked, "Where's Fancy Ingram?"

Miller replied, "When they brought me in, they let him out. That so called judge says he was actin' within the law because he was tryin' to capture a wanted man."

"You didn't see what they did with my rig, did you?" Kinslow asked Miller.

Before Miller could answer, the jailer spoke up, "It's in the big drawer on the right side of the desk and your rifle is in the gun case, yonder."

"Well, thank you," said Kinslow, "that's more like it. Uh, what is your name?"

"Guthrie, Sir. Emil Guthrie."

Kinslow opened the drawer Guthrie had indicated. He found his gun and holster and a couple of other rigs as well. He checked his pistol to make sure it was loaded. Satisfied, he buckled the holster on, checked the other revolvers and found they were both ready to go. He picked what he thought was the best one and tossed it to Miller.

"Mr. Guthrie, would you be so kind as to tell me where they might have put Mr. Miller's horse?" Kinslow asked, far too politely.

Guthrie thought for a moment before answering, "Most likely at Henry's Livery. Its one street over and about four doors down. Not far."

"Emil, I would like you to come along with us and show me where," suggested Kinslow.

"You ain't gonna kill me are you?" asked Guthrie with suspicion.

"Only if you do something stupid," Kinslow said as he retrieved his rifle from the gun case.

They were about to leave when Max Boudreaux spoke up, "You're going to leave me here?"

While Kinslow may have empathized with Max, he was still a stickler for the law. "I'm sorry, but I can't let you out, Mr. Boudreaux. I would be breaking the oath I took."

"You say you follow the law. What does your law say about leaving me to die? You think they are going to give me a chance to tell my side. They'll probably hang me out of spite because you two got away," argued Boudreaux.

Kinslow felt trapped. He'd intended to take Boudreaux to Denver, but the situation had changed. His commitment to his badge wouldn't allow him to let a killer loose, no matter what the circumstances. He couldn't decide on guilt or innocence. That was up to a court. On the other hand, his sense of fair play nagged at him to do the right thing. After all, he'd taken up Miller's cause because he believed him. He took the keys out of the empty cell door, where Guthrie had left them and opened Max's cell.

"Let's make sure we understand each other. You are still my prisoner. I will take you to Denver and you and Ansen can both tell your stories to a federal judge that I know. If you try to escape, I will shoot you. Are we clear?"

"We are clear, Mr. Kinslow. We are very clear," replied Boudreaux, with an undertone that suggested to Kinslow that Max wasn't promising anything. He felt Boudreaux would still hold true to what he said back on the trail. He would try to escape, should the opportunity arise.

Kinslow picked up Knothead and with Guthrie leading the way, they made their way to the livery. There were a half dozen horses in the corral and Guthrie indicated there were several others in stalls inside the barn. Kinslow instructed Miller to watch Boudreaux and Guthrie while he checked inside. He made his way cautiously through the large doorway and hollered out. "Hello, anybody here?" He waited a moment and tried again. There was no answer. He checked the horses in the stalls and concluded neither Miller's nor Boudreaux's mount was there. He thought he recognized Miller's saddle and gear amongst several others on a bench against one wall. He picked up what he figured was Miller's outfit and headed outside to the corral.

"This your saddle, Ansen?" he asked.

"Sure is, and I think my horse is here in the corral," replied Miller.

Kinslow addressed Guthrie, "What about his horse and gear?" he asked, indicating Max.

"Far as I know, his horse should be in the corral here. His tack should be where you found those," answered Guthrie.

Kinslow issued orders, "Ansen, you find your horse and Boudreaux's. Guthrie, give him a hand. Max you come with me. We'll find your gear." Ten minutes later they were mounted and heading out of Fort Collins, on their way to Denver. Guthrie was left tied and gagged to one of the corral posts.

It was nearly dawn when Johnathan Birk came down the stairs from the second floor of the Bristol Hotel. Again, he hadn't slept more than an hour or two. He conceded once Miller was hung, he and Mark could rest in peace. He wouldn't have to get half drunk every night just to dull the pain and get a little sleep. He didn't allow himself the luxury of thinking Mark's death wasn't Miller's fault and Andy's confession about it being an accident, holding any merit. He didn't care. As far as he was concerned, accident or not, Miller was still responsible for this son's death and he was going to pay.

He entered the hotel's tavern, which also served as an eatery. The hotel clerk, who did double duty as the waiter on the night shift, hustled over as soon as Johnathan was seated and was standing ready with pad and pencil to take his order. "I'll have three eggs, cooked hard and some bacon and keep the coffee coming," said Johnathan.

The clerk disappeared through a door at the far end of the bar. Johnathan could hear his muffled voice barking out his breakfast order. He bounced back through the door with a cup and coffee pot in hand. Johnathan was taking his first sip of coffee when Emil Guthrie and another tall, very thin man, who smelled as bad as the livery he worked in, rushed in and stood in front of his table.

Guthrie spoke, "Mr. Birk, Sir — Uh— I'm afraid we have some bad news for you. You see, Amos here — he works at the livery and he come in at his usual time to get the place going for the day. He usually stokes up the fire in the stove and cleans up in the barn before he gets out to the corral. So he didn't see me until —"

"Hell man, will you please get to the point," said Birk in exasperation.

"Miller has escaped, Mr. Birk!"

"Where? How? Who was watching him?"

"That marshal fella jumped me and took him. I didn't see him coming. I swear, Mr. Birk, I didn't stand a chance. He took the half breed Ute, too."

Birk jumped up and all in one motion kicked his chair back and grabbed Guthrie by his shirt front. "You're lying. That lawman is half dead laying in some gully," he said through clenched teeth.

Guthrie replied with a quiver in his voice, "No Sir — I — I swear on my mother's grave, it was him."

Birk released his grip on the terrified Guthrie and gazed upwards toward the ceiling as if looking for inspiration. After a moment, he lowered his head, made eye contact again, and said, "Go get Judge Beams and that useless Quincy for me. Do you think you can handle that much?" He turned to Amos the livery man and said, "Go upstairs and roust my men. Tell them they have five minutes to get down here."

Both men hurried off to their appointed tasks. Birk sat down and the clerk scurried over to refill his coffee cup. Johnathan took the pot from him and slammed it on the table. "Leave it here. Now, let me be," he said.

Less than five minutes later, Amos came back down the stairs, leading a sleepy Sanders, Sanchez, and Trueman. Sanders took a cup from the bar and poured himself a coffee from the pot on Birk's table. "What's up, Boss?" he asked, casually.

"Miller is gone!" spat Birk.

Sanchez and Trueman looked surprised. Sanders didn't blink. He took a sip of his coffee and asked, "So, what do want from me?"

"I want you to finish what I hired you for. Get Miller on the end of a rope," snarled Birk.

"I have already done my part. I figure you owe me fifteen hundred dollars," countered Sanders.

Birk turned angry, "You won't get a dime until Miller swings."

"Same deal?" asked Sanders. "Fifteen hundred alive, five hundred dead."

"Same deal," said Birk.

Sanders took another sip of his coffee and said under his breath, "Maybe I'll just settle for the five hundred."

Birk heard him, but just ignored it. He said to Sanchez and Trueman, "Round up some supplies, get the horses all saddled, and bring them out front as quick as you can."

Birk finished his breakfast and he and Sanders were on their fifth hand of poker, when Judge Beams and Quincy came in. The judge kept looking around the room nervously, as if he expected the ceiling to fall in. When they both got to Birk's table, Quincy removed his hat which vividly displayed his badly swollen nose and the dark purple rings encircling his eyes.

"Good God, Quincy, you look like hell," Birk remarked. Then to Judge Beams, "I want you to write out a warrant for the arrest of Marshal Woodrow Kinslow. Let's see —ah, yes — let's make the charges obstruction of justice and two counts of aiding and abetting felons to escape jail. Sound good, your Honour?"

"Yes. Yes, of course. I'll have them in a few moments," mumbled Beams.

He turned to leave when Birk added, "Oh, while you're at it, you might as well amend the one out for Miller, too. Murder in the first degree which will make it all official and everything."

Taking advantage of the lull, Quincy said, "What did you want to see me about, Mr. Birk?"

Birk paused for thought and then solemnly said, "Well Tom, it's like this. Two prisoners were broken out of your jail by a renegade marshal. You're going to need some help rounding these men up, I'm sure. So, out of the goodness of our hearts, me and the boys have decided to help you out. But we want to make sure this is all legal like, so you'll have to swear us in as deputies."

Quincy rubbed his hand on his stubbled chin before he spoke, "You may have the judge in your hip pocket, Mr. Birk, but nobody owns me."

Just how long do you think you're going to keep your badge? One word from me and the judge will give your walking papers," retorted Birk.

Quincy unpinned the town marshal's badge from his left front pocket, took a long hard look at it, threw it on the table in front of Birk, and said "I've bent the law a little when it comes to your bidding, but I draw the line here. Get someone else to do your dirty work."

As he turned to leave, Sanders make a clucking sound, imitating a chicken. Dick Quincy made the last mistake of his life. He intended to confront the man who just made fun of him and ask him if he wanted a beating. Unfortunately, Tom Sanders did his talking with his gun and as Quincy turned towards him, Sanders put a round hole dead center between Quincy's ringed eyes before he could even open his mouth. Quincy slumped to his knees and then fell face first into the floor.

The click of a pistol being cocked behind him spun Sanders around. He saw Fancy Ingram at the top of the stairs, his gun out and ready. Before either one could do or say anything, Birk intervened. "Whoa, whoa boys! Put the guns away." He looked up at Ingram and said, "Our town marshal just quit. Did you want the job?"

Ingram holstered his pistol and said as he came down the stairs, "Sorry about that, I just get a little jumpy when I hear shooting?"

Sanders took a little longer to make sure there was no threat before he put his gun away. Birk extended his hand to Fancy and said, "Name is Johnathan Birk. You are Mr. Ingram, I presume."

"People call me Fancy. Not sure why, though. Could be I like fancy clothes, or maybe 'cause it's I'm pretty fancy with a gun." He looked at Sanders when he said the last part.

Not long after, Judge Beams hurried in, carrying papers, which Birk assumed were the arrest warrants. He strutted over to Birk's table and tossed the papers in front of him. As he turned to go, he noticed Quincy's body on the floor. "What did you do now? My, oh my. This is getting to be too much," he remarked.

"Mr. Quincy just resigned his position. Pull yourself together, your Honour. We are in this together and we are going to see it through. Now, just more thing you can do and then you can crawl back into your bottle," said Birk.

"What would that be?" asked Beams.

"Swear me and my men in as officers of the court and we will do what needs to be done." Birk then addressed Fancy, "Could use a gun like yours. You interested?"

"Sure. Sounds like it might be fun," replied Ingram.

Birk said, pointing to Sanders and Ingram, "Swear us all in. There will be another two along in a few minutes."

Chapter 11

Kinslow and company stopped to rest and water their horses at a small spring fed creek. "How much of a lead do you think we've got?" Miller asked.

"Don't know for sure, but if I had to guess, I'd say about five, maybe six hours," Kinslow replied. He still had some hardtack and jerky left in his saddle bags which he cut into pieces and passed around and then continued, "I figure we left around midnight. The liveryman will start work around dawn and find our tied up deputy, who will head straight for Birk. Give Birk an hour to get things together and then they will be coming hard."

"Can we outrun them?" asked Miller.

"No, I don't think so."

"Then what are we gonna to do?"

"I'm sorry, Ansen, I don't know. I just don't know." Kinslow paused to think then continued, "Stand and fight when the time comes, I guess."

"Why don't you just give it up?" asked Max, much to Kinslow's surprise. "We could split up and head in three different directions. They won't know who to follow." He paused briefly then added, "There is an old Ute proverb that says a man does not have to do a foolish thing to prove he is brave."

"Where I come from, we call that being a coward," interjected Miller. "'Besides, that's not any Indian sayin' I ever heard of."

"There is often a fine line between bravery and foolishness," countered Max.

Kinslow interjected, "He does have a point, Ansen. Only trouble is, Birk isn't going to let up until he sees this thing through to the end. Sometimes, to save face, a man is forced into foolishness or bravery, depending on the circumstances."

"That is true," concluded Max.

"Mr. Boudreaux, you are certainly a fascinating man. You must've had a very interesting upbringing," said Kinslow.

Kinslow wasn't far from the truth. Max's father was a Frenchmen who trapped the rivers and creeks and once every spring all the trappers would meet on the South Platte for something they called *Rendezvous*. They would sell their furs, get exceedingly drunk, and tell each other lies. It was there he met Max's mother, a beautiful Ute woman. He fell in love with her the first time he saw her. They were married and not long after, they had a baby whom they named Maximillian.

His father was not happy to live in one place and his mother would not leave her family, so his father left and Max grew up as a Ute, learning his people's ways. When he got older, being half white, he wasn't sure where I belonged. He soon came to the realization the only way to make it in the white man's world was to know the white man's way.

His first paying job was a bronco buster for a wrangling outfit. He made a friend there, a white man named Joshua, who taught Max how to read and to use the white man's language correctly. He read everything he could get his hands on; books, newspapers, and even the Bible. After Joshua got stomped by a mean stallion, Max did some trapping, broke horses for the army, and mostly drifted from job to job."

"Why did you take the blame for killing a rapist," Kinslow asked.

"Better that way. They won't bother anyone else, especially the girls, about it," replied Max.

"What if the judge in Denver asks for proof of your story and he just might?" Kinslow asked.

"If we see him, he will just have to take my word for it and that of Woodrow Kinslow, a U.S. marshal and an honest man."

"Truthfully, I'm not sure it will be enough," cautioned Kinslow.

"It will have to be, my friend." Max took a bite of the hardtack and looked off into the distance. Kinslow knew the conversation was over.

"Let's grab forty winks. Horses could use the rest and so could we," said Kinslow, changing the subject.

"I think we should keep movin', Woodrow," said Miller. "Birk will just gain an hour on us if we stop."

"If we don't rest the horses, they will give out and Birk will catch us anyhow. Now get some sleep," ordered Kinslow.

Kinslow tried to doze, but thoughts of a possible confrontation with Birk steamrolling through his mind, wouldn't let him. He looked over at the other two men. It appeared Miller was restless as well, while

Boudreaux was out cold, snoring away. *Well, at least Max and the horses were getting some rest*, he thought.

A few hours later, they were traveling through rolling hills covered with grassy slopes that were dotted with a mixture of ponderosa pines and the occasional small grove of aspen. Thick ridges made up of mostly sandstone and shale ran at various angles across the face of some of the hills. Looking like turrets on a castle, sandstone outcroppings that varied in size from a large boulder to a small barn protruded from the rocky ridges at regular intervals. The elements had eroded some of the larger ones, so chunks of sandstone and shale had broken off the main body, creating large slag piles of loose rock below the ridges.

As he rode, Kinslow couldn't shake a heavy, smothering feeling that Birk wasn't far away. His keen intuition was on the mark as usual. Birk and his posse came to the top of a knoll just in time to see Kinslow and company disappearing over a hill, less than a quarter of a mile away. "We got 'em, boys. We got the bastards!" screamed Birk with excitement, as he spurred his horse into a gallop, with the others quickly following his lead.

The Kinslow bunch had just come off a rise and were headed downhill onto a small flat plain that rose sharply, after a few hundred yards, into another large hill. The sound of gunfire attracted Kinslow's attention. He looked back and it took a moment for it to register that the riders charging down the hill were shooting at him. "It's Birk! Head for the big pile of rocks straight ahead," he shouted as he gently heeled his horse in the ribs. Knothead took up the challenge and reached full speed in a few strides. Kinslow didn't stop until he was safely behind cover. Much later, he would regret not looking back, or he might have done things differently.

He dismounted quickly, with rifle drawn, ready for the fight. He expected Miller and Boudreaux to be right behind him. Such was not the case. Max had split off to the right and had gone down a small, wooded gully. Miller's horse must have stepped on a rock or in a hole, for it was down and snorting in pain. Ansen was thrown clear and was just getting to his feet when Birk drove his horse into him and knocked him back down.

Kinslow levered a shell into the Winchester's chamber and fired quickly at Birk. He didn't take the time to aim properly and the bullet flew over Birk's head. A hail of lead ricocheted all around Kinslow and he ducked behind one of the sandstone slabs. Once positioned, he peeked out in time to see Birk and four others riding back to a nearby small grove of trees. Birk had thrown a rope around Miller and was dragging him. The grove was only a stone's throw from the rock pile, so by the time Kinslow levered another shell into the firing chamber and took aim, Birk and his men were well into the trees.

Kinslow took a deep breath and sat down behind the rock slab. He needed a moment to gather himself and to think. Max Boudreaux had found his window of opportunity and was probably half a mile away by now. Kinslow wasn't worried about his horse. Knothead never strayed far. He would wander about munching on tufts of prairie grass until Kinslow whistled for him.

Ansen Miller was the main concern. Birk had him, but what was his intent? Was he going to carry out the execution here and now, or take him back to Fort Collins for a mock trial? Kinslow figured Birk was going to get it over with and hang Miller now. He needed to find a way to convince Birk the only legal way was to let Miller have his day in court, so all the facts could come out. With that thought in mind, he eased himself to a standing position and took a quick look. There didn't seem to be any activity in the grove. Kinslow hollered, "Birk! Johnathan Birk! We need to talk."

No response came. Kinslow tried again, this time a lot louder. "Birk! We need to talk."

"We have nothing to talk about. I'm going to hang this bastard as soon as he comes round and then we're coming for you," shouted Birk.

"You hang him and I will hunt you down. You can't take the law into your own hands," Kinslow answered with conviction.

"I am the law. Judge Beams deputized us all," Birk replied with arrogance.

"You can't hang him without a trial. What are you afraid of, Birk? That the truth will come out? That your son's death was an accident?" argued Kinslow.

After a lengthy pause Birk shouted back, "Accident or not, he killed my son and he is going to pay."

Kinslow tried a different approach, "What you are doing is just plain murder, not justice. Is that what your son would want?"

"Don't you dare talk about my son. You're not fit to lick his boots!"

"One last time," Kinslow spat out each word slowly with as much authority as he could, "give me Ansen Miller and we can end it here."

Again, there was a lengthy pause before Birk replied, "You want Miller? You can have him."

Puzzled by the sudden about face, Kinslow chanced a longer look from his vantage point. Ansen Miller was being walked out into the open by Birk, who stood directly behind him with one arm around Miller's throat and his revolver jammed into Miller's temple. Birk stopped after about ten paces and addressed Kinslow, "You want this murdering son-of-a-bitch? He's all yours!" Birk pulled the trigger and Ansen Miller died instantly. To add insult to injury, as Miller slump to his knees, Birk gave him a well place boot in the middle of his back to hurry his drop to the ground.

It all happened so suddenly, Kinslow stood stunned with jaw agape. Birk covered the short distance back to the safety of the trees before Kinslow could react. The bullet ricocheting off the rock just above his head, drove Kinslow back behind cover.

"Come out peaceable, Marshal and we won't kill you, I swear," Birk said with just the right amount of sarcasm to let Kinslow know he was lying through his teeth.

With the killing of Ansen Miller, Kinslow lost some confidence in his ability to read Birk. He knew one thing for certain; Birk could not afford to leave him alive, now. He thought, with the odds at five to one, his best move would be to find a way out of here, and quick.

He began to survey his sanctuary. The only way that seemed to offer any hope of leaving without being detected, was to climb to near the top of the rock pile he was using for cover and then follow a shale ledge that ran at a forty five degree angle up the slope of the hill. Bent over, he could use the ledge as a screen, make his way up the hill, and be gone before Birk knew it. The only question was the whereabouts of his horse, but first things first. He would get out of the immediate vicinity and then worry about finding Knothead.

He scrambled up the sandstone slabs and loose shale that made up the backside of the rock formation. He was almost at the top, ready to duck under the cover of the ledge, when a voice he recognized stopped him in his tracks, "Howdy, Marshal. Remember me?" It was Fancy Ingram. He stood on a large sandstone slab with revolver in hand, directly above Kinslow. Ingram wore a wide, satisfied grin on his face as he pulled the trigger.

Kinslow's instincts and exceptional reaction time saved his life. As he twisted and dove to his right, the bullet that would have ripped through his heart tore through the back of his left shoulder and out the front. As he hit the ground, his rifle flew up in the air and as he rolled down the loose shale, he instinctively drew his pistol and squeezed off a couple of shots in Ingram's general direction. The bullets never came anywhere near Fancy, but they were enough to force him to jump down from his vantage point. As a result, a moment or so later when he ventured a look from behind cover, he couldn't see Kinslow anywhere. Unknown to him, Kinslow had lost consciousness and his limp body continued to roll to the bottom of the loose shale and dropped over the edge of a protruding ledge. It was only a short drop of a couple feet, but it was enough to hide him from Fancy's view.

Ingram climbed back atop the sandstone slab again and there he hesitated. He was convinced he'd hit Kinslow. No way could he have missed, he told himself. He scanned the bottom of the rock pile from left to right and back again several times. He caught sight of Kinslow's rifle in the loose shale a few feet below. He fired a couple of rounds at the spot where he thought Kinslow might be. There was no response. Shaking, with little beads of sweat forming on his quivering lip, he edged his way to the rifle, snatched it up, and frantically scrambled back the few feet to cover.

Normally, a professional gunman would make sure his quarry was dead, but Fancy was not the bravest of men. He was full of confidence when he knew he had the advantage, but when the odds were even or maybe not in his favour, he would back down and had done so several times in the past. He wasn't about to go down and crawl among the rocks and let the marshal bushwhack him. It was time to put on the act.

"I got him! I got him! I got that stinkin' marshal!" he shouted as he strutted back to the grove and the waiting men.

Birk's stare sent a chill through Fancy, but he maintained his composure when the boss asked, "How come so many shots?"

Years of lying to cover up his inadequacies had served Fancy well. He replied without hesitation, "Oh, he was quick. I give him that. Quick, but not too smart. I only winged him on the first shot and he ducked behind a boulder. He threw a couple of shots my way and I waited him out and when he made a run for it, bang! Heart shot. I put one more between his eyes just to make sure." He held out the rifle and tossed it to Birk. "Souvenir for your mantle, Mr. Birk, the great Marshal Kinslow's rifle."

Listening to Fancy relate his heroics, Birk had some doubts and was prepared to go check the body until Ingram tossed him the marshal's rifle. He was sure Kinslow would not have given it up if he weren't dead or badly wounded. He sighed and said, "That's it, men. It's done. A fine job. Yes sir, a fine job, indeed."

Sidetracked

Birk mounted and began to ride back in the direction they had come. Sanchez stopped him by asking, "Senor, should we not bury these men? It would be the Christian thing to do."

"Tell you what, Sanchez, you can stay and bury that scum if you want to. Me and the rest of the fellas are heading back to Fort Collins for a little celebrating," replied Birk as he spurred his horse and rode off.

Sanchez didn't have anything resembling a shovel, so he dragged Miller's body by the boot heels to the rock pile. He went through Miller's pockets and put the contents in his hat and set it aside. He folded Miller's arms across his chest and laboriously moved pieces of sandstone to cover him up. It wasn't much of a grave, but it was the best he could do under the circumstances. At least it would keep out the coyotes and wolves.

He stood over the makeshift grave and started to say a prayer. As he began to cross himself, a strong hand grasped his throat from behind, stopping him abruptly. Max Boudreaux asked in a low whisper, "Where are the rest?" as he took Sanchez's pistol from his belt.

"They — they are — gone. They have left, Senor."

"Then what are you doing?"

"I refused to leave until these men have been properly buried."

"Well, aren't you a good little Christian?"

"Senor?"

"Never mind. You said to bury *these* men. Is Marshal Kinslow dead?"

"I believe so, Senor. The young gunman told Mr. Birk he killed him. I have no reason to doubt him."

"Show me where," Max commanded as he jammed the pistol into Sanchez's back and prodded him forward.

Sanchez led Max to the boulder where Fancy had stood and described what he'd heard. Max played the scene out in his mind and began to work his way carefully down the loose shale pile. He ordered Sanchez to follow. Standing atop the ledge Kinslow had fallen under, Max caught site of a pistol in the dirt. As he started to climb down to get the gun, Kinslow's body came into view. Max picked up the pistol, shoved it into his belt, rushed over to Kinslow, turned him on his back, and checked for any signs of life. "He's alive!" he said to Sanchez. "Come here and give me a hand."

Max checked Kinslow's wound, both the entry and exit. The bullet had gone through the back of his shoulder about six inches down from the top, at an upward angle and came out just below his collar bone.

When Max tried to move Kinslow into a more comfortable position, he moaned and his right hand instinctively went up to the wounded shoulder. He slowly opened his eyes and looked up into Max's smiling face.

"Good to see you're still with us, my friend," Max said with total sincerity. He didn't make friends easily because he did not have any respect for most of the men he met in his life time, but Kinslow was different. He was honest, could be trusted, and most of all, he treated a man with the respect he deserved.

"Max, is that you?" asked Kinslow through his pain and blurry vision. "I thought you were long gone."

"I was, but we can talk about it later," Max replied.

Kinslow tried to sit up when he heard Sanchez's approach. Max explained, "It's okay, Marshal. It's Birk's Mexican tracker. He's unarmed." Max saw the confusion on Kinslow's face, so he elaborated, "Looks like he stayed behind to bury the bodies. Not sure if it was Birk's orders, or he did it on his own. I'm guessing it was his idea." Turning to Sanchez, he said, "Help me get him up."

They got Kinslow into a sitting position and Max took another look at the wound. "Looks like it went clean through. Didn't hit anything vital. Looks like a busted shoulder. You'll be your ornery self in a few weeks."

"A few weeks? I can't wait a few weeks. I've gotta get Birk and his men."

"Birk will still be around in a few weeks. Besides, he thinks you are dead." Max grabbed Sanchez by his shirt front and brought them face to face. Their noses were almost touching. "And he isn't going to find out different, is he?"

Sanchez could see in Max's eyes that what he said next could determine whether he lived or died. "Senor, I don't like what Mr. Birk do. I obey him because my family is back at his rancho. I will not say anything about the marshal." He paused a moment and his face brightened as he added, "Senor, I will tell him I buried Senor Kinslow."

Max hesitated. He was ready to choke the life out of Sanchez, but now he had some reservations. Kinslow interrupted his train of thought. "Max, bring him here."

Still holding Sanchez's shirt front, Max dragged him to Kinslow's position and forced him to his knees. Kinslow leaned forward on his good elbow and asked, "What's your name?" "Carlos Miquel Hornando Sanchez, Senor."

Kinslow managed a small smile. "Got any children, Carlos?"

"Si Senor, I have two beautiful little girls."

"Well Carlos, I am going to come for Birk and his men. I will either kill them or take them to prison. Right now, I am willing to go easy on you. Tell Birk I am alive and I will treat you just like him and you will spend the rest of your life in jail, never to hug your children again. Do you understand what I am saying?"

"Si Senor, I do. I truly do," replied Sanchez.

"Fine, now go find my horse. He's on the other side of the hill somewhere
filling his belly," said Kinslow.

As Sanchez raced off, Max looked at Kinslow, smiled, and shook his head. "You are amazing? How did you know to ask about his children?"

"Over twenty years in this business, you learn about men and what is important to them. He won't tell Birk anything unless Birk hears it from somewhere else and confronts him about it."

Max still wasn't convinced. "I think we should kill him here and now and then we won't have to keep looking over our shoulder."

"No Max, he deserves a chance. Scum doesn't usually give a damn about a Christian burial for another man. I think we can trust him."

"I shall bow to the voice of experience," said Max. He untied Kinslow's bandana, soaked it with water from his canteen, and began to tend Kinslow's wound. A few minutes later Sanchez appeared, leading Knothead.

Kinslow unpinned his badge from his vest and gave it to Sanchez. "Give this to Birk. Tell him it's a souvenir for him. Can you do that, Carlos?"

"Si, the lord will forgive me this lie, I am sure."

Sanchez dashed to the grove, untied his horse, mounted, and waved goodbye as he rode away. As Max helped Kinslow unto his horse, he asked, "Where are we going, my friend?"

"To see some friends of mine," replied Max.

Chapter 12

"Who goes there? Come into the light where we can see you," commanded Sanders.

"It is I, Carlos Sanchez," came the tentative reply.

Sanders let the hammer of his pistol down gently and put the gun back in his holster. "You shouldn't be sneaking around. You could get yourself killed."

"I am sorry, Senor. I was not thinking."

Jonathan Birk stepped into the light of the campfire and asked with a hint of suspicion, "So you buried Miller?"

"Si Senor."

"And the marshal?"

"Si Senor."

"Got back mighty quick for having dug two graves, don't you think?"

"No Senor — I had nothing to dig with, so I just cover them up good with stones. I said a prayer for their souls and hurried to catch up to you." He fumbled in his pants pocket, pulled out Kinslow's badge, and said, "A memento for you, Senor," as he handed it to Birk.

Birk took the badge, looked it over, and tossed it into the campfire. Any doubts about Kinslow's death had just dissolved with Sanchez's gesture. He said to Carlos, "Get yourself something to eat. There are still some beans on the fire."

Sanchez helped himself to the food. He felt as though a huge weight had been lifted from his shoulders and he sat down to eat with a contented smile on his face.

Shortly after Sanchez rode away, Max managed to get Kinslow on his horse. As they rode, Kinslow kept slipping in and out of consciousness. Max had bandaged his wounds with a piece of Kinslow's own shirt, put him on his horse and to keep him from falling off, he tied Kinslow's wrists to the saddle horn. As darkness fell, Max made Kinslow comfortable near a fire he'd just built. He put the marshal on a groundsheet with a saddle for a pillow and covered him with a couple of horse blankets. He stayed awake watching over Kinslow for most of the night, but when fatigue finally overtook him, he succumbed to sleep.

Kinslow was still out cold when the sun rose. Max gently peeled back the makeshift bandage and checked the wounds. The bleeding had stopped, but the exit wound looked inflamed. He shook Kinslow awake, made him take a drink of water, and got him back on his horse, tying his wrists to the saddle horn again.

They rode all day, stopping several times for water and to rest the horses. Although he wasn't aware of where they were going, Kinslow wasn't concerned about it because he trusted Max. During moments of consciousness, he was able to determine by the position of the sun that they were headed in a south-westerly direction, into Ute country, most likely. By nightfall, Kinslow had passed out completely. Max checked his wounds again. The entry wound looked like it was healing nicely, but the exit wound by his collar bone looked infected and Kinslow was running a high fever.

Not having a knife, Max took the cartridges out of Kinslow's pistol and shoved the barrel into the coals of the fire. When it was red hot, Max took the pistol out of the fire and without hesitation applied it to Kinslow's exit wound. Although he was unconscious, Kinslow winced from the pain. To be on the safe side, Max put the pistol back in the fire and when it was hot enough, he doctored the entry wound as well. He went into the trees and picked some dry moss to protect the cauterized wounds and then rewrapped the crude bandages. He let Kinslow rest a few hours before moving on.

About noon the next day, Kinslow was regaining consciousness. He was vaguely aware of the sound of several barking dogs and the laughter of children. He could smell wood smoke and the aroma of roasting venison. He tried to open his eyes, but he could only force his eyelids to remain open for a split second at a time. Through these small glimpses, he saw enough to figure out he was in a Ute encampment.

The next time Kinslow opened his eyes, he was convinced he was either in heaven or dreaming, but what a wonderful dream! An absolutely beautiful angel with jet black hair and eyes to match was wiping his brow with a damp, cold cloth. She smiled when she saw his eyes open. He smiled back at her and passed out again.

Two days later Kinslow regained full consciousness. The first thing he saw was a patch of blue through the hole in the top of the tepee where all the poles came together. He recalled the fragmented pieces of memory from the moments of consciousness he'd had in the last few days. He concluded Max had, indeed, brought him to a Ute village. Where? Who's village? He could only guess. Weeminuche tribe, perhaps? He couldn't be sure.

He tried to raise himself up on this elbows. A searing, hot pain ran through his left shoulder and his left arm would not tolerate his weight. He turned gingerly on his right side and used his right elbow and arm to hold himself up.

He surveyed the entire interior of the tepee. There was a small fire in the middle for warmth. In summer, most of the cooking was done outdoors. There were several deer and elk hides scattered about the floor. A large dry log ran the entire length of the rear of the tepee. On it was a deer hide water bottle, several wooden bowls, a couple of blankets, and Kinslow's clothes and gun belt.

Awareness slapped him like an insulted school marm. Clothes! He painfully lifted the corner of the elk robe that covered him and sure enough, he was as naked as the day he was born. He was thinking about his predicament when the flap, which served as a door to the tepee, opened and an elderly woman poked her head inside. It is not certain who was more surprised; Kinslow, who immediately ducked back under the robe and grunted in pain, or the old woman who backed out of the tepee and began shouting something in Shoshone. Kinslow knew enough of the language to recognize *'sick white man'* and something like *'growls like a bear'*.

He wasn't sure what to expect next and when nothing happened for a few minutes, he lifted himself up again, using his good arm, pushed back the robe and tried to stand up. He slid his legs into a fetal position and using what strength he had, he got himself onto his knees and then up into a kneeling position. He put his right leg forward and with a tremendous push, he was up on his feet. He suddenly felt very weak and dizzy and he dropped back down to his knees.

He was catching his breathe, getting ready for another attempt, when the flap opened again and there was the vision of loveliness he'd seen in his feverish dreams. He looked up and grinned and she smiled back. Kinslow suddenly realized he was still buck naked and ignoring the pain, he scrambled back under cover.

The young lady's demeanour took on the air of an irate mother-in-law. She rushed to Kinslow, got him comfortable and then came the lecture. Kinslow listened intently, but she spoke too fast for him to get hardly any of it. Something about him being as smart as a fish and didn't he know he was badly hurt and needed rest.

Kinslow nodded *'yes'* several times as she spoke and when it looked like there was a pause in her rant he said, "Yeah, yeah! I'm alright. I'm fine."

Kinslow raised his eyebrows when she said in English, "You are not fine!"

"Oh, you speak English," he said.

"When I have to," she replied.

Kinslow paused. It was all a big rush, like the water from a summer thunderstorm roaring down a gully. There was so much he didn't understand. "Where am I? Who are you? Where is Max?" he asked.

"You rest. I will get some food and then we will talk," she said as she rose quickly and disappeared through the flap. A heart beat later, the old lady stuck her head in, looked at Kinslow, uttered a disgruntled harrumph, and closed the flap. Kinslow wondered what he'd done to upset her.

Kinslow played with the injured shoulder trying to flex it and move it in different directions. He was pleasantly surprised to discover he had nearly full movement in every direction except when he tried to lift his arm directly above shoulder height. This told him the bullet had missed the shoulder joint and bone damage was minimal. In time, he should have full use of the arm and shoulder. He determined he was weak from the loss of blood and when he peaked under the crude bandage he saw the burnt flesh and realized someone had cauterized the wound.

The flap opened again and in came his angel with a big pot of something, which she set down near the log in back. She picked up one of the bowls and spooned some of the contents of the pot into it. She brought it over to Kinslow and told him to sit up as best he could. She dipped out a spoonful of the contents and proceeded to feed it to him.

He recoiled from the odour. It smelled like rancid bacon fat. The expression of disgust gave him away and the angel said, "It is a soup made from deer fat, berries, and herbs. You must have something to eat. This will help you get your strength back."

The mention of food triggered a hunger response in Kinslow. He hadn't eaten in days and he realized how hungry he was. He thought it can't be that bad. He closed his eyes and let the angel feed him. He was wrong! It was awful, but he kept eating spoonful after spoonful until the bowl was empty. When the angel went to refill the bowl, he quickly declined, insisting he'd had enough. She didn't push the issue.

She knelt down beside him and pulled back the crude bandage and inspected his wound on both sides. She pulled a knife from a sheath tied around her waist, cut the old bandage off, got a damp piece of cloth from the log, and cleaned the damaged areas. She put on some sort of mixture on the wounds and bandaged them back up again with another piece, of what Kinslow thought, used to be his shirt. He wasn't going to ask about the applied medication or the shirt. Sometimes it's better not to know too much.

She rinsed the cleaning cloth several times with water from the deerskin bottle and proceeded to wash his face. He felt embarrassed and protested mildly. She told him to hush up and lay back and enjoy it.

He asked between wipes, "What is your name?"

"My given name is Leonora, but I am called Black Flower, because of my dark eyes."

"Leonora? That's a strange name for an Indian gal."

"My father was a white man and he named both my brother and I after people in his reading books."

Kinslow thought for a moment then it came to him. "Max! Max is your brother!"

"Yes."

"My name is Woodrow. Woodrow Kinslow. I'm a U.S. mar — "

She cut him off and said, "I know who you are and what you are."

"Oh, I see. Max told you?"

"Yes he did. He also told me you saved him from a hanging." She paused momentarily looking at Kinslow for a response and then continued. "You gave him his life and now he has given you yours. A debt repaid, I should think."

"He still has to answer to the law for the killing," said Kinslow.

The anger rose in her voice, "Whose law? White man's law? I spit on white man's law. You call it law, but where is the justice?"

"That's for a judge and jury to figure out," Kinslow replied.

She looked into his eyes for a short time, smiled, and said calmly, "Max said you would be hard-headed about this. That is why he is no longer here."

"Where did he go?"

She smiled again which was beginning to annoy Kinslow. "Nowhere and everywhere. One can never be sure where Max could be."

"I'll find him."

She ignored the last statement. "Are you still going to talk to the judge in Denver for Max?"

Kinslow didn't answer. The silence was awkward. After a moment, Black Flower rose, gathered up the dirty pots, cloths, and bowls and stormed out of the tepee.

For the next few days, the routine was the same. Black flower would come in four times a day to feed Kinslow, dress his wounds, and tidy up after him. She didn't speak to him, even though he tried to make conversation for the first couple of days. By the third day, he'd given up. She obviously wasn't going to talk to him. Women! Didn't matter what race they were, they were still impossible to figure out.

On the fifth day, Kinslow felt his strength returning. He was able to get himself upright and standing, without falling over. He tested his recovery rate several times a day and this was the first time he felt he was making any progress. He made his way to his clothes and started to put the long johns and socks on when he noticed his clothes had been cleaned. The trail dust and campfire stains were gone and they smelled nice. He put his pants and boots on and was looking for his shirt and vest when Black Flower entered.

She was surprised to see him up and about. "Oh, I see you are getting better," she said.

Kinslow turned to her and asked, "Where are my shirt and vest?"

"The clean part of the shirt I have been using for bandages. The vest I burned. It was covered in blood and I could not clean it. I will get you another shirt." She set down the soup and quickly exited.

Kinslow put on his gun belt and tied down the holster. He took the pistol out and checked the chambers — empty. Max certainly was no fool. He loaded the Peacemaker from the cartridges in his ammunition belt and put the gun back in the holster. He checked the derringers and found them both still loaded. He stuffed one in his boot and the other in his pant's pocket.

Black Flower came back with a buckskin shirt and handed it to Kinslow, who checked it over. It was a good heavy deerskin shirt adorned with intricate beadwork. Many hours were spent making it. He handed it back to her and said, "I'm sorry. This is very nice, but I cannot accept it. It's just — well, it's too nice."

"It is Max's shirt. I'm sure he would not mind if you borrowed it."

"Well, in that case, I'll take it." He put the shirt on and it fit perfectly, which was surprising because Max was a much smaller man.

Kinslow spooned out a bowlful of the concoction he'd learned to despise more and more with each passing day. He sat on the log and ate one mouthful, set the bowl down, and said to Black Flower. "Don't suppose a fella could get some real food?"

Without saying a word, Black Flower took the bowl from him, poured the contents back into the pot, and left with it. She returned almost immediately with a bigger bowl, containing a large chunk of meat set atop a good helping of greens of some sort. He ate ravenously. He wasn't sure what the meat was and he didn't really care.

Kinslow spent the better part of a week working his injured shoulder. He forced the healing muscles to full capacity, although the pain was excruciating at times. He chopped wood. He threw rocks. He lifted boulders. He stretched the muscles for hours on end, anything to work the shoulder back into shape. Black Flower would bring him food and sit and watch him work. She would smile whenever they made eye contact, but she never said much, other than the usual pleasantries.

Kinslow was at the camp for over two weeks and he was anxious to get back to business. He wandered around the encampment several times. Everyone ignored him. Most of the men, not wanting to be rude, would give him a polite nod of the head to acknowledge his presence. All of the women would look at him and turn their backs, while the children would just smile and giggle. Kinslow guessed he really wasn't welcome, but Max had obviously left instructions that his friend was a guest and not to be harmed. They would comply with Max's wishes, but it didn't mean they had to be nice to him.

Kinslow thought his shoulder was well on its way to a full recovery and he decided it was time to go. He found Black Flower and told her of his intentions.

She looked disappointed and sensing Kinslow could see it, she smiled and said, "Come with me."

She took him to the far end of the encampment where the horses were tethered. There was old Knothead. The horse snorted with excitement at seeing him and Kinslow was just as happy to see him. Black Flower got his saddle and gear from a willow hut, nearby. He saddled the horse and led him as he walked with Black Flower back to her tepee. She told him to wait while she went inside. Several minutes later she emerged with his saddle bags. Kinslow checked through them before he put them on his horse. Inside, was another shirt like the one he was wearing, minus the bead work. There was also some food, which he took to be the Ute version of jerky and hardtack.

He thanked her for the shirt and food and especially all the care she'd given him, but he emphasised he still had unfinished business to take care of. He asked her where they were in relation to Denver. She pointed to the southeast.

Kinslow stood for an awkward moment, fumbling with the reins and then made a motion to go. Black Flower rushed into his arms and gave him a big hug. He didn't know what to do and after what seemed like an eternity, he lowered his arms and returned the hug. Black Flower turned her face to his and kissed him on the cheek. He let her go and stepped back.

Black Flower asked, "When you are finished what it is you have to do, will I see you again?"

Kinslow didn't answer right away. He mounted and then spoke to her. "I'd like that, but I don't know where this business will lead. We'll see." He turned the horse and rode off without looking back. She stood watching until he was just a speck on the horizon.

It was an uneventful three day ride to Denver. Kinslow went directly to the Federal Building, where he found Judge Jonas Farnsworth, a long time friend and colleague. They small-talked over a brandy and a cigar for a few minutes and then got down to business. The judge listened attentively while Kinslow told the whole story of Birk and the events that had transpired. In his mind, the judge was prepared to talk Kinslow out of any serious charges until he heard the part about the cold blooded murder of Ansen Miller and the attempt on Kinslow's life.

"You'll get all the warrants you'll need, son. I will instruct my clerk to write up whatever you want and I'll sign them for you at once," promised Farnsworth.

"There's one other thing, Jonas. I've never asked you for a favour before, but I am asking now." Kinslow told him about Max's plight and how Max had saved his life. He pleaded with the judge to dismiss the matter with a writ.

"How are we ever going to get law and order into this savage country if we keep turning the criminals loose? People want justice. I — I don't know Woodrow," said Judge Farnsworth.

"People want law and order first. Justice is a luxury that comes later," replied Kinslow.

Pretty deep for you, Woodrow. I didn't know you were a thinker," replied the judge.

"I'm not. You know I have always put the law first, Jonas. Break the law and I bring you in. Justice, I leave to the courts. This case has shown me a lot, though. There are men with power and influence who use the law to their own advantage. Where is the justice in that? No, your Honour, law and justice must go together, hand in hand, for the system to work."

"Sometimes all we have is the law, Woodrow," countered Farnsworth.

"I know, but I have to tell you I won't be the one to bring Max Boudreaux in. I'll turn in my badge before I do that," replied Kinslow with conviction.

The judge looked long and hard at Kinslow with his chin resting in his hand. Then he said abruptly, "Well, if you feel so strongly about it, I trust your judgement, Woodrow. You are one of the best men we have. Based on that trust, I will dismiss any charges against Mr. Boudreaux in this matter."

Kinslow rose and shook the judge's hand vigorously. 'Thank you. Thank you very much, Sir."

After relaying to the judge's clerk what warrants he needed and the contents of the dismissal writ, Kinslow was told it would be a couple of hours before all the paper work was complete. He used the time to go to the Federal Commissioner's Building where the Territorial Headquarters were located. He said hello to some of his colleagues, collected his back pay, and after sheepishly explaining how he lost his badge, was issued a new one.

With money in his pocket, he bought a new hat and vest, a new Winchester, ammunition, food staples for the road, and a couple of shirts, not that he didn't like the ones Black Flower made for him, but they were just too heavy. He preferred something lighter and decided he would save the buckskins for the cold days of winter. He stopped at a local watering hole for a drink of whiskey and a beer to wait out the rest of the time. He nursed his drink as his mind wandered back to the events of the past few weeks and he thought hard on what he needed to do next.

"Another one?" The bartender's question brought Kinslow back to reality. "What? Oh, no thanks. I've got to get going." He paid the bartender and headed for the Federal Building. Judge Farnsworth's clerk had the warrants and the writ all signed and ready to go. There was a note from the judge among the warrants wishing him good luck.

He picked up his horse from the livery, packed up, and headed back to the Ute encampment. Black Flower was very surprised to see him. He felt warm and tingly inside when he saw her smiling as she ran up to greet him. He dismounted, returned her hug, and handed her the writ. "This paper says to the entire world that Max is no longer wanted for killing the white man. The case has been dismissed. He is a free man."

"But Max didn't kill him," Black Flower protested.

"It's alright. I think I know what happened and we'll just leave it there," Kinslow said as he remounted and rode off as quickly as he could. He knew if he looked into those ebony eyes once more, he would stay and to hell with Johnathan Birk and all the rest of it.

Chapter 13

About the time Max Boudreaux was leading Kinslow into the Ute encampment, Johnathan Birk and his men were arriving back at his ranch. Maria Sanchez was waiting on the front porch as they rode up. Carlos scrambled off his horse, ran to his wife, and gave her a huge hug and a big kiss. Birk let them have their moment and then interrupted, "Maria, these men are all hungry. Please fix them something to eat."

"Si Senor," she said and hustled back inside.

"See to your horses, wash up, and come into the house for some food," Birk ordered, as he dismounted and handed the reins to Sanchez. He went into the big ranch house, dusting himself off with his gloves as he walked. He found his way to the porch in the back of the house, where he pumped water into a basin, washed off over a week's worth of trail dust, and changed into the clean shirt and pants Marie had set out for him.

Feeling refreshed, he went to the study where he opened the safe, took out a tin box containing his working cash, relocked the safe, took a cigar out of the humidor on the desk, and poured himself a brandy. He was halfway through the cigar and into his second brandy when the men came in. He beckoned them into the study, poured them all a whiskey, and told them to sit down. He peeled five hundred dollars from a roll of cash and handed it to Tom Sanders, who counted the money and with a puzzled look, asked, "I thought you said fifteen hundred?"

"Fifteen hundred, if we got Miller alive. We didn't, did we?" said Birk, the statement dripping with sarcasm.

"But you shot him! Not me!" countered Sanders.

"Deal's a deal. Besides, I have a proposition for all of you and there will be lots more of this," Birk said, waving a hand full of bills. He turned to Jim Trueman and gave him a hundred dollars. "A little bonus for you, Jim. You earned it"

Trueman thanked Birk, who then handed Sanchez and Ingram each fifty dollars. He looked directly at Sanchez and said, "Thank you Carlos. You can go now."

Sanchez started to object, "But, Senor Birk —"

Birk was getting angry as he interrupted, "You're damn lucky I don't fire you. If you wife wasn't the best damn housekeeper in seven counties, I would. Now, get the hell out."

Sanchez finished his drink, slammed the glass on the table, and hurried out of the room. Birk saw the puzzled look on the other men's faces. "Man's too soft for what we have to do. The burying thing didn't sit well with me," he offered as an explanation.

It seemed to satisfy the other three and Birk continued, "My son's death has opened my eyes. I was willing to go along with this homesteading idea. There is enough land in this country for everybody. If the bastards would have stayed on their side of the river and me on mine, there wouldn't have been a problem, but you let them have an inch and they want a mile. No sir, no more!"

He paused for a moment as if to gather his thoughts. "I plan to get rid of them damn squatters, each and everyone. Drive them out! By any means necessary!" He looked at each of the three men and added, "You can help me and I'll pay you well, or if you don't have the stomach for it, get on your horse and leave now and I won't hold it against you."

He waited for a reaction from the men. Nobody moved. His peripheral vision caught sight of someone standing in the doorway. He turned his head and saw Andy leaning against the doorframe. "How long you been listening?" Johnathan asked.

"Long enough." Andy replied indignantly, "So, Miller is dead? And now you want to get rid of the rest of them."

"Should have done it in the first place. Maybe Mark would still be alive if I had," replied Johnathan, with a touch of regret in his voice.

"Oh, so now it ain't my fault Mark is dead," remarked Andy.

Birk was silent for a moment then he spoke, choosing his words carefully. "Listen Andy, I've been a foolish old man. You are all I have left and a father should stand by his son. I would give anything to take back those things I said on the trail. I'm apologizing and asking your forgiveness, but it won't change my mind about what I've got to do."

Andy walked across the room and extended his right hand for a shake. Johnathan pulled him close instead and gave him a big hug. As Andy returned the embrace, he was facing Tom Sanders, who smiled and winked. Andy reciprocated by forming his hand into an imaginary pistol and shooting Sanders and then he parted from his father.

"All right then, back to business," said Johnathan. Andy poured himself a brandy and sat down in one of the big arm chairs by the fireplace. Johnathan continued, "With the four — I mean — five of us in this room and maybe two or three others who are good with a gun, we are going to drive every homesteader, farmer, immigrant, or whatever the hell they call themselves, out of this valley. I want to put such a fear in them that they will not only leave, but they will advise anyone else who might be thinking about settling here, to move on."

Fancy Ingram spoke up, "Just how do you want it done, Mr. Birk?"

"Let's just say the homesteaders are suddenly going to have a run of bad luck —things like cut fences, mysterious fires, stock dying or disappearing for no reason, crops getting trampled, and such. I will pass the word to the merchants in town that if they want my business, they better not be dealing with any of these people."

"What about the law?" Ingram asked.

"The '*law*' will do whatever I tell them to. Maybe it's a good thing to keep in mind," retorted Birk.

Fancy wasn't sure exactly what Birk meant, but he certainly got the sense it might be a threat.

Birk continued, "We will go on some night time '*visits*' to our neighbours, wearing something to hide our identity. Even if they were to go to the law, who are they going to name?"

"When do we start, Mr. Birk?" asked Sanders.

Johnathan took a long look at Andy, who sat staring and twirling the brandy in his glass, and said, "My son Andy will be in charge. He'll get his instructions from me and you'll take your orders from him. That alright with you, son?"

Andy was totally surprised at his father's sudden confidence in him. "Sure thing, Pa," he replied enthusiastically.

Birk addressed Tom Sanders, "First thing I want you to do is find the Dunn brothers. They usually hole up in Boulder. Tell them I have work for them that would make good use of their talents and the pay is good."

Sanders knew Abraham and Isaac Dunn. There was nothing they wouldn't do if the price was right. They had no conscience, no honour. They could be on your payroll, but if someone offered them more money, they wouldn't think twice about turning on you. Sanders stood up and asked, "Can I grab some grub first, boss?"

"Yeah sure!" Birk said and then yelled to the kitchen, "How's the food coming, Maria?"

Maria scurried into the study, "The food is ready, Senor Birk. I just have to bring it in."

"Thank you, Maria. Well gents, let's eat," Johnathan said as he led the way into the dinning room with Trueman, Ingram, and Sanders close behind. Andy rose slowly. He was totally confused by his father's behaviour. For one thing, his father never had any of the men up to the ranch house for a meal. He would join them in the cook shack, quite frequently, to eat and talk about ranch business, or sometimes just to be sociable, but never up to the house.

Mark's death certainly had changed his father. He was obsessed with vengeance and his own twisted sense of justice. Andy was wrestling with his own conscience. Here was an opportunity to get into his father's good graces, but at what cost? He was finally going to get the attention from his father he'd been seeking all his life and he decided there was no price too high to pay for that.

Two nights later there was a fire at the Miller place. Four riders adorned with makeshift hoods, made from gunnysacks with holes cut out for the eyes, nose and mouth, torched the barn and a couple of storage sheds. Their fight was not with helpless animals, so they ushered two horses, a mule, and an old milk cow out of the barn before setting it ablaze.

As the buildings were burning, they rode up to the front of the house. Still mounted, one of them called out, "Mrs. Miller, come out of the house. We are going to burn it. No need for you to get hurt." He waited a short time and then repeated, "Did you hear me, Mrs. Miller. Best get out here now. It's going to get awful hot in there in a minute."

The speaker motioned to two men to fire the place and as the lit torches landed on the roof, Beth Miller stepped out onto the porch, brandishing a rifle. "Now, what are you planning to do with that Mrs. Miller?" asked the one who seemed to be in charge.

"You're not fooling anyone, Johnathan Birk. I know it's you under that silly mask. You coward! You can't even show your face like a man!" she shouted.

"You want to see my face?" Johnathan Birk said as he pulled off the hood. "Here's my face! Just so you know who you are talking to when I tell you I will be back tomorrow and if you are still here, we will hang you from the nearest tree. Do I make myself clear?"

"You're still all cowards. Big tough men, badgering a woman alone. If my Ansen was here, you wouldn't be so brave," she replied.

Johnathan Birk smirked and said, "Well, your husband ain't here and he never will be. You see, I put a bullet in his head and he's coyote food by now."

Beth Miller raised the rifle clumsily and tried to lever a shell into the chamber. Fancy Ingram shot her twice in the chest before anyone could blink. She stood for a moment than dropped like a stone, face first, off the porch steps, and into the dirt.

"Goddamn it, what in hell did you do that for?" bellowed Johnathan.

"She was going to shoot you, boss. I just thought — "

"I could have handled it. I needed her to spread the word to her friends and neighbours. Damn!" Johnathan sat in silence for a moment and then added "Ah well, there will be other opportunities, I'm sure."

Jim Trueman, who was starting to feel comfortable in his new role, tried to add a bit of humour, "Maybe we should have brought Sanchez along. He could have buried her." Nobody laughed.

The ride back to the ranch was sombre. No one said anything. Andy was in torment. He argued with himself in his mind. He had just witnessed a cold blooded murder and for what? To ease his father's pain? How many lives would it take? He wanted to point his horse east and just keep on riding. Another part of him, felt elated. He was at his father's side, an important part of his father's life now and he wasn't going to do anything to mess it up.

Almost a week later, Tom Sanders was back with the Dunn brothers. Abraham Dunn was a short stocky man. He was clean shaven with long, black, silver streaked hair, which hung down to his shoulders. A little brown derby hat covered his mostly bald head. He wore a red wool shirt, a brown leather vest, army issue pants, Mexican boots, and a Bowie knife strapped across his chest. He carried no pistol, but his weapon of choice was a short, double barrelled, 12 gauge shotgun which he carried in a pouch strapped to his back. Abraham liked to do his work up close and personal.

Isaac Dunn was a taller, more slender man. He had a big handlebar moustache and he still had all of his hair, which he kept short. He wore a big Texas range hat, a buckskin shirt, leather leggings over his army issue pants, and the same Mexican riding boots his brother wore. Unlike Abraham, he used a double rig with the pistol handles pointed inward. He liked to draw both guns at once, cross-handed.

Neither Abraham nor Isaac spoke very much. They were civil, polite, and followed orders. Their loyalty lay with whoever paid the most. It was said they were pure evil with no conscience or remorse and yet, during down time, when he wasn't working, Abraham read the Bible.

One of the stories about Abraham that struck fear in most that heard it centered on an incident in Wyoming. The brothers had been working for a group of ranchers who'd hired them to catch some rustlers. One night, the two brothers and a bunch of ranch hands were in the bunkhouse. Most of the men were playing cards, including Isaac. Abraham sat near the stove reading his Bible, when one of the cowhands decided to have a little fun. He asked Abraham how a man could be a stone cold killer and still believe in God and read the Bible and such.

"I only kills them what needs killin'. Now, let it be," Abraham answered, with just a hint of annoyance in his voice.

The cowhand continued, "Let it be? Hell, I do believe that is about the strangest thing I have ever seen. How about you boys? If old Abraham here can go to heaven, maybe there is hope for us all."

Abraham looked up from his reading. It could have ended there, but the cowpoke made the mistake of snatching the Bible from Abraham's hand. He wanted to see what part of the Bible Abraham was reading. He never got the chance. Abraham's big Bowie knife was stuck to the hilt in his throat and he died before he hit the floor. It is said Abraham pulled the knife out of the man's throat, wiped it off on his shirt sleeve, sat right back down, and continued reading. The brothers were fired the next day, but they did get paid in full.

Sanders brought the Dunns into the ranch house to meet Johnathan Birk. Johnathan shook their hands, motioned them into the study, and when Sanders started to go in with them, he was promptly dismissed by Birk. This didn't sit too well with Sanders. His large ego was bruised by what he thought was a slight.

During the next two weeks, four other homesteads were hit. The story was the same in each case. Five or six hooded riders rode in, burned all the buildings, trampled all the gardens, and ran the stock through any crops which was followed by a verbal warning from one of the riders that basically stated that the homesteader had better be gone the next day, or there would be some killing. Fortunately for the homesteaders, they did not retaliate and there was no one hurt or killed during these raids.

The burned out homesteaders called for a meeting with others of their kind in the valley and they all decided to go to the law. Jed Claxton met with a spokesman for the homesteaders. Claxton listened to the man's story and assured him he would do everything in his power to find out who was doing this. The spokesman, a big burly German immigrant, got angry and said everyone knew damn well it was Birk and his hired gunslingers and the law had better do something about it. Claxton said he could only act on proof and not speculation. The spokesman left disgruntled and was found dead a few days after Jed Claxton visited Johnathan Birk. He had been stabbed in the throat with a large knife of some sort.

Chapter 14

Jed Claxton was enjoying his day. His feet were up on his desk and he was sipping on a whiskey laden coffee when Kinslow came through the office door. Claxton's eyes went as wide as a hoot owl's and he spilt his coffee all over himself, trying to sit up. "Christ, they told me you was dead. Bushwhacked by Miller and the half-breed you was taking to Fort Collins."

"Let me guess where you got the information — Johnathan Birk, perhaps?" said Kinslow.

"Yeah, how'd you know?"

"Lucky guess. As you can see, I am very much alive." Kinslow reached into his vest pocket and took out a handful of folded papers. He shuffled through them, pulled three out, and threw them on Claxton's desk. "These are warrants for the arrest of Johnathan Birk, Tom Sanders, and a young gunny calls himself Fancy Ingram, on charges of murder and attempted murder. The others have no names on them, yet. It will be up to me to write in whatever name I choose when I find out who else was involved."

Kinslow handed another document to Claxton. "This is a writ and it says all charges against Max Boudreaux have been dismissed by a federal judge."

"You can't do that!" retorted Claxton

"I didn't, a federal judge did," replied Kinslow.

Claxton paused. Not knowing a lot about the hierarchy of the judiciary caused him some confusion. "What about the warrant out for your arrest?" he asked.

"I'm on my way to Fort Collins to see Judge Beams right now," Kinslow said, as he picked up all the warrants and the writ and put them back into his vest pocket. "Could be when I'm done with him, his name and yours will be on one of these."

Claxton stuttered, "But — I — What for?"

"I know both of you are in this mess up to your eyeballs. All I have to do is prove it."

Claxton attempted to divert the conversation again. "You don't have to go Fort Collins. The judge is here in town. He always takes a room at Fitzgerald's when he's here."

Kinslow smiled at the news. "That's good to hear," he said as he turned to go. With his back facing Claxton, his keen ear picked up the faint shuffling sound of metal against leather. He stopped and said, "Don't do it, Claxton. It ain't worth dying over."

"Kinslow, you are under arrest. Put your right hand up and drop the gun belt with your —"

Kinslow went down into a squat, pulling his revolver, and spinning his body around to face Claxton as he dropped. Claxton fired, but the bullet went high. Kinslow's shot caught him dead center. Claxton fell to his knees with a surprised look on his face. He lifted his pistol for another try, but Kinslow's second shot blew his heart apart and he slumped down on his haunches, in a kneeling position. Kinslow got to his feet, holstered his pistol, and took the time to lay Claxton's body down on the floor. He removed the badge from Claxton's shirtfront and put it in his own shirt pocket as he left.

Before he proceeded to the Fitzgerald Hotel to see Judge Beams, Kinslow stopped at Maclean's Undertaking Parlour and told the young man working there about Claxton's body. The hotel clerk at the front desk seemed surprised to see him. Kinslow thought all of Colorado figured him for dead. "Judge Beams, what room is he in?" he asked.

"He's in room twelve, Sir, but he's not there now. He's in the dining room having some lunch," replied the clerk.

Kinslow thanked him and went into the dinning room. Recognition took his mind back a month or so to when he and Ansen Miller sat in this very room. Kinslow stood in the doorway and located Judge Beams. He was seated at a small table, tucked away in a corner, almost out of sight. He dropped his soup spoon when he saw Kinslow walking towards him. Beams quickly gained his composure, put a phoney smile on his face, stood, extended his right hand, and said, "How nice to see you, Marshal. May I assume the rumours of your demise are untrue? Please, have a seat."

Kinslow sat and simply said, "Your Honour."

"Well Marshal, what can I do for you on this fine day?"

Kinslow reached inside his shirt pocket, took out Claxton's badge, and threw it on the table. Beams reached inside his suit coat, took out his wire rimmed glasses, and put them on to examine the badge. "What is this?" he asked.

"Belonged to Jed Claxton. He won't be needing it anymore."

"I don't understand," said the judge, even though he had a fair idea of what it meant.

Kinslow took out the warrants and the dismissal writ and handed them to the judge, who looked them over. Beams knew exactly what they were, but he continued with the dumb act. "I still don't understand. Murder? Who was killed? And how do you know Johnathan Birk had anything to do with it?"

"Ansen Miller, a friend of mine, was murdered. He was a U.S. deputy marshal which makes it a federal crime. How do I know Johnathan Birk had anything to do with it? I saw the son-of-a-bitch kill him with my own eyes!"

"But — but — Miller was a wanted man, as were you. I deputized Johnathan and his men to apprehend Miller. If they were forced to shoot him in the process, they had every legal right to do so."

"There's a federal judge in Denver who disagrees with you," said Kinslow as he picked the papers back up.

Beams had that smile on his face again when he said, "Who am I to argue with a federal judge? He definitely outranks me. Consider this matter closed, as far as my jurisdiction goes. Now, about Max Boudreaux, if Judge Farnsworth thinks a dismissal is warranted, then so be it."

Kinslow rose slowly, holding the warrants in front of him. "This matter is not closed — how did you put it? — in your jurisdiction. Before I am through, your name is going to be on one of these. Johnathan Birk will have company up there on the gallows."

"Now, see here —" stuttered Beams.

"I'll be back for you, your Honour. Count on it." Kinslow said it like a promise as he turned and left the room.

Kinslow's next stop was the Mercantile. Abigail was alone in the store and her face beamed when she saw Kinslow. "Why lands sake, you're alive! Everyone says you got yourself killed by them two prisoners of yours. Oh my, it's good to see it wasn't true."

"Well thank you, Ma'am. I need —"

"I told you to stop calling me Ma'am. Abigail's the name."

"Yes Ma'am. I mean — I need some trail supplies — beans, flour, hardtack, some jerky, and some carrots."

"Carrots?"

"My horse likes them."

"Don't have any carrots left. How about some turnips? If he likes carrots, he'll like the turnips, I'm sure."

"Yeah, why not?"

Abigail started gathering Kinslow's supplies. She talked as she worked. "Why does everyone think you died? What happened to those prisoners of yours?"

Kinslow usually didn't like small talk, or answering questions that were nobody's business but his own. Abigail was such a sweet old lady, he made an exception. "As you can see I am not dead and only one of those gentlemen was my prisoner. One of them was my deputy and he was murdered on the trail."

"Oh my, do you know who did it?"

"Yes, I sure do."

There was an uncomfortable pause. Abigail was waiting for more, but Kinslow had said all he was going to say. Abigail broke the awkward silence. "There are a lot of strange things going on around here, lately."

This peaked Kinslow's interest and he asked, "What do you mean?"

"Rumour has it there is a gang of masked marauders riding around burning people's places and warning them to get out. They shot some poor woman dead on the spot. Mrs. Miller, I think her name was."

The color went out of Kinslow's face. "Are you sure?"

"Oh yes. Yes, I'm sure."

Kinslow paid Abigail, thanked her, gathered up his supplies, and hurried out. He packed the goods and gave Knothead a turnip which the horse immediately spat out. Kinslow muttered the word *'fussy'*, mounted, and galloped out of town in a south easterly direction, towards Ansen Miller's homestead.

He rode his mount long and hard and was on a knoll overlooking the Miller place by noon the next day. He tied up his horse, pulled out his field glasses, and surveyed the burnt out homestead. It was only the back end of August and already some of the leaves on the poplar trees were turning color. He saw the charred piles of lumber, which were once buildings, the trampled garden, and a recently dug grave with a crude wooden cross for a marker. He checked the several groves of trees around the area for any signs of life. An old milk cow, her udder full to near bursting, was the only thing he saw.

He was careful not to be seen as he got closer to Birk territory. He was pretty sure Birk didn't know he was still alive, but he knew that between Judge Beams and Abigail, the news may have already reached him. He rode slowly down the hill to what was once the house and looked around. He searched the ground around all the burnt buildings for any signs. It had rained quite heavily a few days before and most of the tracks were undistinguishable. He did, however, notice a fresh set of hoof prints leading to a grove of trees just back of where the house once stood. He stood up in the stirrups and scrutinized the trees with his field glasses. He didn't see anything moving, but he still had an uneasy feeling.

He remained vigilant as he stepped down from his mount to look at the grave. The overturned earth looked very fresh. A wooden cross, the two pieces crudely laced together with a piece of bailing wire, was adorned with a partially burnt piece of plank. Someone had used a hot iron to burn the words '**Beth Miller - R.I.P.**' on it and had used another piece of bailing wire to secure it to the cross.

Kinslow usually didn't let his emotions control him. He'd learned over the years that this was a hard, unforgiving land. He'd seen death too many times to mention and he'd developed a way of dealing with it. He did not allow himself to get personally attached. The only thing he was passionate about was the law. He did the investigations, made any necessary arrests, and moved on. Innocent people like Beth Miller often got killed, but it's just the way it was out here.

Kinslow was a spiritual man. He didn't believe God was the personified old gent with a beard seen in paintings, which hung in churches and cathedrals, but he believed there was something intelligent out there running things. Before he rose from the graveside, he took off his hat, lowered his head, and said a few words to whoever might be listening. He prayed Beth and Ansen Miller would get a better shake than they'd gotten down here.

A deep raspy voice broke up his solemn moment. "Stretch them arms way up high, Mister, and turn around. Make one bad move and you'll be in a grave next to Mrs. Miller."

Kinslow's mind was already working on his next move as he stood slowly and began to turn around. The man had called her *Mrs. Miller*. He showed her respect. Chances were, he was not one of Birk's men. Kinslow turned completely around and saw a short man, five foot five or six maybe, wearing a beat up old Stetson, a blue wool shirt, and pants that were held up by a pair of bright red suspenders. He was pointing a Sharp's Fifty at Kinslow's chest and a short barrelled .44 was holstered on his left hip.

Before Kinslow could identify himself, the man lowered the buffalo rifle and began apologizing when he saw Kinslow's badge. The deep raspy voice didn't sound natural coming out of his small body. "Sorry, Marshal. I didn't know the law was here. I figured you for one of those murdering bastards until I saw you praying over Mrs. Miller. But I still didn't know who you were, so I was just being cautious, is all. Like I said, sorry about that."

Kinslow lowered his arms and took control. "Who are you and what are you doing here?"

"My name is William Stoud. Most folks call me 'Little Bill'." He moved the rifle to his left hand and walked towards Kinslow, extending his right arm.

Kinslow shook the man's hand and said, "Pleased to meet you, Little Bill. I'm Woodrow Kinslow. My friends call me 'Woody'."

"Well, I'd like to be your friend, Mr. Kinslow, once I get to know you. Listen, I got some really bad coffee that might still be warm. Care for a cup?"

Kinslow took hold of his horse's reins and he and Little Bill walked the short distance to a small grove of trees directly behind the burnt out farmhouse. Kinslow was still curious and continued the conversation as they walked. "Little Bill, you didn't answer the second part of my question. What are you doing here?"

"Not much. Just trying to figure it all out."

Kinslow could see this wasn't going to be easy. "Figure what out?" he asked.

Little Bill waved his arm in the direction of the burnt buildings, "Who's doing all of this, of course."

"What makes you so interested?" asked Kinslow.

"Had a contract with a big German fella, Karl Heinrich. He owned a small spread southeast of here. He was catching wild horses and selling them. I was busting them for him."

The lawman in Kinslow asked, "Who was he selling them to?"

"Army took most of them. Sold a few to the Birk spread and some in town."

It seemed as though Little Bill had said all he was going to, but Kinslow kept pressing. "Go on. What happened?"

"Near as I can figure, this bunch of bushwhackers burned Heinrich out about the same time they did this place, or not long after. Told him to get out of the valley or they would kill him. He didn't hesitate. Packed up what he had left in an old buckboard. He hadn't sold all the horses, yet. Told me if I could catch them, I could have them. Even told me I was welcome to the property, if I wanted it.

"I kinda took him up on his offer. Been rebuilding the corrals and was starting to round up the runaway stock, when I come across Mrs. Miller. She was pretty ripe. I figured she'd been lying out there for quite a while. I no sooner finished burying her when you come over the hill."

"I heard there was some trouble and came out to check. Thank you for looking after her," Kinslow said sincerely.

"No problem. Where is Mr. Miller?"

"He's dead. Killed by the same bunch."

"It's too bad. Have any idea who they are?"
"Yes I do. That's why I'm here." Kinslow could see Little Bill was waiting for more information. "I'm convinced it's Johnathan Birk and a bunch of gunslingers he's hired."

Little Bill didn't seem surprised. "Figured it might be something like that. Seen it before."

"Been around have you?" asked Kinslow, without getting too specific. He thought if Little Bill wanted to tell him more, he would.

When they reached Little Bill's camp, he took the blackened coffee pot off the nearly dead fire, picked up a tin cup from the ground, threw out the contents, poured it full of the thick, black liquid, and handed it to Kinslow.

Little Bill said, "I was around for some of the Arizona range wars. Seen a lot of good people killed." He took the lid off the coffee pot and took a gulp from the pot itself. The silence told Kinslow Little Bill had said all he was going to, for now. He wasn't sure how involved Little Bill had been in the range wars, but judging by the buffalo gun and the .44 he carried, Kinslow was sure it wasn't busting broncs.

Little Bill took another swig of coffee from the pot and concluded his train of thought. "I really would like to settle down here. Nice country."

"Birk will just run you out," said Kinslow.

"That's what I figure, too. I reckon we'll have to settle this first."

"We?" asked Kinslow.

Little Bill dumped the rest of the coffee on the fire and said, "Yeah, seems to me like you could you use a hand."

Chapter 15

"What? How the hell can that be? He's dead! I know it!" spat Johnathan Birk.

"He came to me, not two days ago and threatened me. Me! A judge no less," stated Judge Beams, somewhat indignant.

Johnathan Birk still found it hard to believe what the judge was telling him. Kinslow was alive! Then it struck him. He called out from the study entrance, "Andy, come in here!"

Andy emerged from the kitchen almost immediately. "What is it, Pa?" he asked.

"Go find Carlos Sanchez and Fancy Ingram and bring them here," ordered Johnathan. He turned back to the judge and asked, "What else did he have to say?"

"He had a handful of arrest warrants, one for you and one each for a couple of chaps he called Tom Sanders and Fancy — something or other. The rest were all blank and he said he was going to fill in the names as they came up. The scoundrel even said one of them was going to have my name on it!"

"Where's Claxton?" Birk asked. "Let him handle this. There is still a warrant out for Kinslow."

"I'm afraid our friend Jed Claxton will be of no further use to us. Kinslow shot him. Plus, I don't think the warrant I issued will stand up in any court, except for maybe mine."

Birk showed his frustration. "Damn! What do we do now?" It was a rhetorical question that he didn't expect the judge to answer.

The centre of the Birk ranch, including the house, the bunkhouses, a couple of guest cabins, cook shack, corrals, and barns were in a low flat area surrounded on three sides by steep rolling hills. Groves of Trembling Aspen with interspersed patches of pine and spruce, adorned the hillsides. On one of these hills, just west of the ranch, Kinslow and Little Bill set up a vantage point where they could observe all that went on down below, but they in turn could not be seen.

Kinslow deputized Little Bill, who at first didn't want any part of being a lawman and said so, in no uncertain terms. Kinslow was just as adamant that if Little Bill was going to be involved in bringing Birk to justice, it was going to be legal and with a badge on his chest. Otherwise, he could just get on his horse and stay out of it. Little Bill was quite sure Kinslow meant what he said, so he reluctantly agreed to be sworn in, with the hope that none of his friends would ever find out about it.

Little Bill was taking his turn at watch through the field glasses, when he saw one man pushing another one as they made their way from the barn to the yard in front of the house. The man being prodded along seemed reluctant to go and a third man, dressed all in black, followed close behind. His hand was on his pistol and he was nervously looking around. Although he couldn't hear anything at this distance, Little Bill saw the man who was doing all the shoving call to the house. A moment later Johnathan Birk and Judge Beams came out onto the veranda. Little Bill handed the glasses back to Kinslow and said, "Looks like something starting up down there."

Johnathan Birk stepped off the veranda and walked slowly and deliberately and planted himself nose to nose with Carlos Sanchez. "You want to tell me, again, how you buried Kinslow?" he asked.

Carlos knew something was afoot. He didn't know how much Birk really knew, so he played dumb. "Si Senor, I cover him with rocks and I bring the badge to you."

Birk brought his right fist up from his hip and with all the power he could muster, hit Sanchez in the midsection. Sanchez gasped as all the air escaped from his lungs and he crumbled to his knees. Birk let him get his air, stood him up, and asked, "Tell me why someone you buried is up and walking around, then?"

Again, Sanchez played dumb. Again, Birk hit him with the same punch as the first one. Sanchez was expecting it this time, but it still knocked him to his knees. Birk lifted him to his feet a second time. "We can do this all day. You will tell me what happened. How long it takes, is up to you."

Sanchez tried a different approach. "I thought he was dead, I swear. I did not check to make sure. The rocks I put on him were not very big, Senor. He could have easily crawled out of the grave." Sanchez glanced at Fancy, trying to deflect Birk's wrath.

Birk followed Sanchez's gaze and was all set to confront Fancy about his claim of having killed Kinslow. The cornered animal look on Fancy's face and the fact his hand was on his pistol, made Birk rethink his urge to press the issue. He would have to wait for a more opportune moment.

Out of frustration, Birk returned his attention to Sanchez. He drove his huge fist down on the side of Sanchez's cheek. The blow sent Sanchez staggering for a few steps and then he collapsed. He lay in the dust moaning, the blood from a gash in his cheek mixing with the dirt. He tried to rise, but Birk kicked him savagely in the side of the head, knocking Sanchez out cold. Just for good measure, Birk gave him another couple of kicks. One blow connected with full force on Sanchez's jaw and snapped his head back, while the other one missed his head and glanced off his shoulder.

Birk was in a frenzy. He was all set to launch another series of vicious kicks that certainly would have killed Sanchez, but Maria had heard the commotion and came outside to see what it was all about. Realizing Birk would surely kill her husband, she threw herself on Carlos' inert body. Birk dragged her up with one arm and backhanded her, knocking her to the ground.

He turned his attention back to Carlos, ready to continue the attack, when Judge Beams scurried past him, picked Maria up, and said to Birk in the sternest voice he could manage, "Johnathan! Johnathan, stop it! You're going to kill him!"

The judge's voice broke the spell on Birk and he replied, "You're damn right I am."

The judge was adamant. "I won't be a part of this. I'm through covering for you. Good day to you, Sir." He turned and headed towards the buggy he'd arrived in.

Johnathan's attention was now on the judge. "Oh no, you don't." In two of his long strides, he caught Beams and spun him around. "You're not going anywhere. You're in this as deep as I am. Now, get back in the house. We've got a few things to talk about." Birk helped the judge get started with a gentle but humiliating kick to his backside.

Maria was huddled over her husband as Johnathan approached. The distraction by the judge was enough to cool him down a little and he turned to Andy and said, "When he comes to, I want to talk to him." Andy had a worried look on his face that the older Birk picked up on. "Don't worry, son. I'm not going to beat him any more. I need his tracking skills." He gave Fancy a long, icy stare, then turned and headed for the ranch house.

Once inside, Birk ushered the judge into the study. He closed the French sliding doors and offered him a drink. Handing the judge his requested brandy, Birk took a sip from his own glass and looked at the judge with cold calculation. He began to speak in a soft fatherly tone, "Ronald, you and I have been friends for nearly twenty years. It was my money and my good word that got you where you are today."

Beams wanted to interrupt because he knew where this conversation was headed, but something about Birk's demeanour suggested it was not a good idea.

"Do you understand what I am saying, Ronald?" Birk's voice got louder and deeper. Now there was a sense of urgency, of anger, to the tone. "It may have been wrong to do what we did to Kinslow and there may be hell to pay for it, but by God, we are going to finish it and you are going to help me!"

Beams interjected, "Johnathan, you know I'm grateful and I would do anything for you, but he's got the backing of a federal judge. We can't fight that!"

"We'll find this Marshal Kinslow again and this time we'll do the job right. After all, we'll be just carrying out your orders, Judge Beams!" Birk put extra emphasis on the word '*Judge*'.

Beams realized he wasn't going to win the argument with his approach, so he tried another angle. "He's already killed Claxton. He'll kill us all before he's through. I suggest we go to Judge Farnsworth in Denver and tell him it was all a misunderstanding. We could convince him killing Miller was an accident and Kinslow just overreacted? What do you say?"

Birk took another two sips from the brandy tumbler and shook his head slightly. "You know Ronald, I know you don't have any backbone, so I am going to make it real easy for you. I am going to find Kinslow and kill him and you can do whatever you think you need to do, to make the law happy. I will leave it in your capable hands. However, if you cross me, I will kill you, too. Make no mistake about that."

"I'll be going now." Beams said as he set down his brandy glass and walked briskly out of the study, not knowing what Birk was going to do next.

"Remember what I said," Birk concluded as the judge opened the sliding doors and left.

Birk followed him out to the veranda and watched him climb into his buggy and depart. He said to Andy, "Tell the Dunn brothers I need to see them, now!"

Johnathan was putting the finishing touches on his brandy and was all set to pour another one when the Dunn brothers entered. "I have a job for you boys. Fella that just left is Judge Beams. He's become

— ummmh, let's say — a liability. Yes, a liability. I like that word. I can't have liabilities. You need to get rid of that liability for me."

"Yes Sir," was all Abraham Dunn said as he and his brother turned to leave.

Birk added, "Abraham, not the knife. Make it look like an accident — or better still make it look like he shot himself."

Kinslow and Little Bill watched the beating of Sanchez and remained on the hill until Judge Beams came out of the house a few minutes later and left. They watched as Andy summoned the Dunn brothers. Kinslow lowered the field glasses and said more or less to himself, "I swear I know the short stocky one." He made eye contact with Little Bill and added, "I'm sure he is Abraham Dunn which means the taller one is his brother Isaac. They're always together like flies and horseshit. Birk has hired some real scum, Little Bill. These two would kill their own mother for a dime."

"What's the plan, Marshal?" asked Little Bill.

"I've thought it over and we are kinda between the rock and the hard place. The well dressed gent, leaving in the buggy, is his Honour, Judge Ronald Beams. The judge just found out I'm not as dead as I'm supposed to be. He made record time coming over to tell Birk. The fella getting the daylights kicked out of him was Carlos Sanchez. He had a hand in saving my hide when Birk had me dead to rights. I reckon Birk figured out he helped me."

"So what's the problem?"

"I'm sure something went on in the house between Birk and the judge that Mr. Birk is not too happy about. I'm guessing the Dunn brothers have been given orders to shut the judge up permanently. The problem is this, Little Bill — do we go after the judge, or rescue a man who helped save my life?"

"Tough choice. The *Marshal* Kinslow should go after the judge, but the *man* Kinslow, should go get Sanchez. It'll be interesting to see which one you choose," said Little Bill.

"You're a big help," said Kinslow with a hint of sarcasm.

"Doin' my best," replied Little Bill with the same tone.

"I'm going to guess Birk is done with Sanchez for now, so we should go after the judge," concluded Kinslow.

"You're the boss," said Little Bill.

Kinslow expressed his thoughts aloud as they rode. "It won't take long for the Dunn brothers to catch up to the judge. We need to get to him before they do. We'll go cross-country and head them off."

Little Bill didn't say anything. He just nodded his head in agreement. The main road wasn't far from the Birk ranch and it headed almost due west to town. The rolling hills, which made up much of the surrounding country side, ran parallel to the road. Kinslow and Little Bill could easily catch up to the judge and the Dunns and pace them from the hill tops. The disadvantage was that they could clearly be seen from the road by anybody who took the time to look.

Kinslow and Little Bill rode hard until they had the Dunn brothers in sight. At one point they had a pretty clear view of the road for a mile or so and they could see the brothers were gaining on the judge. Kinslow's plan was to ride as hard as they could, get ahead of the Dunns and pick a point where they would come out on the road between the brothers and the judge. They would persuade the brothers to leave and then catch up with the judge and warn him. Kinslow saw this as an opportunity to convince the judge to turn state's evidence against Birk.

Things don't always work out the way they are planned, however. Judge Beams had decided to stretch his legs. He stopped the buggy and was walking about when the Dunn brothers caught up to him. As a result, Kinslow and Little Bill came out onto the road a hundred yards ahead of them, just in time to see the Dunn brothers reach the judge.

Thinking quickly, Kinslow spurred his horse and as he galloped forward, he waved his arms and shouted, "Judge! Judge Beams. It's Marshal Kinslow."

As far as Beams was concerned, there was nothing to fear from the Dunn brothers, but he did not feel the same about Kinslow. He said to Abraham, "He's here to arrest me. You have to stop him."

Abraham Dunn was not the sharpest knife in the drawer. He liked to do things in a logical order. First things first. He drew the short-barrelled shot gun from the pouch on his back, pulled back both hammers and without hesitation fired both barrels, point blank, at Judge Beams. The force, at such close range, knocked the judge back five feet and almost cut him in half.

Next, he turned his attention to the two men on the road. Abraham broke the shotgun and was reaching for two new shells in his vest pocket when a bullet torn his right knee apart. He dropped the shotgun and as he was falling, he saw his brother go flying backwards off his horse. Isaac hit the ground hard with a sickening thud, flat on his back, with a crimson hole in the centre of his chest.

Abraham grimaced from the pain in his leg. After a few seconds, instinct took over. He opened his eyes and began looking for the shotgun. The kick in the jaw from Kinslow's size eleven knocked him on this back. Kinslow bent over and removed the big Bowie knife from its scabbard on Dunn's chest, tossed it as far as he could into the brush, then stepped back and waited for Abraham to get his senses back.

Little Bill made eye contact with Kinslow, who smiled with curious amazement when he asked, "How did you know which man to take?"

"Figured you'd go after the shooter first thing and the other one was already pulling his pistols, so I dropped him," replied Little Bill.

Kinslow looked at the Sharp's .50 in Little Bill's hand and then took a quick glance at Isaac. "That cannon sure does the job, alright. Good work!"

"Doin' my best."

Abraham Dunn was groaning and trying to sit up. Kinslow said, "Looks like our friend is coming around."

"What'll we do with him?" asked Little Bill.

"Good question?" Kinslow rubbed his chin and thought for a moment then continued, "We should hide or bury the judge and our dead friend over there. "Him," he pointed to Abraham, "we stash somewhere and keep as a material witness. Birk will go loco trying to figure out what happened to the judge and his two killers. Make him sweat a little." Kinslow couldn't help but grin.

Little Bill remarked, "It seems to please you some. I mean, making Birk sweat."

"Yeah, you're right. Maybe I am taking this a little too personal."

"Never said that."

"You didn't have to."

"Alright then," Little Bill said to change the subject, "where should we put this coyote?"

"When I ran into Ansen Miller, he was holed up in a line shack way up in the hills along an old high country trail. It's about a two hour ride northeast of Birk's ranch."

"Northeast?" questioned Little Bill. "We'll have to go right past Birk's place."

"No, we'll go up and around it to the north and cut back." Kinslow nodded in Dunn's direction, "We'll fix his leg a little so he doesn't bleed to death and bring him along. We'll get Sanchez and his family and then head for the line shack."

"Just like that?" asked Little Bill.

Kinslow winked at Little Bill and replied, "Just like that!"

Chapter 16

Positioned behind Maria Sanchez, Kinslow held his rein-calloused hand tightly over her mouth, so she couldn't yell out when he woke her. She opened her eyes and tried to struggle, but he had a firm grip on her. The more she fought, the harder he held on to her and the tighter he squeezed the hand covering her mouth. She relaxed somewhat as she listened to his soft voice telling her he was not there to harm her.

"My name is Woodrow Kinslow, ma'am and I am a U.S. marshal. I am going to take my hand away, Mrs. Sanchez. Please don't scream, or you will get us both killed. Do you understand, Mrs. Sanchez? I am not here to hurt you. I am a U.S. marshal and I am here to help you and your family."

Kinslow could feel her body relax and he slowly eased his grip and took his hand away. Maria Sanchez turned in the rocking chair she had been sleeping in and faced him. Kinslow stood and turned up the coal oil lamp on the bureau to his right as he spoke, "Mrs. Sanchez, like I've told you already, I am a lawman. I am here to arrest Johnathan Birk and anyone else who's involved in this business with him. Your husband helped save my life and I am very grateful. I owe him. My partner and I have come to take you and your family to safety, but we must be very quiet and we must hurry."

"I see — yes, I — What do you want me to do?" asked Maria, almost frantic.

"My deputy is waiting with a buggy that will hold you and your family. You need to quietly wake the children and get them around to the back of the barn without anyone seeing or hearing you. I'll bring Carlos there."

Maria rose out of the chair. Kinslow turned his back to her while she changed her clothes. She took a carpetbag out of the closet and put some of the children's clothing, shoes, a hairbrush, and some toiletries in it. She made her way through the old bed sheets, which were hung to serve as a room divider, to where two young girls were sleeping and woke them. Kinslow thought one of the girls was around ten and the other a couple of years younger. Maria made a game of it. She told the children to be as quiet as they possibly could because they were going on a night time picnic and they shouldn't wake their father. He was very tired and had to work hard the next day.

Kinslow made sure they were well on their way to the barn before he went back for Carlos. He woke the injured man gently, ready to clamp his hand over his mouth, as he'd done with Maria. Carlos moaned and slowly opened his eyes. Recognition took a while and then changed to surprise as he tried to talk, "Senor, Marshal —"

"Shhhh, yes it's me. Maria and the girls are waiting for us. They are in a buggy behind the barn with a friend of mine. Do you think you can walk?"

Carlos sat up. He fought his way to his feet, but needed to sit back down on the bed. "I think I can walk with your help, Senor." He stood again on wobbly legs. Kinslow put Carlos' arm around his own shoulder and supported all of his weight, while Carlos put one foot in front of the other. It seemed to be working, so they slowly and laboriously made their way from the cabin to the barn. It was a hundred yards of open ground and if they were going to be spotted, Kinslow figured it would be there.

As Kinslow and Carlos approached, Maria dashed to them and assisted Kinslow in putting her husband into the back seat of the buggy, next to the girls. It was fortunate the judge had expensive tastes and owned a roomy two seat model. Once Carlos and the girls were settled, Maria climbed into the front seat with Little Bill.

Kinslow untied the horses from the fence rail. He mounted Knothead and led Little Bill's roan, stopping at the side of the buggy to make introductions. Maria nodded to Little Bill, who tipped his hat slightly and simply said, "Ma'am."

Maria asked Kinslow, "This carriage, does it not belong to the judge?"

"Yes, it does. I am sure he won't mind if we use it," answered Kinslow.

"The judge, is he helping us, also?" she asked.

Kinslow was trying to keep as much of the dirty business away from Maria as he could. He decided it might be better the other way. "Mrs. Sanchez, Judge Beams is dead. Birk sent two of his gunmen out to kill him. We didn't get there soon enough to stop it."

Maria gasped and then composed herself. "Why don't you just go into the house and arrest Senor Birk? Everyone is sleeping."

Kinslow thought for a moment before answering her question. "It's not just him I'm after. I want everyone connected with the death of Ansen and Beth Miller, but I need time to find out who is involved and gather more evidence. If I take Birk now, the rest will scatter."

He turned his horse and started out across the pasture behind the barn. Little Bill turned the buggy and followed suit. They could have gone quietly through the yard and directly to the road, but Kinslow wasn't taking any chances. They would cut across the fields and double back to the road, well out of site of the ranch.

Within an hour, they were up in the hills at the spot where they had tied Abraham Dunn to an aspen tree. When the buggy stopped, Maria got down and began to tend to Carlos and the girls, while Kinslow and Little Bill went to retrieve Abraham Dunn, who was exactly where they left him. They got him to his feet and onto Little Bill's horse. Kinslow didn't feel it necessary to tie him down as he usually did with most of his prisoners. Dunn wasn't going to do much, or go far with a shot-up knee.

Kinslow said to Little Bill, "I don't understand why he's so quiet. When he heard us coming, if it were me, I'd be making a big ruckus, hoping it was Birk's men looking for me."

Little Bill replied, as a matter of fact, "When we left, I kinda told him he best be quiet. Told him I saw cougar tracks and with his bleeding leg he shouldn't be attracting any attention."

Kinslow laughed. "Oh, you did, did you? Good work."

"Doin' my best," replied Little Bill.

An hour or so after sunrise they were at the line shack. The route along the old trail was difficult for the buggy in several places, but nothing Little Bill couldn't handle. They got Carlos settled in one of the bunks and tied Dunn to the hitching rail outside until they could decide what to do with him.

Kinslow called Maria and Little Bill together outside the shack. He instructed Little Bill to head to town for supplies and gave him some money. He broke down Dunn's shotgun and slid in two shells. He gave Maria quick instructions on how to use it and handed it to her with the suggestion she simply point and pull both triggers, if anybody from the Birk party came close. Maria was hesitant, but Kinslow motivated her by telling her if Birk got a hold of Carlos again, he would kill him and there was no telling what he would do to her or the girls.

He made sure Abraham Dunn was securely tied to the hitching rail, mounted his horse, and said to Maria, "Little Bill should be back by dark. I'm not sure how long I'll be gone, myself. Drive the buggy to the back of the shack, unhitch the horse, and put him in the corral." To Little Bill he said, "If they ask about the supplies, tell them you're going prospecting."

"I've been around the dance floor a few times, Woody," said Little Bill a bit disgruntled.

Kinslow realized Little Bill had used his nickname. So, Little Bill considered him a friend. That was good. Kinslow thought he was going to need a friend in the days to come. "Just the same, no one can know you are connected to me," he said.

"What are you going to do?" Little Bill asked.

"I'm going back to our little perch on the hill and watch Birk sweat a little."

At about the time Kinslow and party arrived at the line shack, Johnathan Birk was having a meeting with his henchmen. "Where the hell are they?" Birk asked nobody in particular.

Tom Sanders looked at Andy, at Jim Trueman, at Fancy Ingram, and back to Andy, before he tentatively asked? "Sorry, Mr. Birk. Who do you mean? Sanchez or the Dunns?"

Birk looked surprised then realized his question could have one of two answers. "Both!" he spat. "Sanchez is probably half way to Mexico by now. Damn that Maria. I thought I had her figured. It's the Dunn boys I'm concerned about. They should have been here last night. I waited up until damn near midnight!"

Andy spoke up, "Pa, they probably spent the night in town and should be back in a day or so."

Birk mulled this over for a moment. "Yeah, you're probably right." He started back towards the ranch house, stopped, and said to Trueman, "See if you can figure out which of the horses Sanchez stole when he left. If we catch that little greaser we can hang him as a horse thief. Sanders, you and Fancy take a ride up the road and see if you can tell what happened to those two lunkheads."

Kinslow settled into the viewpoint on the hill just in time to see the meeting in the yard outside the ranch house adjourn. He watched as Johnathan and Andy went inside, Trueman head to the corral area, and Fancy and Sanders ride up the road towards town. Kinslow guessed they were sent to check up on the Dunn brothers.

He'd just rolled a smoke and was all set to light it, when Trueman came running around the corner of the barn, headed straight for the ranch house. He took the steps up to the veranda in two strides and went inside, without knocking. As Kinslow lit his cigarette, he wondered what all the commotion was all about.

Johnathan and Andy Birk were relaxing over a drink in the study when Jim Trueman entered. He made apologies for having to disturb them and then relayed his findings. "Sir, Sanchez didn't steal any horses. They are all accounted for. But I did find some strange tracks back of the barn, heading across the pasture. Looks like a buggy and two horses."

Johnathan looked perplexed, one might even say confused. "Buggy?"

"Yes Sir," Jim said and then his face brightened and he added, "Just like the judge has. But when he left yesterday, I thought he took the road."

"He did, you — " Johnathan caught himself. His voice softened and he continued, "Thank you Jim, you've been a big help."

Trueman caught the dismissal tone in Birk's voice and left. Johnathan started to rant. Andy wasn't sure if his father was talking to him, to himself, or some unseen entity in the room. He had never seen his father like this before and it worried him.

"That son-of-a-bitch thinks he can double cross me. I made him a judge. If it wasn't for me he'd be sweeping out some goddamn saloon. I'll kill the bastard, myself."

Andy interjected, "Pa, what's wrong?"

"What's wrong? I've been double crossed, son. That good for nothing son-of-a-bitch, who calls himself a judge, helped Sanchez and his family get away and by the looks of it, he took those idiot Dunn brothers with him. Everybody is against me. I can't trust anyone any more."

Andy didn't take his father's remarks personally, like he had before. He knew his father trusted him and wasn't including him in the statement. "Why would the Dunns go with him, Pa? I thought you hired them?"

"Andy, the only thing important to men like them, is money." Johnathan's voice got higher and louder and he was almost shouting as he continued, "Money, money, money! What happened to loyalty? Character? The days of men standing together to fight for something they believed in are gone, boy. They're gone!"

Andy stood, walked to Johnathan, and put both hands on his father's shoulders, from behind "Take it easy, Pa. We'll handle it. You and me."

Johnathan reached up and patted his son's hand several times, "Thank you, Andy. I know I can count on you."

Andy wasn't used to affection of any kind from his father. His lifted his hands from his father's shoulders and said, "Since we don't have a housekeeper any more, I'll go make us something to eat."

Kinslow had been keeping his vigil for several hours. Half a dozen cigarette butts were stacked in a little pile next to the pine tree he was leaning against. The return of Sanders and Ingram caught his attention. He watched as they corralled their horses and went into the ranch house, then decided he should head back to the line shack. He thought about how he would like to be a fly on Birk's wall right about now and he smiled to himself as he rode off.

"What the hell are you telling me?" Birk asked as if he couldn't believe what he was hearing.

Tom Sanders said, "We come to a spot in the road, about an hour out, where it looked like there was a lot of commotion. There was blood in the dirt in two or three places. Lots of tracks."

Fancy Ingram jumped in. "We ain't good trackers, but we followed some into the bush and found two fresh dug graves."

Sanders took the conversation back, "Best we can tell, two riders jumped the judge and the Dunn brothers. We couldn't figure out if the Dunn boys took care of the judge and then got jumped and one of them got killed, or if it's the Dunns buried in them graves and the judge got away —"

Birk interrupted, "Why didn't you dig them up and find out?"

Sanders answered, "Guess we didn't think of it. Sorry, Mr. Birk."

"Christ, I'm surrounded by idiots," muttered Johnathan.

Fancy's hand went to his pistol, instinctively. Andy saw the move and put his hand on Fancy's arm. Fancy turned to Andy and realized what he'd done. Luckily, Johnathan didn't see the gesture.

The older Birk paced back and forth across the study several times. He stopped and it seemed like he found the answer he was looking for. "Andy, get provisioned for a trip to Fort Collins. I want you to find a man named Claude Bassion and offer him any amount of money to come track for us. Tell him we are after rustlers. If you see any men you think might be good in a fight and won't ask too many questions, bring them along, too.

Andy left on his appointed task. Johnathan turned to Sanders and Ingram and said, "You two geniuses get some rest. We have some more night riding to do."

Chapter 17

"We got beans. We got bacon. We got beef jerky. We got flour, sugar, coffee, and for the little ones, we got these." Little Bill pulled two peppermint sticks from his shirt pocket and handed one to each of the children. He emptied the rest of the pack on the crude table while Maria began to put things away on the plank shelves, muttering to herself in Spanish.

Little Bill sensed she was not pleased and asked her what was wrong. She said something about men who lived on the trail having no idea what constituted good food — no onions, no peppers, no fruit, no vegetables. How was she supposed to cook anything decent? Little Bill defended his position by telling her he was only following Kinslow's orders.

To escape the need for further explanation, Little Bill went to check on Carlos. As he came near the bed, Carlos opened his eyes and tried to get up, a look of fear on his face. It dawned on Little Bill that Carlos did not recognize him. "Mr. Sanchez, it's alright. I'm a friend. You know Marshal Kinslow, don't you?" Little Bill waited for an acknowledgement from Carlos and continued, "Well, I'm working with him." He couldn't quite bring himself to say the word '*deputy*'.

Carlos recognized him as the buggy driver and he lay back down and closed his eyes. "He looks a lot better, don't you think?" Little Bill asked Maria.

"Yes, I think he will be fine," she answered.

"Well, I'll just go out and see about the horses and our tied up friend," said Little Bill, ending the small talk.

Little Bill unsaddled his mount, ushered him into the corral, and gave it and the buggy horse some feed. All the while Abraham Dunn, who was still tied to the hitching rail, was pleading to be let loose, so he could relieve himself. When Little Bill was finished with the animals, he directed his attention to Dunn, who said, "You think more of them horses than you do me!"

"You got that right, Mister," was Little Bill's curt reply.

Dunn didn't have a comeback. "Well, are you going to let me piss or not?" he asked.

Little Bill took out the short barrelled .44, cocked the hammer, and jammed it hard under Dunn's chin while he began to untie the rope around his wrists. "You so much as twitch and you'll never have to worry about pissing again." He jammed the pistol into Dunn's windpipe once more for emphasis.

Abraham Dunn liked to work in close. He always got his opponent to come near enough to grab and then the advantage was his. He'd seen his share of tough men, men who thought they were tough, and men who bluffed their way through situations without being either. He put Little Bill in the first category and decided trying anything at this time would not be to his advantage.

With Dunn's wrists untied, Little Bill rose slowly and backed away with his pistol still cocked and trained on Dunn, who struggled to get up and couldn't quite make it. "Don't suppose I could get some help getting up here?" Dunn asked, as if he expected some assistance.

"You supposed right. This is as close as I get," replied little Bill.

Using the hitching rail for support, Dunn managed to finally lift himself up. He unbuttoned his trousers and did his business. When he was done buttoning up, Little Bill ordered him inside the cabin. He hollered to Maria as they were coming in, so she would not be frightened when she saw Abraham coming through the door first.

Once inside, Little Bill directed Dunn to a short wooden bench attached to the wall near the stove, which was used to store a day's worth of firewood. There were a few pieces of wood left on the bench, so Little Bill ordered Dunn to put them on the floor by the stove and to sit himself down in the middle of the bench. He called Maria over to cover Dunn while he tied his wrists back together and put another rope around Dunn's waist which he used to secure him to one of the bench legs.

Dunn just wouldn't let up. "You gonna feed me, or are you planning to starve me to death?"

Little Bill smiled and said, "If it were up to me — Maria, I could use some grub, too. Would you mind rustling something up?"

While Maria prepared a meal, Little Bill rubbed the horses down, chopped some firewood, brought in water, and poured himself a cup of coffee. Dunn complained and whined the entire time. There were only three chairs in the cabin, so when Maria called dinner she loaded up the girls' plates and they sat on the edge of one of the bunks to eat.

Carlos was able to get himself to the table. "This is good to see," said Little Bill. He could see the joy in Maria's eyes.

When he was done eating, Little Bill searched for and found some nails on one of the shelves. He picked one up and using an old horseshoe, pounded it into the cabin wall about eighteen inches above Dunn's head. He lifted Dunn's tied arms and hung them from the nail. He got a plate of beans, sat down next to Dunn, and began to feed him. Abraham took the first bite and then spat it out, all over Little Bill.

Little Bill stood up, brushed the food from his shirt, set the plate on the table, and said to Maria, "Looks like he ain't hungry."

Little Bill, Maria, and Carlos ate in silence. Once the meal was over, Maria told the girls to clean up and wash up the dishes. She poured some more coffee for Little Bill and asked Carlos if he cared for any. Carlos declined and went back to bed. Little Bill rolled a smoke to have with his coffee.

Dunn had tested Little Bill and decided it was going to take a lot more prodding to rattle him. He started in again. "I sure could use a smoke." Little Bill ignored him. Dunn tried again. "Hey Shorty, I said I want a smoke." Little Bill took a long pull on his cigarette and blew the smoke in Dunn's direction.

Dunn was furious. "I'm gonna enjoy cutting your liver out, you little shit!" He took a couple of deep breaths and regained his composure. "Shorty, I can't figure you out. Why did you throw in with Kinslow? You don't look like a foolish man to me."

Little Bill took a drink of his coffee and a big pull on his cigarette, blowing the smoke in Dunn's direction again.

Dunn ignored the gesture and continued, "That marshal is a dead man. He just doesn't know it, yet. Face it Shorty, that big rancher has way too much power and what he wants he will get. Believe me, he wants to drive out all the squatters in the valley and he will stomp all over anyone who gets in his way."

There was no response from Little Bill. He completely ignored Dunn and asked Maria for more coffee.

Dunn wasn't finished. "Shorty, I'm telling you, Birk will get the lawman and you and when he does, I'm going to ask him to let me have you. Oh, I'm so looking forward to it."

Without warning, Little Bill stood, drew his pistol, walked over to Dunn, and hit him across his shot-up knee with the pistol butt. Dunn screamed from the excruciating pain. Little Bill pulled his tied arms off the nail and while Dunn was totally focused on the pain, Little Bill undid the rope around his waist, threw him to the floor, and stepped back.

It took several minutes for the pain to subside. When it did, Dunn pulled himself into a sitting position and asked in a pleading voice, "What the hell did you do that for?"

"I don't like being called, '*Shorty*'," answered Little Bill.

Little Bill ordered Dunn out of the cabin. Dunn used the bench for leverage and managed to drag himself to his feet and out the door. Once outside, Little Bill untied Dunn's hands, retied them behind his back, and then secured him to the hitching rail.

"You leaving me out here? A man could freeze to death, you know," Dunn whined.

Little Bill ignored him and went back inside and as he entered, Maria asked with concern in her voice, "Is it true what he says? Will Senor Birk come after us? Will he kill you and Senor Kinslow?"

Little Bill answered honestly. He didn't know any other way. "I don't rightly know what will happen, Ma'am, but I wouldn't bet against the marshal and me."

Little Bill was on his fifth cup of coffee when he heard the sound of an approaching rider. He quickly stepped outside and around to the side of the cabin where he could not be seen. As the rider came into view, a familiar voice called out, "It's me, Kinslow."

Little Bill stepped out from the shadows and greeted him. "Thought you were going to be gone a couple of days?"

"No need right now. I'll get old Knothead put away for the night and I'll be right in. Hope you got some coffee on." Kinslow noticed Dunn. "Shouldn't he be inside?" he asked.

Little Bill shrugged and replied, "Says, he likes it out here."

Kinslow raised his eyebrows and without saying anything, turned and rode around the back of the cabin to the corral area. When he came inside, there was a plate of bacon and beans with a flour biscuit and a cup of coffee waiting for him.

Kinslow talked between mouthfuls. "Best I can figure, Birk has two things in mind. The first one is finding me. He doesn't have Sanchez as a tracker anymore, so he has to get another one. It should buy us a little time. Number two, I don't think he's done with the homesteaders. I believe he means to drive them all out."

"Yeah, our friend outside mentioned something about it," said Little Bill. "So, what do we do?"

"We need to talk about that," replied Kinslow as he set down his spoon, took a sip of his coffee, and began, "We have to catch the whole bunch of them in the act. I figure we keep watching and when Birk makes his move, we will be one step ahead of him."

"We got enough to get Birk for killing Miller. I mean, you are a witness," interjected Little Bill.

"I owe Ansen Miller and his wife. I figure I got him killed and I'm not going to rest until I get them all."

"Is it justice you're after, Woody, or vengeance?" Little Bill asked in all sincerity.

Kinslow sighed before answering, "I was asked that once before. Sometimes it's hard to tell the difference, Little Bill. Sometimes it's real hard to tell the difference." Kinslow finished his meal in silence.

For nearly a week, Kinslow and Little Bill kept watch from their outpost on top of the hill, overlooking the ranch house. On the second day, one of Birk's cowhands rode slowly up the hill towards them. Little Bill thought for sure they were going to be spotted, but the rider stopped about fifty yards below them, dismounted, rolled and smoked one, and then rode back down the hill.

On the fifth day, Andy Birk and four other men rode into the ranch yard. Kinslow used the field glasses to get a closer look. "Looks like this is it, Little Bill. Birk will hit one of the homesteaders soon. Let's go!"

Little Bill asked as they mounted, "Where we going?"

"To get some help," was all Kinslow said.

As Kinslow and Little Bill rode out, Johnathan Birk poured drinks all around. Andy thought his father seemed happier and more jovial than he'd been for some time. "Andy, why don't you introduce these fine gentlemen," suggested Johnathan.

'*Fine Gentlemen*' were hardly the words Andy, or anybody else for that matter, would have used to describe the four men standing in Birk's study, each with a glass of whiskey in his hand.

Claude Bassion was in his mid thirties. He was a very tall, thin man who stood six foot, five inches tall and he may have weighed a hundred and seventy pounds, soaking wet. He had high cheek bones and very dark eyes that suggested some Indian blood in his veins. He had been a scout for the army since he was a teenager and now he hired himself out as a guide and tracker. Anyone who knew anything about that sort of business said he was one of the best.

Mike Billings was the opposite of Claude in stature. He was about five foot seven and a little on the dumpy side. There wasn't much to know about Mike, except he was dependable, but he liked to argue about everything. If you told him it was sunny out, he would say he was sure it was going to rain.

Milt Hartley was a drifter in the truest sense. He couldn't hold a job down for very long. Milt liked to drink and to talk. The more he drank, the more he talked and the more he talked, the more trouble he caused. Mostly, the talk was about all the great and wondrous deeds he'd done. They were all fabrications, of course, and Milt always got challenged. Trouble ensued and Milt usually ended up moving on.

Matt Cox was the quiet, silent type who you could seldom read or understand. He'd had a few scrapes with the law, had served some time, and he didn't mind the dirty work to earn his pocket change.

Andy did the introductions and the men, each in turn, shook hands with Johnathan, who said "Have a seat, gentlemen," as he refilled his brandy glass.

The men all found a place to sit while Andy took up his usual position, leaning on the fireplace mantle. Johnathan cleared his throat and spoke, "Gentlemen, you are here because you are interested in possible employment. You should know what the job's about before you make up your mind." He looked at each of the men for any signs of apprehension. He saw none.

Johnathan continued, "To put it in simple terms, there are people squatting on my land who have no right to be there. They have no right to lay claim to this land I worked and built up with my life's blood over twenty years." He got very emotional at this point. "They have no right to this land that has claimed the lives of my dear wife and my oldest son. They have no right even if the goddamn Government says they do! Our job is to drive them out by any means necessary!"

The men in the room started to stir uneasily with the tirade. Claude Bassion, the tracker, spoke up, "I'm a tracker, Mr. Birk. What do you need me for?"

"To track, of course." Johnathan could see Claude was waiting for more. "Seems there are a couple of fellas who have taken it upon themselves to protect these land grabbers. You need to find them for me, so we can eliminate the problem."

"I don't do no killing. Tracking, guiding — I find them for you, but I don't kill nobody," insisted Bassion.

Johnathan felt his stomach knotting up. He wanted to go over and slap Bassion, but common sense took over. He needed a tracker. There were lots of other men to do the dirty work. "Fine, you find them. We'll take care of the rest," he said.

Johnathan looked at each man in the room again, "Alright, anybody here who doesn't have the stomach for it, I'll give you five dollars for your trouble and you can leave now. If you stay, the pay is a hundred a month and a thousand dollar bonus when the job is done."

No one moved to go. Johnathan said to Andy, "Get these men settled in one of the bunkhouses. Move Trueman, Sanders, and Fancy into the same bunkhouse with them and move the ranch hands into one of the others. I want all these men together." To the men he said, "Get yourselves settled and something to eat. I'll be over later to formulate some plans. Thank you, gentlemen."

That evening, Johnathan and Andy Birk held a strategy meeting around the common table in the bunkhouse. Johnathan gave them a synopsis of events that had occurred to date. Of course, the narrative was completely from his perspective and embellished, to say the least.

He told them how the homesteaders were robbing him blind. They were killing cattle for their own use, putting up fences to stop his stock from getting to water, and just being a pain in the neck. He told them how his boys came upon Ansen Miller killing a calf and when challenged, Miller killed his oldest boy with a shotgun. He told them how he'd gone to the Miller place, how Mrs. Miller tried to shoot him, and how she was killed in self defence.

He went on to describe how he'd heard all the homesteaders had formed a vigilante group and were threatening to burn him out. In self defence, he'd struck first and burned out four places closest to the ranch and it was in his best interests to drive out the other half dozen or so squatters who had settled in the eastern part of the valley.

He did some fancy twisting of the truth to fit Kinslow into the picture. Seems Kinslow was a friend of Miller's from years back. He deputized Miller and while Johnathan and several of his men were camped out, on the way back from Fort Collins, Kinslow and his posse had jumped them. There was a big shoot out. Ansen Miller was killed, the marshal was wounded, and Johnathan and his men escaped. Kinslow got some judge in Denver to make up some trumped up warrants and he was out in the hills somewhere waiting to make his move.

"So you see gentlemen, we have a fight ahead of us, but we have right and justice on our side and we shall prevail," Johnathan said like he truly believed what he was saying.

There were nods of assent and sounds of approval throughout the group. Johnathan stood up and concluded by saying, "You men introduce yourselves, if you haven't done so already. Get some rest and be ready to go to work tomorrow night." To Claude Bassion he said, "See me in the morning. I will tell you where you can start looking."

Chapter 18

Little Bill was amazed at the marshal's foresight. Kinslow said this would be the night something might happen and sure enough, he was right. They had returned to the hillside lookout and weren't there for more than a couple of hours, when a large group of riders gathered in front of the ranch house to listen while Johnathan Birk stood on the veranda barking orders.

Little Bill was glad they didn't have to wait too long. It had rained steadily all day and if Little Bill hated anything in this world, it was sitting in the rain. At first light, they had ridden to the homestead of Liam and Sean O'Connor, Irish immigrants who came to America to make a new start for themselves and when they discovered they had just given up one life of tyranny for another, they were somewhat disillusioned and angry.

Kinslow related his theory about Birk trying to drive the rest of the homesteaders out of the valley. According to Kinslow, Birk had started with the places closest to his ranch and was working his way east. Kinslow figured the O'Connors were next and that it would be soon.

The brothers said they would be watchful and were prepared to fight. Kinslow suggested they lay low for a few days and not get themselves killed, but the brothers would have no part of it. They would fight for what was theirs.

The four of them sat down and over coffee and a shot of Irish whiskey, they discussed various strategies to use against the Birk raiding party, when it came. Kinslow voiced his concern about the odds. He was convinced Birk had anywhere from seven to ten men. To stand a chance against so many guns, they would need more help, or the element of surprise. They didn't have the time to rally the other homesteaders, so a stand at the O'Connor place, it would have to be. They devised, what they thought would be a good plan and then Kinslow and Little Bill rode back to the lookout above the Birk place.

As soon as they saw the gathering in the ranch yard below, Kinslow and Little Bill knew the moment was at hand. They mounted quickly, rode hard along the hill tops, and came out on the main road, a couple of miles ahead of the Birk party. Kinslow didn't like to work his horse this hard, but sometimes it was necessary. An hour or so later, they were galloping up to the O'Connor cabin.

"It's Marshal Kinslow and Bill Stoud," Kinslow hollered as they rode in. Liam O'Connor stepped out from behind a huge pine directly behind Kinslow and Sean did the same from behind a similar tree to Kinslow's right. They were both well armed and ready for a fight. Kinslow stepped down and barked an order, "They're about twenty minutes behind us. Let's get into position."

The O'Connor place was almost perfect for a trap. The trail up to the homestead left the main road, went east for a short distance, doubled back on itself westward across a small stream, and then disappeared into a grove of pine trees. Unlike most homesteaders, who cleared their little piece of heaven to plant grain or other crops, the O'Connors ran a small cattle and horse ranch and had left most of the trees standing to act as windbreaks.

The cabin was built on a small rise with a steep knoll behind it. Anyone approaching it was surrounded by large pine trees on both sides. The trees on the left had not been touched and the grove extended past the cabin and part way up the knoll. The trees on the right were thick as well, up to within a hundred feet of the cabin, where they had been cleared to make room for storage sheds and corrals.

To sum up, it was like a small box canyon. Once in the yard, Birk would be surrounded on three sides. Kinslow's plan was to use this to their advantage. The idea was to be patient and let the riders come all the way into the yard, where they would be sitting ducks. Kinslow thought it through carefully. He figured Birk and his men would challenge anyone in the cabin to step out. They would try several times and when it was obvious no one was coming out, they would react, either by opening fire, or throwing lit torches, or both.

Kinslow stationed the O'Connor brothers in the grove of trees to the left of the cabin, while he and Little Bill found a spot in the trees to the right. Kinslow would start the shooting and Little Bill would join in. Once the raiders' attention was on them, the O'Connors were to open fire from their side. "Pick a target with your rifle, shoot, and then empty your pistol into the crowd, get on your horse, and get the hell out of here," were Kinslow's final instructions.

Kinslow hoped this guerrilla tactic would confuse and scatter the raiding party and if they were lucky, they might even inflict some damage. The point was to let Birk know he was in for a fight.

They quickly put their mounts in place for a hasty retreat and took up their positions. It was still drizzling and it made the waiting cold and uncomfortable, but they didn't have very long to wait. Kinslow was right again. About twenty minutes later, they could hear the sound of many riders coming up the wagon road.

As they came into the yard, the raiders were in three distinct rows. Three of them, Johnathan Birk with Andy on his right and Tom Sanders on his left, made up the front row. A few feet behind them, from left to right, were Milt Hartley, Claude Bassion, Jim Trueman, and Fancy Ingram. Matt Cox and Mike Billings brought up the rear. Kinslow recognized most of them. They were brazen and no longer felt the need to wear any type of disguise. Overconfidence — Kinslow liked that.

A few feet from the cabin, Johnathan Birk yelled out, "You in the house, come out. I want to talk to you."

He waited for a five count and said again. "This is your last warning. Come out unarmed and you will not be harmed."

Once again, he waited a few seconds then drew his pistol and fired three shots into the door. Getting no response, he gave the order and everyone starting firing into the cabin, mostly through the windows.

After another momentary pause, Birk said, "Burn it down." Sanders and Andy Birk threw lit torches into the cabin through the shot-out windows. At the same time, Kinslow took aim at Mike Billings and fired. Billings dropped from his horse like a rock, dead before he hit the ground. Kinslow didn't intend to kill the man. He'd aimed for the shoulder, but because of the dim light and the man's horse moving at the wrong time, Kinslow's bullet hit Billings in the head. Little Bill fired a second later. By this time, the whole group had reacted to Kinslow's first shot. Consequently, even though Little Bill didn't have the same reservation about killing a man that Kinslow had, he ended up firing at a moving target, shot high, and just wounded Matt Cox in the shoulder.

A hail of bullets came towards the spot where Kinslow and Little Bill had just been standing. They were already on the run for their horses, shooting blindly behind them as they ran. Little Bill went down, moaned, and then got right up again. As they ran, Kinslow asked. "Are you hit?'

Little Bill replied, "Just a nick."

"Where?"

"Nowhere vital. Keep moving."

As soon as the raiding party started towards Kinslow's position, the O'Connors let go from the other side. Liam sported a Spencer carbine which he fired at the man closest to him. The shot tore Milt Hartley's liver to pieces and he would die soon after. Meanwhile, Sean O'Connor let go with his ten gauge shotgun, quickly reloaded, and fired again. He'd loaded the shells with bird shot and nails. The flying shrapnel did considerable damage. Johnathan Birk got hit in the cheek with a nail and Jim Trueman's left arm took a hit. On the second shot, Sean didn't aim the shotgun and fired low. Several of the horses got small nicks and cuts.

Just like Kinslow and Little Bill, as soon as they had fired the initial shots with their rifles, the O'Connor brothers drew their pistols and while running for their horses, shot blindly backwards at Birk and his men. Nobody was hit but two of the horses were badly wounded.

Kinslow's plan worked like a charm. Confusion reigned in the yard. By the time Birk re-established order and they had waited sufficient time to ensure the ambush was over, Kinslow, Little Bill, and the O'Connors were half a mile down the road, well on their way back to the line shack.

Johnathan Birk took stock. Two men dead, himself and two others wounded, and a couple of horses that would have to be put down. He stood in the middle of the yard with the burning cabin behind him and the drizzling rain running down his face, mixing with the blood oozing from the nail in his cheek. He opened his eyes wide and screamed to the heavens in frustration.

The others watched with a feeling of unease and apprehension. Johnathan lowered his head and asked no one in particular. "Whose place is this?"

Andy came closer to his father and answered his question, "Two Irishmen, Pa. O'Hara? O'Connell? — no, O'Connor. That's it! O'Connor."

"They are dead men!" Birk stated emphatically and then softened his tone when he said, "Bassion, check both sides of the road for sign before the rain washes everything away. I want to know how many there were and which way they went and make it quick."

Bassion tied his horse to one of the corral rails and began his search. He preferred to work on foot under these conditions. It was too easy to miss something from the back of a horse, especially when the only light was from the flaming farmhouse.

Birk, in the mean time, shot the two badly wounded horses and was giving orders. He wanted the bodies of the two dead men taken back to the ranch for burial. Andy argued there were no horses to put the bodies on. The O'Connors had turned all their stock loose and Birk's group had no spare horses, having just shot two.

Johnathan did not want the bodies to lead back to him, so he said, "Then bury them in the bush, but be quick about it."

Andy found several shovels in the barn, tossed one to Sanders, one to Fancy, and the three of them buried the dead men in a couple of shallow graves well inside the pine grove . Just about the time they were finished, Bassion returned.

"Well, what did you find out?" demanded Birk.

Bassion was precise and to the point. "There be four of them. Two on each side of the road. From what I see, they shoot and then run. Horses be tied for quick get away. They come out on the main road and head west."

"West? Where?"

"I do not know, but I will follow them and see where they go."

Bassion got his horse and rode off into the rain. Birk took one more look around and ordered, "Burn the rest of it." He mounted and watched to make sure the barn and two other smaller buildings were well ablaze before he gave the order to leave.

A few hours later, Kinslow and party arrived at the line shack. The rain had stopped an hour before, much to the delight of Little Bill. As soon as they were within ear shot of the shack, Carlos came running out. He was frantic and trying to talk, half in Spanish and half in English. "Senor Kinslow, he's gone. I am so sorry. Forgive me, I am so sorry."

Kinslow dismounted and approached the excited Mexican. "Slow down, Carlos." He waited until Sanchez was calmer and then added, "Now, tell me what happened."

Carlos swallowed hard and began, "This bad man Dunn, he say he have to relieve himself. I say no. He say he have to go bad. I say pee in your pants. He say it's not pee. Maria holds the gun while I untie him. I take him to the little house out back. He go in. Pretty soon he's making funny noises. I ask what's wrong. He say he sick. I go to open the door of the little house and bang, the door hit me and knock me down. When I get up and point the gun, he is gone from my sight. I am so sorry, Senor."

"Was he on foot?" asked Kinslow.

"Si Senor."

"How long ago did this happen."

"Maybe, four or five hours, Senor."

Kinslow looked back at the others. "Even with his gimpy leg, he's probably half way back to Birk. We better clear out and fast."

Liam asked, "What do you want us to do?"

"There's a buggy out back of the shed and a horse in the corral. Get it ready for travel and then come in and help us pack up."

Little Bill grunted a couple of times as he dismounted and Kinslow remembered he had been shot. "Where did you get hit?" Kinslow inquired. "Let me have a look at it."

"Don't worry about it. I'll be fine," replied Little Bill, sternly.

Kinslow couldn't understand Little Bill's reluctance. "Look, if you're wounded, let's get it fixed up. Now, where are you hurt?"

"I got shot in the ass! Okay? You still want to look at it?"

Kinslow couldn't keep the smile off his face when he said, "If I have to."

Once inside the shack, Kinslow did check the wound. It probably hurt Little Bill's pride more than it did his hind quarters. The bullet had ploughed a furrow about a quarter inch deep and three inches long, along one cheek. The bleeding had already stopped and Little Bill was no worse for wear. Kinslow poured some whiskey on it as a disinfectant. Maria offered to do the doctoring, but Little Bill would have no part of it.

While the O'Connor brothers got the buggy ready to go, the rest of them packed up the food and gear and in half an hour, they were on their way. They decided to head for the mining camp where Kinslow had stopped a few weeks ago. Kinslow figured it to be about five or six hours along the ridge trail.

By using the high trail, they would bypass the town of Greeley, but the higher trail would be rough with the buggy, but not impossible. They wanted to stay off the main road, which was down in the valley. Also, the higher trail offered them vantage points every few miles from where they could check to see if the Birk bunch had picked up their trail.

Kinslow's plan was simple. Get the Sanchez family to relative safety and he, Little Bill, and the O'Connor brothers would go back and carry the fight to Birk. Kinslow wasn't sure how they were going to do that. Because Birk had an expert tracker, it was imperative they get to the mining camp and be well on their way back before the tracker got too close. This way they could make it very difficult for him to find where they had left the Sanchez family. Kinslow doubted if Birk even cared about the Sanchezs anymore, but he wasn't going to take the chance he might.

While the Kinslow party headed for the mining camp, Andy Birk attended to Matt Cox's shoulder and Jim Trueman's arm. Both men had been lucky. Cox's wound was a deep graze. The bullet had hit at such an angle that it glanced off his shoulder blade. Trueman's arm had some bird shot and a couple of nails that needed to be taken out and the wounds cleaned up.

Johnathan Birk had already pulled the small nail from his cheek and he wasn't receptive to any care and attention at the moment. He and the rest of the men gathered in the study, muddy boots and all. Johnathan poured drinks all around. He was still somewhat unsure of what exactly had happened at the O'Connor place. Johnathan didn't like not knowing things. He liked to be in full control at all times and when he wasn't, he was like a bear with a sore hind end.

The sound of hoof beats caught Johnathan's attention. A few seconds later, Claude Bassion came running into the ranch house.

Johnathan met him half way to the study and asked, "What did you find out?"

"I lose their trail. Too much rain, too much tracks. Be better in daylight."

Johnathan paced for a time and then addressed the group. "Anybody know for sure who ambushed us?" He looked around the room at each man. No one said anything. "I'm thinking it was either a bunch of them dirt pushers got some guts and jumped us, or it's that damn marshal and his friends," he concluded.

Andy, who had just finished wrapping Trueman's arm, spoke up. "I think the marshal and one other man talked the O'Connor boys into joining up with him."

"Then, where the hell are they?" asked Johnathan.

"I don't know, Pa. Camped up in the hills somewhere, I should think."

Johnathan thought about what Andy said and replied, "You know, I think you are right, my boy." He turned to Bassion and said, "Mr. Bassion, here's where you earn your pay. Get a couple hours of shuteye and then I want you out there at the crack of dawn and don't you come back until you can tell me where those bastards are!"

Chapter 19

Johnathan Birk had finished his steak and eggs and was working on his third cup of coffee, which wasn't anywhere near as tasty as Maria's. Willie filled in adequately as a cook, but Johnathan thought he'd better find another housekeeper after all this squatter business was finished. Andy usually didn't eat in the mornings, but he was keeping his father company at the breakfast table, lately.

Both of them had seen Bassion off about an hour earlier. Johnathan was more civil than he was previously and suggested the tracker pick up the trail back at the O'Connor place. Bassion agreed and set off as dawn was breaking. Johnathan put his arm around Andy's shoulders as they walked back into the house. "Well son," he said in a fatherly manner, which made Andy feel good inside, "Let's go in and figure out how to finish this business."

Willie had just bought out a fresh pot of what he called coffee, when they heard a commotion in the yard. They both rose and went to see what all the noise was about. Two ranch hands were supporting Abraham Dunn between them, with a shoulder under each of his arms and the cowboy on Dunn's wounded side also supported his shot-up leg, to take the pressure off it.

Dunn was hollering "Mr. Birk! Mr. Birk!" His face lit up when he saw Johnathan emerge on the veranda.

"Bring him over here boys," ordered Johnathan. Dunn was soaking wet and covered in mud and Birk really didn't want him in the house. He directed the cowboys to bring him up on the veranda and sit him in one of the chairs that was handy.

"Mr. Birk, I got away. Yes sir, I did," Dunn said as he sat down.

"Got away from who? Slow down and start at the beginning," said Johnathan.

A small crowd of cowhands and wranglers had gathered to see what was going on. Birk dismissed them with a remark about how he wasn't paying them to stand around. When they were all gone, Birk turned his attention back to Dunn and told him to continue.

"Me and Isaac, we caught up to that judge fella a couple of miles down the main road. We was all set to conclude our business when we got jumped by two fellas. I killed the judge, figuring Isaac could handle the two bushwhackers. This little fella blew poor Isaac in half with a .50 and the tall one shot my kneecap all to hell before I could reload."

Birk interrupted the narrative, "Was the tall one wearing a badge?"

"Yeah, sure — I think. Yeah, a badge. You're right, he was wearing a badge."

"Not the sharpest knife in the drawer," mumbled Johnathan to himself and then he said aloud, "Did you recognize the smaller man?"

"No sir, but he ain't no cowhand. Not the way he handled himself."

Another unknown element that didn't sit well with Johnathan. "Where did they take you?" he asked.

"To a line shack up on the ridge over yonder." Dunn pointed to the north, behind the ranch house.

Birk shook his head, "Right under our goddamn noses! Are they there now?"

"No sir, just the Mexican you beat the hell out of and his family. I knocked him on his ass and got away. I come straight here, Mr. Birk."

Birk was momentarily surprised. It must be Carlos Sanchez. He thought Sanchez should have been half way to Mexico by now. He regained his composure and said to his son, "Andy, get some boys to take Mr. Dunn to the bunkhouse and get him some grub and dry clothes. Tell Sanders and Ingram I want to see them, pronto."

Johnathan went back in the house and sat down at the dinning room table. He was just getting comfortable when Tom Sanders and Fancy Ingram came rushing in with Andy close behind them. "You wanted to see us, Boss?" asked Fancy.

"I sent the tracker back to the O'Connor place to pick up the trail of the bushwhackers who jumped us last night. He should be on his way back in this direction by now. Head him off and take him up to a line shack about five miles north of here. Andy will go with you. He knows where it is. Tell the tracker to start there. Be careful boys, they might still be there. If they are, don't you three take them on alone. If they've moved on, let the tracker find them. In either case, you three hightail it back here. We got business to tend to tonight."

Andy Birk, Fancy Ingram, and Tom Sanders had intercepted Bassion and took him to the line shack that Abraham Dunn had spoken of. There was no one there, but there were definite signs it had been recently occupied. Bassion easily picked up the Kinslow party's trail. He dismissed Andy, Fancy, and Tom and told them he would back when he found Kinslow and company. Andy bid him adieu and the three of them headed back to the ranch.

It was mid afternoon when Kinslow and party arrived at the mining camp. Little Bill rode in slowly and looked around carefully. Seeing nothing, he gave the all clear. They hadn't stopped since they left the line shack, some thirty miles back. People and horses were tired and hungry, but Kinslow insisted the animals be taken care of first.

Meanwhile, Maria had set up shop in the big rectangular building. The stove was nice and hot and she and the girls were in the midst of preparing a meal. When the men came in, Maria ordered them to sit and informed them the coffee would be ready in a minute. Kinslow took the opportunity to gather them all together. "Sit down, everyone. We need to figure out our next move."

Carlos began to help Maria and Kinslow said, "Carlos, sit down. This concerns you, too."

Kinslow started by addressing the O'Connor brothers. "Looks like you're in this mess through no fault of your own. Way I see it, you have several choices. You can leave and try your luck somewhere else and nobody would blame you if you do. You can go back and stand up to Birk and likely get yourselves killed, or I'm hoping you'll join us and bring Birk and his men to justice."

The brothers didn't even hesitate. Liam spoke for both of them, "We have been fighting tyrants and oppressors all our lives, Mr. Kinslow. One more don't make much difference. Count us in."

Kinslow made eye contact with Little Bill. "This could get rough before it's over, Little Bill. I won't hold you to anything. You can move on if you've a mind to."

Little Bill seemed upset that Kinslow thought he would even consider leaving. "Never once in my life have I ever started something I didn't finish and I aim to finish this."

"Good, that makes four of us. Now — "

Carlos interrupted, "What about me, Senor Kinslow? I too, am not going to run or hide from a fight."

"Sorry Carlos, you need to look after your family. They need you more than we do," replied Kinslow"

At that moment the door opened. In the blink of an eye there were four guns cocked and pointed at the two men silhouetted in the doorway.

Kinslow recognized a familiar voice, "How 'bout me, Mister Marshal? Can you use my help?"

As the two men stepped through the door, Kinslow's eyes lit up and he almost ran forward, his right hand extended. "Max, you old son of a gun! It's good to see you." Kinslow paused to look over the man who had come in with Max. "And who is your friend?" he asked.

"His name is Nicossa. He is my brother."

Kinslow extended his hand to Nicossa, who wasn't sure what he was supposed to do, but having just seen Max shake hands, he did the same. Nicossa was dressed in full native attire except for the boots and an English Derby hat. His long black hair, flowing out from under the hat, was adorned with an intricately beaded ring that sported two eagle feathers. It gave him a unique look, to say the least.

Before Kinslow could ask any more questions, which he was prone to do, Max added, "He is my half brother on my mother's side. He doesn't speak much English."

Kinslow wasn't satisfied, "What brings you to these parts? Were you looking for me?"

"Not really looking. I knew we would meet again some day and it is good it is so soon after we parted. My brother and I often ride the high trails. We saw the smoke and I recognized your horse in the corral. We thought we would say hello."

"Well come on in. Find a seat. Maria will have some grub ready in a bit. Stay awhile and have something to eat," said Kinslow.

Max and Nicossa came in and stood near the table while Kinslow introduced them to Little Bill, the O'Connors, and Maria. Kinslow neglected Carlos since he and Max knew each other. Max, however, introduced Carlos to Nicossa and added something in Shoshone.

After introductions Max said, "My friend, I stood outside listening because I did not know if you were with friends or in trouble. I heard what you said about Birk. You are still trying to get him?"

"It's a lot worse now, Max. Let me tell you about it." Kinslow brought him up to date as Max listened intently.

Max translated everything to Nicossa and then they carried on a conversation for awhile. When they were done talking, Max said to Kinslow, "We would be honoured to help you in your quest."

"Why?" asked Kinslow.

"I have seen Black Flower and she has told me how you talked to the judge in Denver and made me free. I will repay the debt."

"You don't owe me a thing. Hell, you saved my life!"

"I also promised Black Flower if I found you, I would tell you she awaits your return."

Kinslow chuckled and asked, "And did you promise to make sure I got there?"

Max didn't answer. He just smiled.

Maria had some food ready and everyone took a plate, or bowl, or whatever was handy and helped themselves. There was plenty of coffee to go around and Sean O'Connor shared some of the whiskey he had in a flask. "Just for such an occasion as this," he said as he poured.

With everyone fed, Kinslow went back to business. "The only way we are going to beat Birk is to take the fight to him. We can't meet him head on. We figure we incapacitated, if not killed, three or four of them, already. Two for sure. We counted nine at the O'Connor place. That leaves seven and God knows how many more cowhands will tie in with him. We are outnumbered, so we have to hit and run and wear him down."

Kinslow looked around the room for any disagreement or input. Liam O'Connor spoke, "What about asking the homesteaders that are still around to join the fight?"

Kinslow replied, "We can try Liam, but don't count on anybody else. I'm guessing most of them have families and to them, the families come first."

Liam didn't see it that way. "Damn it Woodrow, you're telling me they won't fight for what is theirs? What kinda of men are they?"

"Don't judge them too harshly, Liam. They are men with options. Most men won't stand and fight until they run out of options. Human nature being what it is, most of them would rather move on than do battle."

Kinslow waited for anyone else to add their piece. No one did, so he continued. "Alright then, let's get ready to move out. We will take the same high country trail back in the direction of the line shack. This will keep Birk's tracker on our trail and away from Carlos and his family."

Carlos spoke up, "Senor, are you very sure me and my family will be safe here?"

"Well, nothing is ever one hundred per cent for sure, but I am pretty certain. Why?" asked Kinslow.

Carlos cleared his throat, took a deep breath, and stuck out his chest, "Because I am coming with you. I have, as you say, run out of options. I am not going to be bullied any more. I, too, want to fight this tyrant."

"This isn't going to be easy, Carlos. In fact, some of us are likely to get shot up or even killed. What will happen to Maria and the girls if it's you?"

"Maybe I can not shoot or fight like all of you, but I know this Mr. Birk well and I know how he thinks."

Kinslow thought for a moment and then said reluctantly, "Alright, but when the shooting starts you high-tail it out of there. You hear me?"

Carlos seemed delighted, "Si Senor."

That being settled, Kinslow moved on. He directed his next question to the O'Connors, "How many homesteaders are left and who do you think we should talk to?"

Sean and Liam looked at each other and then Liam said, "There were nine or ten places in the valley and Birk has run off four of them, five if you count us."

"What can you tell us about the ones that are left?" Kinslow asked.

Liam spoke again, "As far as I can tell, there are five farms east of our place that Birk hasn't hit yet. Patty McQuire is next to us. He's got a wife, two sisters, and about six kids. He's scared as hell. I wouldn't count on him.

"There's an older man, a Swede I think, with two young sons next to McQuire. They run a logging operation and a sawmill. The other three are all German people who just come over from the old country. Never met 'em. Don't know much about 'em."

Sean added, "We sold a couple of horses to one of them. Deitrich was the name, I think."

Kinslow said, after mulling over the information, "We should persuade McQuire to leave for a while and talk to the Swede and the German folks and see it they are willing to fight. If not, then it looks like it's up to us."

Chapter 20

When Johnathan and Andy Birk came through the cook shack door, Abraham Dunn, Fancy Ingram, Tom Sanders, Jim Trueman, and Matt Cox were choking down the last bits of what Willie loosely called supper. Johnathan positioned himself at the end of the long table. He made eye contact with Matt Cox and asked, "Mr. Cox, how is the shoulder? Can we count on you to do some hard riding tonight?"

Cox swung the sore arm in a complete circle to show Johnathan he had full use of the shoulder. It hurt like hell, but he wasn't going to let the boss know. "Feels good, Mr. Birk."

"How 'bout you, Jim?" asked Johnathan.

Trueman rubbed the bandage on his wounded arm, "Right as rain, Boss," he replied.

Dunn, feeling left out, jumped in quickly, slapped his wounded leg, and said, "If someone can set me on a horse, I'll be fine, too."

Johnathan gave him a long questioning look and then continued, "Alright, then, I am sure we will have use for your talents, Mr. Dunn. Gentlemen, we have a window of opportunity here. Kinslow and his rag-tag band are somewhere in the hills, with Bassion on their trail. They shouldn't give us any trouble while we conduct some business tonight. We are going to hit a few homesteads and burn them out. I am sure this will convince the rest of them to leave."

He paused and rested his fists, knuckles down, on the end of the table, "And then my friends, we are going to find this burr under my saddle, this pain in my backside, this marshal who thinks he can run me, and we will plant him and anyone we catch with him."

Johnathan searched each man's face for any sign that might show a lack of commitment. He didn't see any.

"Half an hour. Be ready to ride," he said as he and Andy left to get their mounts. Twenty minutes later, all of the men were ready to go. They rode their horses hard and were at the McQuire homestead in short order.

As they rode into the farmyard, in the fading light they could see something was not quite right. Andy, who was in the lead shouted, "They burned it out themselves, Pa!"

As they looked closer, they could make out the remains of several buildings burnt to the ground. Some of the larger timbers of the house were still smouldering.

Johnathan looked around cautiously. He was a little jumpy because of what happened at the O'Connor place. Any trees that might provide cover were out of range for even a rifle. He relaxed and laughed, "Well boys, I'll be damned if the little Irishman didn't take our advice and move on. Looks like he saved us the trouble of burning it down." He didn't show it, but he was angry that McQuire had burnt his own place. He wanted to do it himself.

"That's fine. On to the next one," shouted Johnathan.

Andy wanted to say something about resting the horses for a few minutes, but his father was well on his way before he could get a word out. The rest of the men looked at each other and when Andy said, "Let's go, we better catch up to him," they rode off at a gallop after Johnathan.

Ollie Nystrom came to America from his native Sweden with his wife Olga and their two young sons Mathew and Nicholas. They were enthralled by the land of opportunity where it was said a man could be anything he wanted to be. All it took was a dream and a lot of hard work to make it come true. They landed in New York and traveled cross country by train and then by wagon to the forty acres of land the U.S. Government said they could have by simply building a home and living on it.

It was a dream come true. Ollie built a two room cabin with plans to expand it to a nice house, once they got a business going. He spent the last of their money to buy the saws and equipment needed to set up a small lumber mill. The boys were twelve and thirteen and could help with the timber cutting and milling of the logs, while Olga ran the household and helped with the business when she could.

Then it happened. Olga was kicked in the head by one of the mules. She never did recover and passed away a few weeks later. Her death devastated Ollie and the boys, but life goes on. They grieved and then got back to the business of living.

Now, two years later, they faced another crisis — a greedy rancher who was trying to take away what they had built. Ollie decided he wasn't going to run or be driven out. He had heard about the two

Irish families. The O'Connors were burned out and the McQuires had moved on the next morning.

A week or so earlier, Ollie had been talking to Hans Deitrich, one of the German homesteaders to the east of his place and Hans told him if Birk wanted his land and that of the other two German families, he could have it at a fair price. They didn't want to stay where there was going to be trouble.

Ollie thought he was prepared for Birk. He kept a Spencer rifle he used for deer hunting, loaded and leaning by the door. He had a 12 gauge shot gun loaded with bird shot, as well. When he heard the riders coming into his yard, he stepped out onto the porch with rifle in hand. He had given the shotgun to Mathew, who was now fifteen and considered a man in his father's eyes. Together, they stood while Birk and his men approached. Nicholas was told to stay inside.

Ollie firmly believed there would be no gun play. He would state his position and when Birk saw how committed they were, he would move on. Ollie had instructed Mathew not to point the shotgun, just to hold it at his side.

As Johnathan got close enough to see that Nystrom and his son were armed, he halted the men, leaned forward in his saddle and spoke directly to Ollie. "Mr. Nystrom, I want you off this land by morning. If I have to come back to tell you a second time, I will burn it and bury you in the ashes. Do I make myself clear?"

"Yah, very clear, Mr. Birk, but me and my boys, we are not going nowhere. We work hard to build what we have. My Olga is buried on this land."

Johnathan replied through gritted teeth, "If you're not gone by morning, you can join her." Looking at the rifle in Ollie's hand, he said "What are you going to do with that, Nystrom, take on all of us?"

"I don't want no trouble. Now, I want you off my property, please."

"You really want to die over this piece of dirt?" asked Johnathan.

"Why do you want to kill me over this *'piece of dirt'*, as you say?" retorted Ollie.

Johnathan paused to think about the question for a moment. Nystrom had caught him off guard. He leaned forward in the saddle and spoke very deliberately "It's not the land. It's what it represents. It took me twenty years to build up what I have. I fought wolves and cougars that were killing my stock. I fought rustlers, Indians, and horse thieves who were stealing it. This land cost me my wife and son and

I'll be damned if a bunch of pig farmers are going to come in here and crowd me out! Until morning then."

He wanted to say much more, but thought he would leave it there. As Johnathan turned to go, Mathew, who was uncomfortable holding the heavy shotgun, began to switch hands. Fancy Ingram noticed the movement and thinking the kid was going to shoot, he drew, fired, and hit Mathew dead center in the chest. Mathew looked at his father, his eyes wide with complete surprise on his face. He managed to get the word '*Papa*' out, before he fell over dead.

Ollie was stunned. He turned to the riders, rage in his eyes and as he lifted the Spencer, Fancy fanned his pistol and shot him three times in rapid succession. The cabin door opened and Nicholas stepped out. He was frightened and crying as he bent over his father. After a moment he stood up and glared at Johnathan. It was the most hateful look Johnathan had ever seen in his life and he had seen a few. Johnathan cocked the hammer on his pistol and shot young Nicholas twice.

There was utter disbelief among the men, except for Fancy, who had a big grin on his face. Andy gathered his composure and said, "Jesus, Pa, what the hell did you do that for?"

"Just saved us the trouble of having to kill him a few years from now when he comes back for revenge," answered Johnathan, without emotion.

There was something in his father's logic but Andy, never for a moment, thought his father capable of the cold blooded murder he just witnessed. He looked around and saw that Trueman and Cox were in the same state of shock. Abraham Dunn wore an amused smile on his face. Sanders sat in his saddle completely passive. One could never tell what his state of mind was. Then there was Fancy Ingram, still grinning from ear to ear. '*He's actually enjoying this*,' thought Andy.

The sound of Johnathan's bellowing voice broke the tension. "Well, what are you waiting for? Burn it! Burn it all!" he screamed.

Andy stayed mounted while Fancy and Sanders dragged the three bodies inside the cabin and lit it up. He watched as Trueman and Cox set fire to the other buildings and the big pile of logs that had been stacked for milling.

At this moment, Andy regretted his decision to come back to his father's house after he had left him on the trail a few weeks back. He felt a strong urge to just ride and let his father sink to the bottom of this quicksand pit of insanity by himself. He knew his father was over the edge, but he didn't know what he could do about it, or even if Johnathan would listen.

Johnathan, who had dismounted, looked up at Andy. "What's the matter? No stomach for it?"

"Pa, you murdered that kid."

"Murdered? Murdered? No son, you got it all wrong. I'm just killing a different kind of vermin."

"These ain't coyotes, Pa. The boy wasn't any more than thirteen — fourteen years old and you shot him for what?"

Johnathan was next to Andy's horse in two strides. He reached up and pulled Andy from the saddle and threw him to the ground. He drew his pistol and stood over his prone son. Andy could see the rage mixed with the hate in his father's face.

Johnathan went into a tirade, "For what? Is that your question? For what? You ungrateful little bastard, I'll tell you for what!"

Johnathan grabbed a handful of Andy's shirtfront and lifted him to his feet. In one motion he holstered his gun and backhanded the boy as hard as he could. Andy went down hard. Johnathan walked over to him and picked him up by the shirtfront again. He took another backhand swing. This time, Andy blocked it and pushed his father away, using both hands on his father's chest. The move caught Johnathan by surprise and he stood for a moment before he headed back towards his son. Andy was ready for him. Every punch Jonathan threw, Andy would block it and push his father away. With every block and push, Johnathan was getting more and more frustrated until he drew his pistol and pointed it Andy again.

"What Pa? You gonna shoot me? Just another varmint, am I? You know what? I don't care. Go ahead and pull the trigger." Andy spread his arms, stuck out his chest, and looked right into his father's eyes. They both stood poised in time for what seemed an eternity when Andy let his arms down and walked back to his horse and mounted.

"Where you going?" asked Johnathan.

"As far away from you as I can."

Johnathan cocked the pistol and said, "No you don't! You are going to stick with me until this business is finished."

Andy called his bluff. "You won't shoot me, Pa. I know that."

Johnathan sighed and replied. "You're right." He turned to Ingram and said, "Fancy, if he tries to leave, shoot him."

Andy could see the sickly smirk was still on Fancy's face and he knew this crazed killer would gladly follow his father's orders.

"Alright, the next one," shouted Johnathan.

They all mounted and rode towards the Deitrich homestead. Hans Deitrich's story was a lot like Ollie Nystrom's. Hans, his wife Greta, and his younger brother, Ludwig had come all the way from Germany to start a new life in the land of milk and honey. They joined a wagon train in St. Louis, where they became fast friends with two other German families with the same plans. As they travelled cross country, the three families got to know each other quite well. They decided they would homestead together and had settled in three adjoining forty-acre slots east of Ollie Nystrom. Hans and his family were in the homestead just east of the Nystrom place; Franz Gruber, his wife, and their young daughter in the next one and Helmut and Elsa Metzger, a young couple, were in the farthest one east.

Hans had heard rumours of trouble in the past few weeks. Ollie Nystrom had told him how Birk was driving all the settlers out of the valley and how he was going to stand and fight. He, Ludwig, and Greta invited the Grubers and the Metzgers for a meal and they all decided they did not want any trouble. There was still plenty of land available in the west and they would sell out to Birk, if he offered a fair price. Hans and Ludwig thought they had it all figured out.

It was past midnight when Hans heard the sound of riders coming into the yard and he thought it was very late for someone to come calling. He slipped his pants and boots on and went to roust his brother. Greta awoke and asked him what was going on. Hans told her not to worry and to go back to sleep.

By the time the riders were near the house, the two brothers were on the steps leading to the veranda, ready to greet their guests. Hans took the liberty of filling his pipe. He lit it and looked up as the riders stopped directly in front of him. He took a pull from the pipe, blew out the smoke, and said, "Good evening, Gentlemen. What can I do for you?"

Birk said, "You have until tomorrow to get off this land. If you choose not to go, we will burn you out." He started to turn his horse.

"We will go, Herr Birk. We are asking five dollars an acre. I speak for the Grubers and the Metzgers, also. It comes to two hundred dollars for each homestead. We all think it is a fair price."

Birk didn't know who the Grubers and Metzgers were. Hell, he barely remembered this man's name, but he guessed Hans meant the other two homesteaders. He turned his horse back to face Hans. "Five dollars an acre? Fair price?" Johnathan was irate and he shouted. "Why the hell should I pay you for my own land?"

"I am sorry, Herr Birk, but you are mistaken. This is Government land which has been opened to settlers. It is ours by law and if you want it, you must pay for it."

Johnathan thought for a moment, reached into his vest pocket, drew out a twenty dollar gold piece, and threw it in the dirt. "My price is fifty cents an acre. Consider yourself paid in full."

Hans picked up the coin and said, "The price is not acceptable. I will consider this a down payment. Please don't trespass on my property anymore unless you are willing to do business."

Johnathan Birk snapped. He drove his horse into Hans Deitrich and knocked him to the ground. Ludwig lunged off the steps, grabbed Johnathan by the arm, and was attempting to pull him from his horse. Fancy's shot nearly tore the top of Ludwig's head off. He dropped beside his already prone brother. Hans looked up with fire in his eyes. As he was rising, Johnathan pulled his revolver and shot him twice in the chest.

Once the shooting started, Greta looked out the front window and realized what was happening. She crawled out a side window and started running for the barn. Tom Sanders saw the motion, spurred his horse, and caught her before she could reach safety. He lifted her up by the back of her dress, threw her across his saddle horn, and rode back to the front of the house, where he dumped her on the ground next to her dead husband and brother-in-law. "What do you want to do with her?" he asked.

Fancy had already drawn his pistol when Johnathan stopped him. "I want this one alive." Everyone could see the disappointment on Fancy's face.

Johnathan looked down at Greta and ordered her to stand up. He leaned over his saddle horn to be closer to her. "I'm leaving you alive, so you can tell your friends down the road what happened. I'll be back tomorrow night to burn their places and they better be gone."

Johnathan continued to look at her to make sure she understood when Greta spit in his face. Johnathan dismounted and punched her as hard as he could in the solar plexus. She went down and Johnathan spat on her and remounted.

"Burn it," Johnathan ordered. He looked at Andy, expecting another confrontation. Andy just sat silent. He met his father's gaze and Johnathan saw a look of sadness and pity. This bothered him more than if Andy had gone off on another rant.

Chapter 21

A Colorado sunrise is one of the most awe inspiring sights a person can possibly witness. The blended pinks, yellows and deep oranges on a canvas of dark grey and purple clouds can make a man believe that God had gotten up this very morning and decided to do some painting. Claude Bassion was about two hours east of the mining camp, where Kinslow and his party were holed up. If he'd known that he was this close to them, Bassion probably would have continued after dark, rather than stopping for the night. He tied up his bedroll, ate a big piece of jerky and a small hardtack biscuit, saddled his horse, and was on the trail without ever noticing the splendour in the sky.

Woodrow Kinslow stood on the boardwalk in front of the building they now called home. He rolled a cigarette, lit it and while he smoked, he took in the kaleidoscope of color on the eastern horizon. Little Bill, moving behind him, broke his reverie. Kinslow tossed him the makings and Little Bill rolled himself a smoke. He took a couple of pulls before he said, "Beautiful morning."

"Sure is. Like the Sioux say *'it is a good day to die',*" Kinslow responded and then added, "We should get going."

A short time later, Maria had them all fed, the horses were watered and their bellies were full, as well. As they saddled up and headed out, Kinslow wasn't sure what the day would bring, nor did he have a definite plan of action. The first thing he wanted to do was talk to the remaining homesteaders and see if he could convince them to stand with him against Birk.

A little over an hour later, they were on the high trail atop the hills following the ridge. Kinslow was in the lead and as he came around a corner where the trail made a sharp turn, he saw a rider coming towards him. Claude Bassion looked up, saw Kinslow, quickly turned his horse around, and tried to spur him into a gallop. The sudden turn caused his horse to stumble and the sideways motion threw Bassion to the ground. By the time he realized what happened, Kinslow was next to him with pistol drawn and cocked.

"Not a move, friend. I am a U.S. marshal. I need to know who you are and your business here on this trail."

Claude took a moment and then replied as he sat up, "I'm just on my way to Fort Collins."

"Why did you run?" asked Kinslow.

"Didn't know who you was. Lots of bad men in this country."

By this time, the rest of the group was crowded around. Max stepped his horse forward to get a better look at the man on the ground and said to Kinslow, "I know of this man. His name is Claude Bassion. He is a very good tracker. Could be he works for Birk."

"Is this true?" asked Kinslow.

Bassion took a long time before answering, "Yes, it is true. But — but — uhh — I only track. I tell this Birk fellow, I no shoot nobody. Tracking is all I do."

"And I'm supposed to believe you." said Kinslow, sarcastically.

"It is true Monsieur, I swear on my dear mother's soul."

Max interrupted, "He speaks the truth, Woodrow. It is known he tracks, but does not kill. Religious man, it is said."

What Max had just said gave Bassion an idea. He rose with his hands in the air, slowly lowered his right arm, reached inside his buckskin jacket, and withdrew a small leather bound book. He showed it to Kinslow and said, "See, New Testament."

Kinslow holstered his pistol and dismounted. He approached Bassion and asked, "What are doing up here? Are you tracking us?"

Seeing no need to conceal the truth any longer, Bassion replied, "Yes. Monsieur Birk say to find you."

"Well, you found us. Now what?"

"I don't know. I am thinking it is up to you."

"Tell me about Birk."

"What do you want to know?"

"What did you do for him? What do you know of his activities the last few weeks? Probably most important, what are his plans now?"

"I have not been with Mr. Birk very long. Few days, maybe. Only tracking I do is to find the peoples who shoot at him. Another man — Abraham Dunn is his name — I think. He come back and tell Mr. Birk you are at the line shack. Yesterday and now today, I track you from there"

With Kinslow listening intently, Bassion went on to describe the aftermath of the ambush at the O'Connor farm — who had been killed, who was wounded, and how upset Birk was. He gave Kinslow a full account of who was in the raiding party. He went on to say how Birk was making plans to confront the rest of the homesteaders in the valley. He related how he thought Birk was going crazy and how his men were becoming worried.

Bassion finished with, "That is all I can tell you."

Kinslow moved in closer until their faces were inches apart. He looked the tracker in the eyes and said, "I am going to give you a break, mostly because my friend Max vouches for you. I don't ever want to see you again until this business with Birk is finished. If you go back to Birk, we will arrest you and you can hang with the rest of them. Do you understand me?

"Yes Monsieur, I do," replied Bassion with conviction.

"Now, where can I find you if I need you as a material witness?" asked Kinslow.

"Fort Collins is my home."

Liam O'Connor rode ahead and caught Bassion's horse, which had stopped to munch on some ryegrass not far from where it had dumped its rider. Bassion thanked Kinslow for the second chance to which Kinslow replied that he should be more selective about whom he hired out to and Bassion rode off in the direction of Fort Collins.

Kinslow addressed the men, "From what the tracker just told us, we might be too late. I think we should still visit the rest of the people and see what's what for ourselves. What do you fellas think?"

Everyone agreed, without argument, it was the best thing to do. It was an all day ride just to reach the O'Connor place and then a short trip between each of the remaining homesteads. It was a quiet, reflective ride, each man alone with his thoughts on what lay ahead.

It was late afternoon when Johnathan Birk called together the dozen or so hands who worked the ranch for him. "Boys, I called you all together to clear the air about a few things and to give you an opportunity to earn some extra money. Five, six years ago the Government of this fair land figured they needed more people to make things work, so they opened up all the land south of the river to settlers. Now, I abided by this. I was some upset because, even though that land ain't part of the ranch, we have always used it to graze our cattle.

"I was willing to be a good neighbour and I was, until they killed my son, Mark. My two boys caught that son-of-a-bitch Miller killing a calf and when they challenged him, he shot Mark in cold blood! In cold blood, goddamn it!

"I was willing to let the law handle it, but boys let me tell you, that is one crooked marshal we got in this territory. I think he's after the ranch. He's already killed Sheriff Claxton and Judge Beams and he is organizing the sodbusters to come after me.

"I need your help. We have already started a campaign to chase the squatters out of this valley. You may have heard rumours about us killing folks and such, but let me tell you fellas, we didn't shoot first. We only defended ourselves. Now, it is time we drove the rest of them bastards out and then we need to go after this renegade marshal and his gang. Who's with me?"

The hands were split right down the middle. Six of them shouted enthusiastically, while the other seven were either very quiet or shook their heads in disbelief.

Birk was seething inside at the lack of commitment. He expected most, if not all of the hands, to rally behind him. He pointed to the men who had voiced support and told them to step to one side. He instructed the remainder to see Andy about their back pay and they all had two hours to gather their gear and get off his ranch.

"The rest of you be ready to ride after dinner," he commanded.

Kinslow and company bypassed Birk's ranch by staying high on the ridge trail and then cutting back down to the main road, once they were several miles past the ranch. About the same time Birk was giving his rally speech to the cowhands, Kinslow and his group arrived at Ollie Nystrom's place. They dismounted and began to look around. Sean O'Connor checked the spot where the house had once stood. The stench of the burnt bodies caused him to empty his stomach. Kinslow and the others rushed over to see what the matter was. They all had a good look at what Sean had seen. There was complete disbelief on all their faces.

A short time before, they had been at the McQuire homestead and had seen that the farm was destroyed. They were relieved not to find any bodies. They were totally unprepared for the gruesome sight before them.

Kinslow stated with conviction, "Dirty, murdering bastards." He looked at the rest of the group, "I'll make you all a promise right here and now. Everyone responsible for this is going to pay. As God is my witness, they are going to pay."

A short time later, they were riding into the Deitrich place. One would have thought the atrocities they had just witnessed at the Nystrom farm would have lessened the shock, but it didn't. When they saw the burned out buildings and the charred bodies, it intensified their feelings of horror and anger.

The rage inside Kinslow grew. He would not rest until Birk and his killers were dead, or behind bars for the rest of their lives. If it was the last thing he ever did, he was determined to make it happen.

As they rode into the Gruber's yard, every one of them felt relief to see the buildings still standing. There was still uneasiness amongst the men because everything was too quiet. They apprehensively checked the house and outer buildings for any sign of life. The place was deserted.

Liam O'Connor said, "Looks like they cleared out. House is empty. Stock is gone." Kinslow said, "Thank God! Birk hasn't got here yet." He gathered his thoughts and asked Liam, "How many more homesteads?"

"Just one. Metzger is their name, I think."

"We need to go warn them," said Kinslow.

"I think they already know. In fact, I would bet they are well on their way by now. These families were close friends. I'm sure they are traveling together," said Liam.

Kinslow needed to make sure they were out of harm's way. "How far to the last place?" he asked.

"About two miles, I figure," replied Liam.

Kinslow addressed them all, "Humour me, fellas. I gotta make sure." He turned his horse back to the road and set off.

A little while later, they were at the Metzger farm. Just like the Gruber's, the place was deserted. It looked like they had packed with a sense of urgency. Food staples were all gone. Spilt flour on the kitchen floor had not been cleaned up. A couple of broken lanterns, a large pot, and some homemade furniture were discarded. The bedding and mattresses was stripped from the beds, but the frames and slats were left behind.

As daylight was fading, Carlos Sanchez lit one of the lanterns and went to inspect the tracks left in the yard. Kinslow watched him intently and gave him his head. When it looked like Sanchez was done, Kinslow asked, "What do you see?"

"Looks like two wagons, Senor. Five, maybe six people. One is a child. Three extra horses."

The others gathered around, looking to Kinslow for direction. "Way I figure it, Birk is going to hit these last two places some time tonight. I'd like to surprise him again. We've got to play hit and run with that outfit, or box them in. We wouldn't stand a chance in a head-on fight. Too many guns."

He paused so they could all digest it. Max translated for Nicossa. Kinslow saw this and asked Max, "Is he alright with this?"

Max told Nicossa what Kinslow had asked. Nicossa approached Kinslow and said in broken English, "Nicossa do battle for you, for Max." The look in his eye told Kinslow he could count on him.

"How about the rest of you?" he asked.

Little Bill spoke up with authority, "You don't need to worry about any of us, Woodrow. We are in this as much as you are."

Kinslow didn't have to ask the O'Connor brothers or Sanchez. Their nodding heads of assent told him all he needed to know.

From a tactical perspective, if it came down to a choice, the Gruber place was the better one for another ambush. The Metzger farm was mostly open land. Helmut Metzger had cleared what trees there were, so he could use the land to plant crops.

Franz Gruber, on the other hand, did not clear much of his land. The house and out buildings were still surrounded by scattered groves of trees, which were not as thick as those at the O'Connor place where they had set up the first ambush, but they would still provide good cover.

They rode back to the Gruber farm as quickly as possible and got into position. There were three groves of trees skirting the road leading into the farmyard. The plan was to spread out on both sides of the place, not unlike the ambush at the O'Connor's. The difference here was to force the Birk outfit to take cover inside the house. To accomplish that, timing was going to be critical. They couldn't start firing until the Birk outfit was close to the house and once the shooting started, it would then become the only obvious choice for cover. Once the Birk outfit was inside, Kinslow would have them right where he wanted them and the advantage would be his.

They didn't have long to wait — two cigarettes worth. Kinslow thought Birk would have been a little more cautious, based on the ambush at the O'Connor place. Birk either was confident in the number of men with him, or his sense of purpose blinded him to any concerns about another ambush, because he rode into the farmyard as if he were over for afternoon tea.

The light from a broken lantern flowed through the front window pane of the cabin and wood smoke columned from the chimney. Johnathan called out several times, but no one answered. He ordered Fancy to dismount and check the cabin out. Fancy peered through one of the windows and informed Birk that it was empty. Johnathan dismounted and the rest of the men followed suit except for Tom Sanders. Birk noticed he was still mounted and asked him why. Sanders told him he didn't have a good feeling about this and cautioned Birk about another trap.

Kinslow couldn't hear what was being said and he didn't like the fact that Sanders was still mounted. The yellow lantern light wasn't enough to make out Sanders clearly, but enough to silhouette him. Kinslow stationed himself at the far side of a gulley, about thirty yards from the right side of the house. He sighted his rifle on what he figured to be Sander's shoulder and fired.

The slug knocked Sanders off his horse and almost on top of Birk. Pandemonium broke loose. The rest of Kinslow's men fired into the Birk gang. There was not enough light to see any targets. It was blast away and hope you hit something. Birk's men fired wildly in return at the trees where they thought the shots were coming from. Johnathan yelled at them to take cover. They all ran for the door and quickly squeezed into the house. One of the horses charged around the corner of the building in the opposite direction of the firing. All the other frightened mounts followed him to safety at the back of the cabin.

Part of Kinslow's plan was to let things quiet down a little, make Birk think they had left, and then let them have it with another volley. He wanted to continue this action several times, until Birk came to the realization there was no way out. Then it was wait and see what Birk did next.

As soon as they were in the house, Andy doused the lantern and they all took up positions at the two windows and the door. There were eleven of them in the house, so there wasn't room for everybody at the windows and door. Tom Sanders lay out in the yard with a bullet in his back along with one of the ranch hands, who had been killed by a shot to the temple. Fancy Ingram and Jim Trueman opened the front door a few inches. Fancy stood while Jim crouched down, so they could both see out the door at the same time.

Andy and two of the hands were clustered around one window, while Matt Cox and Abraham Dunn were at the other. Johnathan sat down at the crude table while the remaining three hands stood milling about, not sure what to do.

Andy knocked out one of the glass panes with his pistol. Cox, seeing this, did the same to his window. All was quiet, too quiet. "Do you think they are still out there, Pa?" Andy asked his father."

"How the hell should I know? Why don't you step outside and find out?" came the curt reply.

'*He's not going to be any help,*' thought Andy, as he looked out the window in all directions and then fired a shot at the grove of trees to his right. A hail of bullets from the trees on both sides of the house was the response.

Fancy Ingram gave a maniacal little laugh and said sarcastically, "Call me crazy, but I think they're still out there."

Chapter 22

There are some days when things just go right and today seemed to be one of those days for Kinslow. The landscape at the Gruber farm was very similar to the O'Connor place, an ideal setup for another ambush. The roadway leading up to the Gruber farmhouse was flanked on both sides by scattered dense groves of trees, consisting of white poplar intermixed with the odd fir, spruce, and pine. One such grove ran parallel to the road and continued beside and beyond the right side of the farmhouse. Twenty five yards short of the house, a shallow ravine, which ran perpendicular to the road, split the grove in two. The trees nearest the house were offset further from the road than the ones on the far side of the gully. It was a perfect vantage point to cover both the front and right side of the dwelling. Kinslow stationed Max and Nicossa on the side of the gully nearest the house, while he and Little Bill found cover on the other side of the ravine.

The grove of trees on the left side of the road did not extend as close to the house as those on the right. It stopped forty yards short. The trees had been cleared to put up some corrals, open ended stock shelters, and a vegetable garden. The shelters and corrals were on the side of the house, while the garden occupied the space between the building and the trees where Sanchez and the O'Connor brothers had taken up their positions. From this vantage point, the entire left side of the farmhouse was covered.

The front of the house had one door in the middle, flanked by a fairly large window on each side. There was a smaller window on each side wall, while the back wall was completely solid, save for the fieldstone fireplace and chimney.

There wasn't much left inside the farmhouse. There was a small stack of firewood by the fireplace and a crude wooden table with two chairs to match. Johnathan Birk sat in one of the chairs facing the doorway and relit the lantern. There were no separate rooms per say, but a large area had been split in two with either an old blanket or sheet used as a partition. The rope used to hang the divider had been left behind. There were two wooden bed frames, one in each of the makeshift rooms — one was large and the other was fairly small. Without knowing who had lived there, one could have guessed it was a couple with a small child.

Other than the lantern, there was nothing useable in the cabin. There were a couple of empty sealer jars on some plank shelves, a broken axe someone had been working on, and a completely worn out pair of boots under the table.

Kinslow originally thought a tactic of hit and run was the only way he could beat Birk. He thought the continual harassment would wear Birk down to the point where he would leave the protection of his ranch and try to find Kinslow and end it. Every time they hit Birk, they would inflict some damage — wound, or even kill some of his men. Morale would deteriorate and Birk's men would lose the zeal for the fight. Once Kinslow got Birk and his men away from the ranch, he knew he stood a better chance of arresting them.

Kinslow and his men looked over the Gruber place before they took up their positions. The original plan was to keep Birk pinned down in the farmhouse for most of the night, firing a volley once in a while to keep him and his men awake. Just before dawn, they would send a volley at the house and then leave. Their horses were all tethered well into the trees about a hundred yards back down the road. Every night after that, they would hit the Birk ranch until he finally got fed up and came out after them.

However, Kinslow saw the opportunity in the present situation. Birk and his men had taken the bait; hook, line, and sinker. They were all trapped in the farmhouse and even though Kinslow and his men were outnumbered, they now held the advantage. Kinslow told Little Bill of the change in plan. "We got them right where we want them. This is as good a place as any to finish it. I'll go tell the others."

Kinslow made his way across the gully to Max and Nicossa. He directed his instructions to Max, "This is it my friend. We are going to try and finish it here and now. We will keep firing every once in a while and drive them crazy. Take your lead from me. I'll fire one shot and then we will each shoot twice, all at the same time. In that way, they can't tell for sure where the shots are coming from.

"At some point they are going to try and break out. Tell Nicossa to concentrate on the side window. You focus on the front window on this side of the house and Little Bill and I will take care of the front door. If for some reason, it looks like we are going to be overrun, I will yell '*pull back*'. Head for the horses and we will meet at Miller's place. Don't kill your horses. You'll have lots of time. It will take them awhile to round their mounts up."

Kinslow doubled back, crossed the road, and found Sanchez and the O'Connors. He relayed the same message to them. "Carlos, you cover the side window. Sean, take the front window and Liam, focus on the front door." He found his way back to his position with Little Bill, took out his pistol and fired a shot. A split second later a hail of bullets hit every window and the front door of the farmhouse.

Abraham Dunn chose that moment to look out his window. A bullet caught him in the throat and tore his jugular apart. One of the hands standing with Andy, by the other front window, got shattered glass in his face and his right eye was cut up pretty bad. Everyone else instinctively moved behind the cover of the walls, or hit the floor. Johnathan hadn't moved through it all. It looked as if he wasn't aware of any danger, or he just didn't care.

The shooting from outside stopped as quickly as it started. Andy moved from his spot by the window to the opposite side of the table from his father. He looked into his fathers glazed eyes and saw a far away look. Johnathan didn't seem to be in the room with them.

"Pa! Pa!" Andy said loudly, trying to get his father's attention.

Johnathan came out of his stupor and acknowledged Andy. "What's going on, boy?"

"They got us pinned down, Pa. We can't move."

"Who's got us?" Johnathan asked. He looked at Andy as if he really didn't know and then his face brightened as his memory returned. "It's the goddamn marshal. How many do you figure there are?"

"We don't know, Pa. Seems like quite a few, judging by all the shots fired at us."

"Jesus, you don't know nothing! Where's Sanders?" asked Johnathan.

"He got hit in the first barrage. He's out in the yard bleeding to death," replied Andy.

"Dunn? Where's Dunn?" screamed Johnathan.

"Over by that win —" Andy started to point to the spot where he knew Dunn to be. His eyes diverted to the floor where Dunn lay in a very large pool of red.

Cox, who was still at the same window, said to Andy, "He's a goner."

A desperate, sorrowful moan came from the yard. Sanders screamed through his pain. "Get me out of here. I've been killed. I'm bleeding bad. Help me for Christ sake!"

Johnathan headed for the door. He opened it barely a crack when a single gunshot rang out followed by another swarm of bullets coming through the windows and the door. A flying splinter stuck in Johnathan's throat, just under his chin. He reached up and pulled it out, took a look at it, and threw it on the floor in anger. He closed the door and walked to the window where Dunn lay bleeding out. He positioned himself so he was hidden behind the wall and yelled out the window "Marshal! Marshal, you hear me? I want to talk."

After a slight pause, Kinslow yelled back, "We got nothing to talk about."

"No sense anyone else getting killed on either side. We can come to an understanding about this whole thing," offered Birk.

" Nobody getting killed over here. How you doing on your side?" asked Kinslow, sarcastically.

Johnathan saw red, "You son-of-a-bitch, I swear I'm going to watch you die slow!"

A single shot rang out. The men in the house had learned that the shot was followed by many more and they all hit the floor. They weren't wrong. Another hail of bullets hit the windows and the door.

A few seconds later, Kinslow could be heard. "It's easy, Birk. I have warrants for you, Andy Birk, Fancy Ingram, Tom Sanders, Matt Cox, Jim Trueman, and Abraham Dunn. Come out one at a time, unarmed, and start walking down the road. I don't care about the rest of you."

"And if we don't?" came the questioning reply from Johnathan.

It was a little over an hour until dawn. Kinslow would lose some of his advantage in the daylight. "You got one hour and then we burn the place down around you. You can die choking in the smoke, or get shot to pieces as you come out. It's your call," Kinslow replied.

Another single shot followed by a barrage drove the men in the house to the floor again. Andy rose and positioned himself by the other window. "Marshal, it's Andy Birk. Sanders is the man wounded in the yard. Dunn is near dead. What will happen to the rest of us if we surrender?"

"That's not up to me. I'll take you in to Denver and the courts will decide."

Johnathan was next to Andy in two strides. He grabbed a huge handful of Andy's shirt, literally threw him to the floor, and stood towering over him. "Nobody's going anywhere, especially you, you little coward!"

Johnathan took out his pistol and haphazardly fired a shot through the window at no target in particular. The response, of course, was the single shot followed by the deluge, through which Johnathan stood over his son, exposed to the flying lead.

Andy stood up and looked his father right in the eye and said, "I ain't no coward. You've gone plumb loco. You're going to get us all killed."

Johnathan took a full roundhouse swing at Andy, but Andy saw it coming and blocked it. Johnathan stepped back and swung again and just like the first punch, Andy blocked it with ease. Johnathan stopped, looked around at all his men, and sat back down at the table.

Andy followed him and continued, "Pa, I am not a coward. I just think we have to play along with this marshal until we can come up with something better. He's smart, Pa and we have to be just as smart as him, if we are going to get out of this alive."

All eyes were on the father and son. Johnathan said with all sincerity, "Have you got any ideas?"

Andy answered confidently, "If we look at our situation, he's got us boxed in on three sides. What he won't figure is us coming out the back. We need to bust through the back wall before he sets the place afire."

Fancy Ingram jumped up from his spot at the front door and almost ran to the back wall, followed by several others. They discovered the wall was as solid as a fortress. It was constructed of heavy fir and spruce logs with clay and prairie grass for filler. Jim Trueman approached with the broken axe in his hand. A foot or so of the handle was broken off, but it was still useable as a hatchet.

Fancy chortled with his maniacal little laugh again and asked, "What are you going to do with that, chop your way out? Christ, we'll be here 'till next Tuesday."

Andy approached Jim and took the axe. He turned it over so the hammer side would hit first and he gave the fireplace wall a good whack. Nothing happen on the first swing, but three swings later, the stone Andy was hitting, gave way. He handed the axe to Percy Maines, a big strapping cowhand who doubled as the ranch blacksmith. Two good swings from Percy and the inner wall of the chimney began to crumble.

The outside wall of the chimney was much thicker than the inside one, but it was still no match for Percy. In less than half an hour, he had knocked out a hole big enough for them to crawl through, one at a time. The men all began to crowd around the opening, wanting to be the first to get out of the trap. Johnathan stood and said, "Hold it! We want this to be a surprise."

Johnathan singled out Dusty Forbes, his best wrangler and Ned Pullman another hand good with horses. "You two sneak out the back and gather up enough mounts for all of us." He addressed the rest of them, "When these two fellas have the horses ready, we will mount up and split into two groups, so we will be coming from both sides of the house at the same time. We will ride at full gallop down the road, which will surprise the hell out of them. We should be well past them before they realize what has happened."

As if in answer to Johnathan's orders, the single gunshot sent them all to the floor just before the place was peppered. Again, Johnathan stood where he was, unnerved by the lead flying all around him.

Kinslow checked his pocket watch and said, "Half an hour to go."

"Are we really going to burn them out, or is it just a bluff?" asked Little Bill.

"We can't bluff, Little Bill. If we don't follow through with our threat, any ultimatums we offer in the future won't hold water. I'm hoping they will buy it and either break out of the house or surrender."

"Where do we set the fire?"

"Back wall, I figure. I can get there without being seen."

Kinslow gave it another twenty minutes before he started to wind his way through the trees to the back of the house. In the meantime, they had fired a couple more volleys. When Kinslow reached Max and Nicossa, he told them of his plan. Nicossa said something to Max, who relayed it to Kinslow. "He says he heard a hammering sound coming from inside. It stopped a few minutes ago."

Kinslow asked Max, "Did you hear anything?"

"Yes, just barely. It was a thumping noise, like somebody hammering."

Kinslow was thinking about what the noise could be as he manoeuvred through the trees. He made his way to where he was directly across from the back of the farmhouse. The eastern sky was just beginning to show signs of dawn approaching. As he got closer, he could see men mounting horses, getting ready to ride. Before he could react, the riders split into two groups; one came almost directly at him and turned at the corner of the house and the other group went around the other side of the building. The two groups of riders converged in front of the house and rode hell bent for leather down the road, shouting and shooting.

By the time Kinslow's men realized what had happened, Birk and his riders were well down the road. Little Bill stepped out and fired a couple of shots at their backs. He thought he saw one rider fall.

Kinslow, Max, and Nicossa converged on Little Bill. A minute or so later, Sanchez and the O'Connor brothers joined them. Liam O'Connor asked, "What the hell happened?"

"They got out the back somehow. Let's have a look," replied Kinslow.

As they all started up the road back toward the house, a shot rang out and a spray of dirt rose up a few feet in front of them. They all scattered and took up positions in the edge of the trees. "Let 'em have it!" Kinslow yelled. Once more, the house was deluged with bullets.

"Hold your fire. I give up," came a voice from inside.

"Come out, one at a time with your hands over your head," commanded Kinslow.

The front door of the house opened and a lone man came out, tentatively. It was Frank Jeffers, the ranch hand whose face had been all cut up from flying glass earlier. Birk had left him behind, either by design to slow Kinslow down, or perhaps there just weren't enough horses.

Kinslow told Jeffers to lay face down on the ground and instructed Little Bill and Max to make sure there were no other surprises. Little Bill, Max, and Nicossa checked the house and all around it. "Looks like three dead. These two," Little Bill pointed to the bodies of Tom Sanders and one of the ranch hands face down in the yard, "and our friend, Mr. Dunn, inside." He looked at Jeffers on the ground and asked Kinslow, "What are we going to do with him?"

Kinslow ordered Jeffers on his feet and asked him. "Who are you?"

"Name is Frank Jeffers."

Well, Frank Jeffers, how long have you been with Birk?" Kinslow was fishing. He wanted to know if this man was a gunman or a ranch hand.

"Nigh on three years. He pays good and the work ain't too hard. Beats trail herdin'."

"And now you are killing folks?"

"I swear, Marshal. I didn't shoot anybody. I was just following orders."

Kinslow mulled it over for a moment and then said to Jeffers, "I believe you. You find something to dig with. You bury these men and then I don't ever want to see you again. If I do, I will either shoot you or take you to be hung. You understand me?"

"Yes Sir! Thank you, Sir." Jeffers stood still as if there was more to be said.

Kinslow told him to get going and then called his men together. "We can't let up. We have to keep after Birk. Way I figure it, the odds are just about even, now."

Liam O'Connor asked, "What do you think he is going to do now?'

"I really don't know for sure. We shot them up pretty good. He'll most likely head for the ranch house to regroup."

Little Bill remarked, "His place is out in the open and built like a fortress. We'd never get close."

Max spoke up, "Nicossa and I can get close, come night."

Kinslow looked at Max and his face lit up. "That gives me an idea. We don't need to get them all. We just need to get Birk."

"What do you mean?" asked Little Bill.

"We don't go after them right now. Let them sit and wonder what we are up to. Tonight, when its nice and quiet, Max and Nicossa will go in and bring Birk out. We take him to Denver for trial. The rest may try to rescue him, or maybe not. If they do, the fight will be out in the open and the fact we have Birk will be in our favour. They can't get too close."

"It's a long shot, but what else can we do," commented Sean O'Connor.

"I thought you wanted them all?" remarked Little Bill.

"I do. We get Birk to Denver then I'll be back for the rest," replied Kinslow. "Who knows? We may still get them all if they come after us."

They got their horses and set out. A few moments down the road, they found the body of Matt Cox. Little Bill was right. He did hit one of them. Kinslow galloped back to the farm yard. Jeffers was just returning from the barn with half a shovel. The handle was broken in two and had been left behind.

"One more body down the road for you," said Kinslow. "By the way, do you think you can you say a few words over them?"

"I sure can, Marshal," replied Jeffers.

Chapter 23

"Christ! Not once, but twice! Twice! What the hell happened?" Johnathan Birk ranted, as he lifted the dinning room chair he was leaning on a foot off the floor and slammed it back down hard. He looked into the faces of the seven men who remained of the twelve he'd taken to the Gruber farm. There was Andy, Jim Trueman, Fancy Ingram, and four of the six ranch hands who had volunteered to go. They lost Tom Sanders, Abraham Dunn, Matt Cox, and two of the ranch hands.

When Johnathan's steel gaze met Andy's eyes, Andy stood up and spoke his mind. "It's your fault. Please don't get mad Pa, but you are not seeing clearly. You are so hell bent on driving the homesteaders out you don't see anything else. You're not thinking things through."

Andy tensed, waiting for a torrent of rage from his father. Johnathan digested what Andy had just said and replied, surprisingly calm, "You may be right, my boy. You may be right. I underestimated this Kinslow. He's a real burr under the saddle."

"What are we going to do about him?" Andy asked.

"I can't spend the rest of the summer chasing him around the country side. Our best bet is to call in some markers in Denver. I know a few influential people in the Government and I think I can convince them to help us get rid of this son-of-a-bitch."

"What do you mean, Pa? Why would they go after a lawman?"

Johnathan replied with whimsical amusement, "Why boy, this Kinslow has gone renegade. He's got himself a gang and he's burned out or scared off all of my friends and neighbours and last night he attacked me and killed five of my men. He is trying to drive me out, too."

Fancy Ingram was delighted. "Why if that ain't the dangdest thing I've ever heard!" he remarked and finished with a snicker.

Sidetracked

Johnathan seemed pleased that this killer thought highly of his plan and it seemed to encourage him. "Yes sir, we'll get the army in here and I may even get to see Kinslow hang."

Willie came through the dinning room entrance and announced breakfast was served. He carried a platter of steaks and another of eggs and set them on the table. The men were all pretty hungry and they quickly filled up their plates. Willie departed and soon returned with a huge pot of coffee, plunking it on the table. His job was to feed the ranch hands their three squares a day whether they were at the bunkhouse or out on roundups or trail drives, so he was a little disgruntled with having to play housemaid.

Johnathan was the last one to help himself to the food and coffee. He filled his plate and sat at the head of the table. Between mouthfuls, he said, "Get some rest today and be ready to ride first thing tomorrow morning. We're headed for Denver."

From a vantage point, high on one of the knolls behind the ranch house, Kinslow and each of the men in his party took turns watching the Birk place with the use of the field glasses. They were looking for any sign of movement at all — anything that would indicate Birk was on the move. It was a bit rough. The morning air was cool and Kinslow had said no fires. He didn't even want anyone to light up a curly, for fear the smoke would be seen from down below.

Shortly after Kinslow's group settled in, about half a dozen men came out of the ranch house and headed for the bunkhouse. A short time later, Johnathan Birk came out onto the porch and lit a pipe. He leaned against one of the posts and enjoyed his tobacco as he looked all around. At one point, he looked directly at the spot where Kinslow and his men were hunkered down. Of course, he didn't see anything, but it still gave Sanchez, who was on watch at the time, an uneasy feeling.

They continued to take turns observing as the day dragged on. Kinslow finally relented and let Liam have a smoke, only because he wanted one, too. The daylight gave way to twilight and still there was nothing happening.

Kinslow called all of his men together and asked, "Max, do you really think you and Nicossa can pull this off? Can you get Birk out of there without anyone noticing?"

"It will be as easy as stealing Kiowa ponies," stated Max, proudly.

Kinslow didn't think that would be an easy thing to do either, but he didn't push the issue. "Alright then, we will give them a few hours longer to get settled for the night and then go to work."

About the time Max and Nicossa were making their way quietly down the hill to a grove of aspen, about fifty yards in back of the ranch house, Johnathan Birk, unable to sleep, made his way to the bunkhouse. He knew some of the men didn't sleep much either and would still be up and about, playing cards or swapping lies. He needed some company right about now.

Max and Nicossa led their mounts, including an extra one for Birk, the last few hundred yards or so to the aspen grove. They tied the horses up and made their way cautiously and quietly to the back of the ranch house. Max tried the back door and discovered it to be unlocked. They entered and found themselves in the kitchen.

They made their way through a set of swinging doors that led into the dinning room area and then into a hallway. A lantern, set very low, was burning on a small night table. The hallway led into a large sitting room with a fireplace, which still contained glowing embers. Beyond the sitting room, a set of fancy glass doors opened into the library and games room.

A few steps further down the hallway, beyond the entrance to the sitting room, there was a set of stairs, leading up to the second floor, the bedroom area. Max and Nicossa made their way up very cautiously, setting each foot slowly and deliberately on each stair. At the top, there was another small hall table with a lantern burning very low, probably used to light the way for anybody who got up in the night. In the dim light they could see four closed doors.

Max, with knife drawn, gently opened the first door on his right. When his eyes adjusted, he saw the contents of a bathroom — a cast iron tub in the middle of the floor, a wash stand with jug and basin, a dressing mirror, and a couple of chamber pots. It was a long way to the outhouse, if one needed to go in the middle of the night.

They moved swiftly and quietly to the first door on the left. Max slowly opened the door, holding the knob open to prevent any clicking noise as it closed. It was an unoccupied bedroom with a single bed, a mirrored dresser, a chair, and wash basin and jug. In the second room on the right was a double sized bed along with the same furniture the first bedroom contained. The covers were pulled back and the pillows were rumpled, indicating someone had just slept in the bed. The last room, the second one on the left, was occupied. The sleeper's back was to the door, so Max couldn't see clearly who it might be. He assumed it was Johnathan Birk.

With Nicossa on his right flank, Max knelt on the bed beside the sleeping man, clamped his left hand tightly over the man's mouth, and shoved the knife point into the man's throat, with just enough pressure to avoid penetration.

Andy woke with a start. Max pinned him to the mattress, so he wouldn't struggle and hurt himself and then said, "Quiet, Mr. Birk. I am not here to hurt you, but I will kill you if you try to give us away."

Max relaxed his grip, got off the bed, drew his pistol, and cocked the hammer back. "Now, get dressed very quietly. You're coming with us."

Andy put on his clothes and boots and Max and Nicossa led him out into the hall with Nicossa in the lead, Andy in the middle, and Max behind him with his pistol jammed in Andy's back. Once out in the light of the hall, Max realized they had the wrong man. He turned Andy around and asked him, "Who are you?"

"Andy Birk," was the reply.

Max put two and two together and asked, "Where is your father?"

Andy pointed to the bedroom across the hall. Max recalled it was the one with the slept-in bed. As Max instinctively glanced to where Andy had pointed, Andy saw an opportunity and tried to take a swing at Max, who saw it coming. He blocked it with his left arm, and at the same time brought the barrel of his pistol down hard on the side of Andy's head, who went down in a heap. Max stood listening for a moment to make sure the noise hadn't attracted any attention. He picked Andy up, threw his limp body over his shoulder, as if he was burping a baby, and told Nicossa to lead the way.

They made it back to the horses without incident. Max tied Andy's body across the saddle of the spare horse and they walked the animals a couple of hundred yards before they mounted and rode away.

Back atop the knoll, Kinslow was anxiously waiting for them and when he saw the body across the horse he said with some delight in his voice, "You got him! Good work."

Max shook his head and replied, "Yes and no."

Kinslow's good mood faded, "What do you mean, *'yes and no*?"

"Well we got Birk, alright. It's just — well, we got the wrong one."

Kinslow long-strided to the horse with the body on it and lifted Andy's head by the hair, so he could see his face. He looked at Max, let Andy's head fall, and while he walked back, he was thinking. "This is Birk's son, but it can still work. We can take him to Denver and that will still draw Birk into the open," he said.

Little Bill spoke up, "Woodrow, I disagree. It does change things."

"How so?' asked Kinslow.

"Well sir, with the original plan of taking Birk senior to Denver, the rest of the gang, except for maybe his son here, wouldn't have the drive to push too hard to save him. But if we try taking Birk junior, papa is going to be real determined to get his boy back and with him leading the way, his men will fight hard."

"I still don't see what difference it makes," countered Kinslow.

"We don't know how many guns Birk has. We could be outnumbered something fierce. We need a place to make a stand and trade the kid for Birk senior."

Kinslow wrestled with the idea Little Bill had just put forth. It made sense. They would have better control of the situation. "I like it," he said. "And I know the perfect place to hole up."

"Where?" asked Little Bill.

"The mining camp," replied Kinslow.

Sanchez interjected, "Senor, my family is at the mining camp."

"I know, Carlos," Kinslow replied. "You are going to take them somewhere else as soon as we get there."

"Where, Senor?"

"In the next valley to the west, there are some miner's shacks by the creek. You and your family put up there for a few days. By that time, we'll either have this business wrapped up, or we'll be dead."

"Si Senor, I will take them there and be back as quickly as I can."

"No you won't! You're responsibility is to your wife and daughters. You'll stay put."

"But Senor, you will need me."

Kinslow closed the distance between himself and Sanchez until he was right in Carlos' face. "No Carlos, we don't need you as much as your family does. If fact, you just might be in the way. I can't concentrate on saving my own skin, if I have to worry about yours. Now, do as I say."

Sanchez was hurt and Kinslow could see it. He didn't want to be so overbearing, but sometimes he needed to be.

"Pretty rough on him," commented Little Bill.

"Yeah, but it's for his own good," responded Kinslow.

Realization of what Kinslow had just done, struck Little Bill. He smiled and thought to himself of how he was getting to like this man more and more.

Kinslow directed his attention to Max. "Max, do you think you can sneak back into the Birk place without getting noticed?"

"No problem. What do you want me to do?"

"Leave Birk a message." Kinslow searched one of his saddle bags and took out one of the warrants, from which he tore off the back page. He pulled out a stubby piece of pencil, sharpened the tip with a pocket knife, and wrote: *'Birk, have your son Andy. Will trade him for you. Will be at mining camp where you tried to jump us before. You have 48 hours – Marshal Woodrow Kinslow.'* He folded the page and handed it to Max. "Slip this under the front door and hurry back. We will be on our way to the mining camp."

It was well after four in the morning when Johnathan Birk stumbled through the front door of the ranch house. He was too drunk to notice the piece of paper lying on the floor, just inside the door. He'd been playing stud poker and drinking cheap whiskey most of the night and the only thought on his mind was to lie down and get some sleep.

A few hours later, Willie McCoy, having fed the men, was entering the ranch house to make breakfast for the Birks. He noticed the paper on the floor, picked it up, read it, and ran upstairs hollering, "Mr. Birk! Mr. Birk!" at the top of his lungs. He rapped on Johnathan's bedroom door loud and long. He could hear some mumbling and cursing from within.

A few seconds later, the door flew open and there stood a dishevelled Johnathan, holding onto the door knob with one hand and his head with the other. "Christ, what's with all the noise?"

Willie handed him the note. Johnathan read it twice, pushed past Willie, and opened Andy's bedroom door. Seeing only the rumpled bed, he said to Willie, "Go roust everyone and tell them to be ready to ride in thirty — no, make it twenty minutes."

Willie rushed out on his appointed chore and Johnathan threw some water on his face and through his hair. He got dressed quickly, saddled his horse, and was in front of the bunkhouse just as some of the men were starting to come out.

"What's going on, boss?" asked Jim Trueman.

"That goddamn Kinslow has Andy. He's holed up in that mining camp about twenty miles west on the old high trail." He paused momentarily and continued, "Today is the day we finish this. Get mounted! Bring your night gear, some food, and plenty of ammunition!"

The sun had been up for a short spell, when Kinslow and party descended from the high trail down into the mining camp. Maria Sanchez and her two daughters were waiting on the steps of the main building that they had been calling home for the last few days. Carlos jumped from his horse, dashed to her, gave her a big hug, and then he embraced each of the girls in turn. He told Maria, in Spanish, about what had happened and that they needed to leave right away.

Andy regained consciousness about an hour out from the ranch. Kinslow was kind enough to allow him to sit up, but he was well secured to the horse with his hands tied to the saddle horn and his legs tied together underneath the horse. Kinslow took the reins of Andy's mount from Liam O'Connor and said, "You men get a bite to eat and try and get a couple of hours sleep while I look around."

"What ya gonna do with him?" Sean O'Connor asked, indicating Andy.

Kinslow smiled and replied, "We'll tuck him away somewhere, safe and sound. Some place where he won't be in the way."

Little Bill said, "You have no intention of trading the kid for the old man, do you?"

Kinslow was surprised at Little Bill's insight. "Not if I don't have to," he replied as he turned and rode off down the main street with Andy in tow. At the west end of the camp, he followed a creek up the mountainside until he saw a tunnel. He dismounted, took Andy off his horse, and pulled him just inside the mine entrance where he tied the young Birk securely to one of the shoring timbers.

"My father is going to kill you and then hang your carcass on a tree and let the ravens pick at you, you son-of-a-bitch," Andy said to Kinslow as he walked away.

Kinslow turned back to face Andy and replied, "I sure hope he gets close enough to try, son. I surely do."

Chapter 24

Kinslow rode back and forth through the abandoned mining camp in a zigzag pattern, committing everything he saw to memory. During their peak, many isolated mining camps, including this one, were the size of small towns. They were nameless, because in most cases they never lasted long enough to develop any form of civic government. After a year or two at best, the miners and those who made a living from them, moved on to the next rumoured gold or silver discovery, leaving behind a collection of hastily constructed clapboard structures and a myriad of sapling frames, once used to support canvas tents.

As he rode, Kinslow was deep in thought, trying to figure out a way to deal with Birk, when an idea came to mind. He remembered hearing of how the Blackfoot in northern Montana would force stampeding buffalo over a cliff to their demise and how the Chiricahua Apache in New Mexico would chase wild horses into a box canyon and then close a makeshift gate behind them. He recalled how the Lakota Sioux employed a similar tactic when dealing with a foe in battle. They would leave an apparent opening or avenue of escape which the enemy would willingly take, only to find themselves suddenly surrounded with no way out. Kinslow hoped to set up a similar scenario for Birk, using the buildings of the mining camp and the main street as his box canyon.

After nearly a half hour of riding, Kinslow covered the entire area. There were two trails coming in from the east that led directly into the camp. One was a high alpine trail that followed the tree line and the other was down on the flat. Once the lower trail was established, the higher one was seldom used except by those who didn't want to be seen. This was the route Kinslow had used a few weeks back to escape from Birk's clutches.

Anyone entering the camp from either the west or the east would travel down what passed for the main street, along which the only permanent or semi-permanent structures stood. The first building anyone saw as they came in from the east was on their right side, adjacent to the fenced pasture Kinslow and company used the first time they were in the camp. It was set back from the main street and the other structures by twenty feet or so. It was a false-fronted, clapboard shack that was once a bathhouse. A crude wooden sign that read, *"regular 25¢   clean water 50¢   hot water 75¢"*, still hung above the doorway.

A small laneway separated the bathhouse from the principle building of the camp, a large one storey, crimson coloured, box-like structure, approximately sixty feet long by forty feet wide. Double doors served as an entrance and there were two large windows, one on each side of the big doors. The first time Kinslow was in the camp, he didn't pay any attention to the colour of the building. It was near dark and with Birk hot on his trail, he had other things on his mind. *Now*, he thought, *there had to be an interesting story behind that choice of colors.*

The big red building was probably used as a central community or meeting hall and would have likely doubled as a church on Sundays, provided there was a preacher in camp. This was where Kinslow and Miller took shelter a few weeks ago and lately it served as home for the Sanchez family. Another small laneway separated the red-box building from another large false-fronted structure. *"Dunnigan's"* was painted in white across the front. At one time, it was, most likely, a saloon or gambling hall, or both.

On the left side of the street, directly opposite the red box building, were a freight office, an assay office, and a general store, each in turn separated by a narrow laneway. At the end of the street was a small cabin with a sign on the front door that simply read *"Eats"*.

Behind these structures, was a line of trees that ran parallel to the buildings and directly behind the trees, were row upon row of make shift tent frames thrown together with pine poles and bailing wire. At the rear of the tent area, a crude wooden bridge crossed a ten foot gulley with a small, rocky, dried up creek bed running through it. The bridge led to what appeared to have been a blacksmith shop with an attached barn, surrounded by several partitioned corrals.

To the west and north of the main structures was another area strewn with dozens of tent frames. A few hundred feet further, the trail crossed yet another flowing creek and continued west into the next valley where the remnants of human occupancy didn't look much different from the ones in this valley. Just before the trail crossed the creek, a smaller pathway branched off to the right and followed the creek part way up the mountain to where there were several exploratory tunnels dug into the hillside. Kinslow had stashed Andy Birk in one such excavation.

"Good, good. This just might work," remarked Kinslow to himself as he dismounted in front of the big red building and went inside. Maria had made a pot of beans, biscuits, some coffee, and set them on the table. She, Carlos, and the girls were busy packing things up for their exodus. The O'Connors were asleep on the floor, Little Bill sat at the table with his feet up, sucking on a coffee, and Max and Nicossa were enjoying some of Maria's fare.

Kinslow rousted the O'Connors and brought everybody in tight around the table. He took out his pencil, tore another page from the back of one of the warrants, and drew a crude layout of the camp. "I'm guessing Birk will take the main trail into town which will put him about here." Kinslow indicated the spot at the head of the main street with the bathhouse on the right and the freight office on the left.

Pointing to the different buildings on his layout, Kinslow continued. "I'll be on the west side of the bathhouse. Once they ride past me, I'll move to the east side of the shack which will put me behind them. Little Bill, you take up a spot on the west side of the freight office. We'll have them in a cross-fire. Liam, you use the assay office for cover and Sean, you set up shop by the store, here. Max and Nicossa, you fellas take cover on the roof of the saloon. Your job is to keep anyone from escaping the trap on the back side.

"When I think Birk and his men are in the right position, I'll step out and give him a chance to surrender. Little Bill, Liam, Sean, you all cover me and if anyone of them goes for their gun, start shooting. Max, this is very important. No matter what happens, no matter how much shooting you hear, do not leave your post. If you do, you give them a way out. If things go right, the only cover left for Birk will be this big building we're in now. We force him in here and then wait him out.

"Couple of other things — I want Birk alive, if possible and I just want to say this could get ugly before it's over, so if anyone wants to pull out, say so now. No one will think any less of you if you choose to go."

Kinslow gave them a moment to think about it and then looked around at all of them. Not one of the men showed any signs of wavering. Little Bill spoke, "Woody, not to doubt your idea, but what makes you think Birk is just gonna ride into town?"

"He thinks he has come to trade for his son. I am sure he is convinced that he is in control of the situation and his arrogance will be his downfall," replied Kinslow.

A short time later they were all biding Carlos and his family goodbye. Kinslow said, "Give it a few days and come back and have a look. If we aren't dead in the street, you'll know it's safe. If we are, you better head out of this territory."

Sanchez removed his straw sombrero and shook Kinslow's hand. "Thank you for everything, Senor. We shall never forget you."

Max and Nicossa gathered all the horses and turned them loose in one of the corrals, west of the blacksmith shop. When they got back to the main building, Kinslow went over the plan again. Every one loaded their weapons, checked them one last time, filled up their cartridge belts, and stowed extra ammunition in the handiest pocket. Kinslow tossed Nicossa one of the rifles they had collected from the fight at the Gruber place.

There was an uneasy quietness in the room. No one spoke much. Kinslow said "Good luck, men," as they walked out the door and that was about the extent of it. They each took up their assigned positions and waited nervously for Birk to show up.

They didn't have to wait long. Just shy of a couple of hours later, Birk and his men came charging down the main trail just as Kinslow predicted. They stopped just short of the buildings. Kinslow removed his hat and stole a look around the corner of the bathhouse. Counting Birk, there were eight of them. To Kinslow, this was a pleasant surprise. He expected many more.

Johnathan Birk was being very cautious. He'd already walked into a trap twice and they weren't going to get him a third time. He instructed one of the hands, "Herrington, ride ahead to the end of the street and back."

Dave Herrington reluctantly rode slowly down the main street, one hand held the reins and the other, his cocked pistol. His eyes switched rapidly from left to right and he scrutinized every doorway, window and rooftop. He came to the end of the street, opposite the west end of the saloon and turned back. "Looks good, Boss. Didn't see a sign of anybody," he said as he got closer to Johnathan.

Still, Birk proceeded cautiously and the rest followed. When they were between the red box building and the freight office, Kinslow stepped away from the corner of the bathhouse and hollered "Birk!" The entire group turned their horses in unison, in the direction of the voice. "Johnathan Birk, I have a warrant for your arrest. All of you, dismount, drop your gun belts, and you may live to see another sunrise."

Several of Birk's men had their pistols drawn and were just waiting for some sign from Johnathan to open up. Johnathan pushed his horse through the pack until he was in the front, facing Kinslow. "Where's Andy?" he asked.

"He'll be just fine until our business here is done," replied Kinslow.

"What business might that be?" asked Birk, smugly.

"I am taking you and anyone else that was involved in your killing spree, to Denver to stand trial for murder."

Johnathan Birk paused for a moment and then said as he drew his pistol, "The hell you are!"

Kinslow fired a shot and ducked behind the corner of the bath house. He wasn't aiming at anyone in particular. It was more of a signal for the rest to start firing. Little Bill and the O'Connor brothers opened up, shooting randomly into the crowd. Kinslow fired several shots from his vantage point.

The result was complete mayhem. Everything happened at once. Frightened horses snorted and rose up. Dusty Forbes was hit twice in the chest and was dead before he hit the ground. Percy Maines threw his hands up to his face as he fell from the saddle; a bullet had torn out his right eye. Ned Pullman's horse was shot dead and tumbled head over heels. Ned never had time to jump and was crushed under the falling animal. A bullet grazed Jim Trueman's cheek. Another shot went through Johnathan Birk's ankle and ricocheted up into his mount. The horse went down, throwing Johnathan as it fell.

The instant the shooting started, Willie McCoy turned his horse, spurred it hard and was laying low in the saddle as he galloped back down the road in the direction from which they had come. Kinslow's well aimed shot caught him dead centre between the shoulder blades, knocking him off his mount. Dave Herrington reacted quickly, as well. He charged in the opposite direction, directly down the main street, past the corner of the saloon and he thought he was home free when Max's shot knocked him out of the saddle. He hit the ground hard and after a dazed moment, he sat up. He started coughing hard and spit up the bubbly, deep crimson coloured blood that indicated a fatal lung shot.

Fancy Ingram's strong penchant for self preservation served him well. He leapt from his horse and dashed for cover next to the freight office, on the opposite side of the structure from Little Bill. Jim Trueman kept his wits about him and shouted at Johnathan, "Stand up, Mr. Birk." Once Johnathan struggled to his feet, Trueman leaned over to one side of his mount and with his arm extended, lifted Johnathan into the saddle behind him in one smooth, easy motion. He raced his horse past the east side of the freight office, nearly knocking Fancy Ingram over. He raced through the row of trees and the tent area and when he caught sight of the blacksmith shop and the barn beyond the bridge, he headed straight for them, dismounted, and helped Johnathan inside the barn.

As quickly as the shooting had started, it was over and the street was quiet, except for the snorts of pain coming from Johnathan Birk's wounded horse. Fancy Ingram was in the back of the freight office, hugging the walls, hoping to make his way from building to building and down the street without being noticed. As he stepped into the alleyway between the freight office and the assay office, he caught a glimpse of Little Bill at the corner of the building on the street side. He took careful aim and fired.

Little Bill caught movement out of the corner of his eye and started to turn back towards Fancy just as he pulled the trigger. As a result, the bullet didn't hit Little Bill square in the middle of the back, as intended. Instead, it created a deep furrow across the width of his shoulder blades. However, the force of it knocked him face down in the dirt. Little Bill groaned, turned over, and tried to get up. Fancy pushed him back to the ground with his left boot on Little Bill's chest. Fancy chortled and aimed his pistol at a spot between Little Bill's eyes. Thinking fast, Little Bill put his arms over his face and started pleading for his life.

Fancy raised his pistol slightly and said with a mouthful of sarcasm, "And I thought Little Bill Stoud was such a tough hombre. If you could only see yourself now, blubbering like a little baby."

The distraction provided Little Bill with the opportunity he was hoping for when he started the crying act. In one swift motion, he swung his left leg hard, knocking Fancy's right leg out from under him. The instant Fancy hit the ground, Little Bill lifted his right leg and drove his boot heel as hard as he could into Fancy's face, knocking him half unconscious. Several more well driven boot heels finished the job. Little Bill rose to his knees, drew his .44, and ended Fancy Ingram's miserable life with a shot to the heart. "Laugh now, you back shooting bastard," he uttered as he put away his gun.

Little Bill was getting to his feet as Kinslow came around the corner, gun drawn. He saw Little Bill standing and the body of Fancy

Ingram on the ground. He noticed Little Bill's blood soaked shirt and as Kinslow holstered his gun, he asked, "You hit?"

"Yeah, in the back," answered Little Bill.

Kinslow stepped behind Little Bill and inspected the wound. "Looks like it's just a deep crease, my friend. You'll be as good as new and you'll have a nice scar to show the ladies."

Little Bill asked, "Are we done here?"

"Just about. One hand and Birk headed towards the corrals. They won't get far on one horse. The rest of the bunch are on the ground."

Liam and Sean O'Connor joined them. Liam was all excited. "Birk and another fella are holed up in the barn," Kinslow said as he pointed to the corral area.

Kinslow walked quickly westward down the street to where Max and Nicossa could see him and waved them in. While they were waiting, Kinslow rolled a smoke and passed the makings to Little Bill, who in turn rolled one and passed it to Liam.

When Max and Nicossa arrived, Kinslow filled them in on the situation as it stood. "You all take positions around the barn and blacksmith shop and don't let those two get out. I think Birk is hit and I am not sure who is with him. I'm going to go get the kid."

Kinslow got his horse from the corral and asked Sean if he could borrow his as well. It was a little over half a mile to the mine where he had left Andy. When he got there, he approached cautiously, pistol drawn, but there was no need. Andy was still secured to the post where he had left him.

Andy was quite nervous. "What's all the shooting? What happened? Where are you taking me?" he asked in rapid succession.

"It's over, Andy. Your father's men are all dead and he's holed up in a barn with one other fella. Wounded, as far as I could tell. I need you to convince him it is over and the best thing he can do is surrender," Kinslow said.

"You go to hell!" spat Andy.

Kinslow grabbed him by the scruff of the neck and put him on Sean O'Connor's horse, mounted his own, and ten minutes later they were back with the others.

Jim Trueman was watching Kinslow's men manoeuvre into position. He figured if there was any hope of getting out, it had to be soon. He said to Birk, "Boss, they are surrounding us. I think we should go now."

Birk replied, "I'm not going anywhere, Jim. My foot is shot to hell and I would only slow you down. You go ahead, if you think you can get away."

Trueman hesitated, trying to decide whether to go or stay. "Get going, I said," Birk stated with authority.

Trueman kicked a couple of planks out of the wall that separated the barn from the blacksmith's shop. The O'Connor brothers had worked their way to the back side of the barn to block any rear exit. Upon hearing the noise, Sean approached. Trueman eased himself through the opening and stood for a moment inside the blacksmith's shop, letting his eyes adjust to the brighter light. Sean, not expecting anyone in the shop, exposed himself in the doorway and Trueman shot him twice in the chest. He quickly made his way out of the building and as he emerged, Liam O'Connor emptied his pistol into Jim Trueman.

On the opposite side of the barn, the shots got the attention of Kinslow and Little Bill. They drew their pistols and were about to go investigate when Johnathan Birk squeezed through the partially separated barn doors. He was using a rake for a crutch to keep any pressure off of his mangled ankle. He advanced until he was about twenty feet from Kinslow.

He stood erect with an egg-sucking smirk on this face. "Now you've done it, you son-of-a-bitch. I got lots of friends in high places and by the time I'm through with you, everyone will believe you're responsible for all of this. You and your rag-tag bunch will be the ones swinging at the end of a rope."

Five shots rang out from behind Birk and he fell forward, face down in the dirt. Liam O'Connor stood behind him with an empty, smoking pistol in his hand. He kept pulling the trigger, even though the gun was empty. Tears were streaming down his cheek. Kinslow advanced cautiously, calling Liam's name. When he got within arm's length, he reached out and slowly took the gun out of Liam's hand.

Liam looked up into Kinslow's eyes. "They killed Sean, Woodrow. The bastards killed my baby brother."

As Kinslow walked towards his distraught friend, Andy Birk, unnoticed by anyone, ran over to his father's body, turned him over on his back, and began hysterically crying out "Pa, Pa", repeatedly. At about the time Kinslow was taking the gun out of Liam's hand, Andy took his father's pistol out of its holster and had it trained on Kinslow's back. Just as he was about to squeeze the trigger, a shot from Little Bill's .44 took the back of his head off and he slumped down across his father's body.

Kinslow whirled around with his gun in his hand. He saw Little Bill's pistol smoking and Andy dead. He looked back at Little Bill and his eyes were asking what happened. "I had no choice, Woodrow. He had you dead to rights with his daddy's pistol."

Kinslow walked deliberately to the bodies of the Birks and lifted Andy off his father. Sure enough, there was a pistol in Andy's hand. Kinslow holstered his Peacemaker, looked at Little Bill, and said, "Thanks."

He returned his attention to Liam O'Connor, who was on his knees, sobbing. Woodrow Kinslow had come to a crossroads in his life. He'd always been a stickler for the law. The law was his mistress and if you broke it you paid the price. The law was the only thing that mattered, the only thing that gave him purpose. Liam O'Connor killed an unarmed man and this same law said he must arrest a friend, a man who had just seen his only family killed.

Somehow, Little Bill understood his dilemma. "What now Woodrow?" he asked.

Kinslow thought, for what seemed an eternity, reached into his vest pocket, took out the warrants and tossed them on the corpse of Johnathan Birk. He looked into Max's eyes and said, "Think I'll go see this little black-eyed beauty I know."

Max Boudreaux just smiled.

The End